WITHOUT A TRACE

WITHOUT A TRACE

A SARA VALLÉN THRILLER

CECILIA SAHLSTRÖM

Translated from Swedish by Emma Ericson

Podium

WITHOUT A TRACE

1998

Come on, buddy, let's go see Mummy."

The boy looked up. He was curious. Smiling. The stranger stood in front, gesturing to him to be quiet.

"Mummy."

He took the stranger's hand. It looked so soft. In the other hand, the boy saw the ice cream and reached for it.

"Not now," the stranger whispered.

The boy was wearing a thin spring jacket with yellow ducks on it. He had his eyes on the ice cream as it moved back and forth in front of his round little face.

The gate opened slowly, and they walked out together. The boy didn't say anything. He just wanted the ice cream.

Before he knew it, the stranger picked him up and gave him the ice cream. He licked it eagerly.

They walked up to a bluish-grey car and the stranger opened the door to the passenger seat. The stranger buckled the boy into a car seat that looked very similar to the one in his parents' car. There was a teddy bear inside the car. The little boy picked it up with his free hand.

"Eddy," he said.

The stranger nodded, walked around the car, and sat down behind the wheel. The car started and the little boy sat there with his ice cream. He looked happy, and the ice cream dripped down his chin onto his jacket, making the yellow ducks all sticky.

When the boy had finished the ice cream, he started to cry.

"Mummy," he snivelled.

"Soon," the stranger said, and stroked the boy's hair. "There, there."

A couple of minutes later, the boy fell asleep.

"You're speaking to the police," the operator said calmly. He assumed it wasn't anything too exciting. In his experience, most people who called the emergency services misjudged how serious their situation was.

"My son, my son . . ." a voice said on the other end of the line.

"Yes?" the operator said, and stifled a sigh.

"My son is gone. He's been kidnapped!"

The operator sat up straighter. "What's your name?"

"Molly Altenius. You must come right away. My son has been kid-napped," the woman screamed.

"What's your son's name and where are you?" *Hysterical woman*, the operator thought.

"My son's name is Karl-Axel Altenius. He's two years old, and he's gone missing from his preschool in Linero. I'm there now." The woman took a deep breath and the operator could hear she was trying her best to sound composed. *I better take this seriously*, he thought, and sat up even straighter.

"I'll send a car," the operator said, and asked the woman to stay on the line while he directed two units to the preschool, including the sergeant's car. *Another case well-handled*, he thought.

When the police arrived at the preschool, they were met by an agitated crowd. A young preschool teacher and an equally young teacher's assis-tant stood next to the mother on the playground outside the school. They all looked confused and scared. The sergeant talked to them to get a better idea of what had happened, and then he called Lund to ask for more resources as well as a forensics unit.

"How could you let Karl-Axel disappear like this? How could you?!" Molly Altenius sobbed desperately. Her hair was a mess and her make-up was smeared across her face. Her chin trembled.

"We didn't let him disappear," the teacher said, defending herself while her colleague cried. "We didn't let him go anywhere with anyone else. We'd been outside. And suddenly, he was gone. We have fifteen children to keep track of." She sounded as devastated as she looked.

"But he's gone, and you let it happen. That's a fact."

"There is no point arguing now—we have to act," the sergeant said, looking serious.

The three women looked at him. The teacher's assistant kept crying.

A moment later, another unit arrived at the school, as well as the K-9 unit. The dog sniffed the missing boy's clothes, and one of the teachers took the boy's photo down from the wall. Then the dog took off to search the playground and the surrounding area.

"Do you think Karl-Axel would react negatively if anyone other than you or your husband came to pick him up from school?" the sergeant asked Molly Altenius, who paced back and forth on the playground.

"I don't know. I guess so. Maybe not if he was tempted by something. I don't know." Her eyes welled up.

"I understand. Have you called your husband?"

Molly nodded.

"I have to go look for him," she said.

"It's better if you stay here. Let the police do the looking."

The sergeant took a moment to think and decided to call for a couple of extra units to look for witnesses. Then he returned to talk to the rest of the staff.

"Do you think the boy could've opened the gate on his own?" he asked.

"No, I really don't think so. It's always locked," the preschool teacher said.

"Is it possible someone forgot to close it? The boy isn't here, so he must have left the area on his own, or with someone else." The sergeant gave them a stern look.

The teacher's assistant trembled and seemed to be in shock. The sergeant saw an adult-sized jacket on one of the hooks on the wall and brought it over. He draped it around the shoulders of the teacher's assistant and gave her a friendly look.

"It's good to keep warm. Shock can affect you more than you'd think," he said, and turned to the teacher again. She squirmed.

"I guess it's possible that someone forgot to close the gate, but I really don't think so. It's a well-rehearsed routine."

Just then, the dog handler returned. He stopped in the doorway while the dog waited outside.

"Jackie followed the boy's scent to the car park over there and to one of the empty parking spaces. Then nothing. We're probably looking at a car that took off."

"Not good," the sergeant said. "Then we can almost assume someone drove off with the boy."

"Yes, I think you might be right. Either way, there isn't much more we can do here," the dog handler said, and waited for further instructions.

"We'll have to assume someone took Karl-Axel away from here," the sergeant said. Then he picked up the dispatch radio and closed the door behind him before he called all available units.

"The boy, Karl-Axel, has probably been taken somewhere by car. The dog followed his scent to an empty parking space in the upper right corner of the car park. Make sure you talk to as many people as possible," he ordered. "And knock on every door in the surrounding area. We need to talk to everyone. Understood?"

1

PRESENT TIME

Chief Inspector Sara Vallén paced back and forth in the corridor. Her lips moved but she didn't make a sound. She counted her steps and each time she reached ten, she turned so suddenly that her long curls flew up into the air. She hated waiting. Especially for others. She would never be late like this. *An appointed time is an appointed time*, she thought to herself. Commissioner Beatrice Larsson, on the other hand, seemed to consider time to be something more elastic. She was rarely—if ever—on time. It bothered Sara. But she never said anything. Instead, she kept counting her steps.

A moment later, Sara heard the distinct sound of high heels on the stairs. The glass doors opened and Beatrice Larsson entered, dressed in a fur coat. Her hips moved from side to side as she walked and Sara couldn't stop herself from giggling. Beatrice Larsson could be described as many things, but she wasn't coquettish. She was tall and powerful. And just like that, Sara wasn't annoyed anymore. After all, it was hard not to like Beatrice.

"I know, I'm late," Beatrice said, and winked at Sara, who laughed.

"Well, I must say you're not the most punctual person I know. But I forgive you, once again."

Beatrice shrugged her shoulders, opened the door to her office, and walked in before Sara. She hung her fur coat on a hook next to the door.

"It's too humid to be wearing fur today," she said, and pointed at the armchair by the round table in the corner. Sara sat down.

"It's time for your annual performance review," Beatrice sighed, and reached for a document on the table in front of them.

"Yeah," Sara answered.

"We'll talk about the different aspects of your performance in the usual manner," Beatrice said, and tapped her pen against the table.

"Yup."

Sara didn't expect much from the meeting, at least not in terms of a pay rise.

The meeting went on for about an hour before Beatrice shot Sara a serious look and tapped her pen against the table again to signal that the meeting was over. And Sara didn't really have anything to add. She had received both a raise and praise for her hard work.

"Thanks," she said, and stood up. When she had opened the door to leave, she turned to her boss to tell her that she was worried about how things were developing within the police force. But when she realised Beatrice was already busy reading something seemingly important on her computer, she changed her mind and decided to leave it for a later time. Everyone was bored with talking about the consequences of the restructuring anyway. It was better to focus on the future.

The police station was peaceful and almost completely quiet. The sky was grey and lay like a frozen blanket over people's souls. Most of Sara's colleagues were out on assignments, except for Jörgen Berg, who had called earlier that morning to tell her he wasn't feeling well. Sara went into her office and had a look at all the cases she was supervising. A month ago, Beatrice Larsson had managed to convince Malmö to let Torsten Venngren and Jonny Svensson work in Lund as she wanted to keep her major investigation team together. The deal was that Malmö would also have access to the team whenever they needed. Both Torsten and Jonny had been happy with the decision. Torsten had told Sara he wanted to work closer with her, and Jonny was lazy and probably thought it would be easier that way. At least that's what Sara thought. She smiled to herself. She had felt more comfortable working alongside Jonny lately. She thought he seemed happier, nicer, and more engaged, which she had also told him.

She leaned back in her chair and stretched out like a cat. She even made a cat-like sound. She knew she should go through her email, as well as all the documents on her desk. Official letters, invitations to surveys that needed to be answered, and law amendments were spread across the desk in unorganised stacks. She knew keeping her documents in order wasn't one of her strengths. At the top of one of the stacks was a list of cold cases. She read through the list without much enthusiasm. There were other things she should focus on, things she had procrastinated doing.

"How much paperwork can one police station produce?" she exclaimed just as Torsten passed by her office with his jacket thrown over his shoulder. He stopped outside her door.

"A lot, it looks like," he laughed. "I remember when we thought the computer would mean a paperless working environment . . . I honestly think we've never had as many documents lying around as we do now."

"Maybe we were lazier before, but as soon as we installed the computers, we started using paper like never before. We print everything as if we're scared of forgetting things if we don't get it onto a physical piece of paper."

"You might be on to something. Do you need help?"

"No, I need to deal with this on my own. I'm incredibly good at collecting documents. I don't throw anything out and I don't file anything."

"I see," Torsten laughed. "By the way, how was your performance review?"

"Well, I was pleasantly surprised by the pay rise. At least Beatrice is trying."

"Sounds like something to be happy about?"

"Maybe, but I think I'd better focus on my stacks here," Sara said.

Torsten nodded and walked towards the stairs.

"I'm on my way to follow up on an anonymous tip," he said. "I'll be back in an hour."

"See you," Sara said, and blew him a kiss. He blew a kiss in return.

Sara turned her focus back to her mountain of documents and sighed.

She started with rearranging everything on the table in new, more organised stacks. Then she picked up a document and read it. Then she picked up another one and another one and another one. Every couple of minutes she had to stand up and stretch a little. She had made some impressive progress when her phone rang. *Thank God,* she thought, and answered the call.

"Sara Vallén, Major Crimes, Lund Police Department."

"Hello, this is Sergeant Kristian speaking," a familiar voice said at the other end of the line.

"Hi there," Sara said curiously.

"This is a bit strange, but do you remember that boy who went missing from his preschool in Linero twenty years ago?"

"Well . . ." Sara said, and thought about it for a while. "I've heard about the case, but I'm not up-to-date with the details."

"Okay. Because the police up in Falun received a tip. The tip is interesting from a couple of different angles."

Sara urged her colleague to go on.

"The tip was regarding a man with known Nazi sympathies. The caller told us this man and his wife are regularly visited by men from the Nordic Resistance Movement . . ." The sergeant paused for a second.

"Yes?" Sara said impatiently. Sara knew the sergeant well and appreciated his meticulous work. But he was also a bit too slow for her taste. Every cell in her body tingled when things moved too slowly.

"Yes, sorry," the sergeant said. "The operator who took the call understood it as if the caller was a neighbour of this Nazi. But anyway . . . Well, the caller told my colleague about a sticker on the man's mailbox. The sticker says *Folktribunen,* which is a magazine that no longer exists. But the Nordic Resistance Movement used to publish it. At least I think so." The sergeant fell silent again.

"I see, but what does this have to do with the missing boy?" Sara took a deep breath.

"Well . . ." the sergeant continued.

Sara sighed.

"I know you're impatient, so I'll get to the point. The caller told us he lives close to the Nazi but when my colleague asked him to tell him where that was, he didn't want to tell us. He's probably trying to stay anonymous. People who call in with tips are normally quite nervous. Anyway, my colleague asked the caller why he had decided to call now. The caller told my colleague that he was passing by the Nazi couple's garden one late afternoon after dark when he heard them argue. He was standing behind a hedge so he couldn't see them. This was where the caller accidentally gave away that he was in fact the Nazi's neighbour, by the way. The fight was about the couple's son. According to the caller, the man shouted something like: 'You went all the way to Skåne to steal someone else's child. You're insane.' Apparently, the man also said he never wanted the child in the first place. The caller didn't think much about it at first, but later he recalled the couple acting strangely one spring twenty years ago. My colleague asked more questions about the couple and the caller told us that years ago—you see, he's lived in the same house for ages . . ."

Jesus, Sara thought.

". . . you don't have to take notes on this."

"I'm not taking notes," Sara hissed. "Please, continue."

"Years ago—twenty-two years ago this September—they had a child. A son. The caller bumped into the mother a couple of times as she took the boy for a walk. A year later, maybe in November, something must have happened. Because suddenly, they pulled all the blinds and stopped leaving the house. One day, they stepped out with a bunch of suitcases. The caller said this must have been in April or May. After that, he didn't see them for months. He couldn't say exactly how many. He suspects they went somewhere. In hindsight, the caller thinks they left to cover up the fact that they had kidnapped a child. A while later, the caller and his family moved abroad and rented their house out. Years later, they returned home. The caller hadn't really thought about his neighbours for years, but when he heard them arguing about their son a couple of days ago, it all came back to him. He told us the argument turned quite chaotic after the man had accused his wife of stealing a child. In return, the woman screamed something about her husband being a murderer. Then she didn't say anything more. The caller stayed behind the hedge until things calmed down and then he hurried back to his house. When he passed the gate, he saw the woman following her husband up the stairs to the house. Apparently, it looked like they had calmed down at that point."

Sara inhaled sharply.

"My colleague took the tip very seriously and started looking into missing children in southern Sweden. He found the Karl-Axel Altenius case and realised the time of his disappearance fitted right into the caller's story. Also, he saw the boy still hadn't been found."

"Wow, what if—" Sara said, then interrupted herself. "Do we know what family we're talking about here?"

"Our colleagues in Falun will get back to us about that. They keep track of the Nazis up there, so it shouldn't take too long to find out who they are. And in this case, we're looking for a whole family, which limits the search quite a bit. This could obviously be a long shot, but still."

"Right, but still . . ." Sara's heart was racing and her whole body tensed up. It was a wonderful feeling. The best.

"I assume you've written a memo about this? Would you send it over? I also want the reference number for the case with the missing boy," she said.

"I've already uploaded the memo to the case file," the sergeant said, and gave her the case number.

"Super. Thanks."

After the call, Sara opened the case file in their filing system and printed it out. She was still on edge and felt one of her eyelids start to droop. She opened her eye wider to regain control over it. It was uncomfortable when her eye acted up and she knew it bothered others too, as it made her look pompous. But she couldn't help it, and it happened especially at times when she felt tense. She went into the archive and found the boxes from 1998 belonging to the case with the missing boy. She was glad the boxes were still in there and hadn't been moved to the National Archives, which would have meant a lot of extra work.

"Jesus, look at all this paperwork," she complained to herself. Then she thought about how much she preferred reading on an actual sheet of paper compared to reading something on a screen. She took a seat behind her desk, and as she read through document after document in the case file, she quickly realised she wasn't as restless when she cared about what she was reading.

"I'm back now."

Sara looked up and saw Torsten standing in the doorway.

"Great; there has been a development related to one of the cold cases," she said, and asked Torsten to have a seat.

"Oh, really? How exciting," Torsten said, and chuckled.

"This time, we might actually be on to something interesting," Sara said.

Torsten pulled out a chair and sat down next to Sara.

"A two-year-old boy went missing in 1998 and was never found. How is it even possible?"

Torsten looked down at his hands.

"I worked that case," he said quietly.

"Why are you whispering?"

"I'm ashamed," Torsten said, and looked into Sara's eyes.

"Are you trying to tell me you're the only one who has ever failed an investigation?" Sara smiled at him.

"No, but this case was something out of the ordinary, and the fact that this child, Karl-Axel . . . You see, I still remember his name . . . The fact that he was never found . . . It was horrible. And it completely destroyed the mother. I wonder if she ever recovered."

"It must have been hard on you," Sara said, and kept looking at Torsten. She told him about the anonymous tip and his face lit up. Even if his eyes were still full of regret about the old case, she could see the fire in them.

Torsten was one of the best officers on the force, and he took failure much harder than most people. *That's the downside of everyone trusting in you and you putting too much pressure on yourself,* Sara thought. She smiled again and stroked the back of his hand. On the outside he looked calm, but she knew he was restless and eager to get started. She didn't have to tell Torsten about the importance of being methodical, as working methodically was another one of his strengths.

"What did you find last time, then?" Sara asked curiously.

"Nothing. At least nothing that led to any conclusions," Torsten said, and frowned. "But I remember this feeling . . . I don't know how to explain it, but I felt like I was chasing this elusive shadow that disappeared every time I tried to catch it. Do you know what I mean?" Torsten asked Sara.

Torsten was usually a man of few words and Sara was surprised by his language.

"I know that feeling very well," she said, and frowned too.

Torsten stared off into space. It looked like he wasn't thinking about anything at all, but Sara knew that wasn't the case.

"I spent a lot of time wondering how a child could go missing like that without anyone seeing or knowing anything. I thought the most likely explanation was that someone close to the child had something to do with it. But we couldn't find anything at all to go on. I was probably asking the wrong questions. Today, maybe I would've asked different ones," he said after thinking about it for a second.

"Probably. But things might have turned out the same anyway."

"I know. It's just that I wasn't a very experienced interrogation officer back then. I couldn't wrap my mind around what had happened."

"Well, that doesn't sound like you at all. It doesn't sound like the Torsten I know."

"Maybe not, but I've grown a lot since then." Torsten rolled his eyes.

"It looks like a difficult case, and I can imagine it was a challenge to find the right method."

"Yes, you're right. But we tried a bunch of different approaches and asked the same questions over and over again. We just couldn't find a way forwards. And I couldn't shake the feeling of that elusive shadow."

"Either way, we have a new lead to follow up now. Together with the police in Falun, of course. We'll see where it takes us. But I have a good feeling about this. I'm not sure it's an actual hunch or just hope though." Sara watched as Torsten ran his hand through his hair like a comb. *What a wonderful person*, she thought. She loved him. Not in the same way as she loved Anders, but still. An impulse made her run her fingers through her own curls. *Pacing*, she thought.

"We need to find a new angle," Torsten said, and Sara noticed something familiar in his gaze.

"I understand a child can go missing. Do you remember that girl who was supposed to be picked up by her grandfather, who accidentally picked up the wrong child? Things like that can happen. But it's very uncommon that a child goes missing without ever being found. I've only really heard of cases like that in other countries," Sara said.

"I think I've been blaming myself for all these years, although I've never said anything about it. I worked so hard but couldn't produce results. I still can't believe we never found that boy, dead or alive."

Sara didn't want to take part in the blame game so she decided not to say anything.

They kept reading in silence. Sara was looking for clues.

"I'm looking for mistakes," Torsten said, and looked up.

"That's where we're different, you and I."

Sara got up and left Torsten alone. She saw him move his index finger up and down one of the documents. He was obviously affected by the unsolved case. She too found it especially difficult to work cases involving children as she couldn't help identifying with the mothers.

Sara wanted to speed up the process of assigning a prosecutor to the preliminary investigation, so she sent the case off electronically for random allocation. Once that was done, she picked up the phone and asked the secretary to speed up the process.

2

Torsten read through the documents in the case file until his eyes started hurting. He leaned back, closed his eyes, and tried to look back in time. Although he tried his hardest to see something that he had missed back then, nothing happened. No visions appeared to him. No clarity. As he tried to remember every word of the interrogations, he twisted one of his curls between his thumb and index finger. His hair was almost completely grey now and he noticed it had taken on a less-soft texture.

I wish I grew less soft with age too, he thought. He had always been a softy. He was just as tall and gangly as he had always been and he didn't have a pot belly like most men his age. He smiled to himself before he continued reading about the boy and his parents. The parents who never got their son back.

That uneasy feeling of the elusive shadow . . . Maybe they were finally about to turn the shadow into something less elusive—something they could touch. He allowed himself to feel hopeful for a second.

Torsten was on his way out of the office when he heard Rita enter the station. She stomped her feet and jumped up and down a couple of times.

"It's bloody cold out there," she said to Torsten, who aimed a bleak smile her way and asked her to come with him. She followed him without asking questions and shook her head like a dog to dry her wet hair. It was damp and cold outside.

Sara's face lit up when she saw Rita entering her office together with Torsten. Torsten had noticed how close the two women were. Their relationship wasn't like the relationship between himself and Sara. They knew each other in a different way. He felt slightly jealous, even if he knew how much Sara liked him too. Maybe he wasn't really jealous of their relationship per se, but of the fact that women seemed to have the ability to get close to each other on all levels, developing deep and emotional bonds. Male relationships were different—at least those he had experienced.

Rita walked up to Sara and leaned in for a hug. Torsten felt left out. *How silly*, he thought, and forced himself to shake it off.

"A two-year-old boy went missing in 1998. He was never found. We've received an anonymous tip from Falun that might give us a new angle. I've reopened the case," Sara explained.

"Wow," Rita said, and shook her head again. "Holy crap."

"I need you to get involved too. Torsten will brief you." It was an order. Torsten and Rita both looked serious and nodded.

"Make a plan and we'll present it to the prosecutor. Maybe you have one already, Torsten?" Sara asked, and turned to Torsten.

"I think we should start by questioning the mother, Molly Altenius, again. We also need to talk to her husband, Staffan Ehn. I must have missed something back then. After that we must focus on Falun. I'll call them again to see if they can tell us what family the tip was about."

"Okay, sounds good. Did you call them already?" Sara asked. "Altenius and Ehn, I mean?"

Torsten shook his head and scoffed.

"When would I've had time to call them? And by the way, shouldn't we talk to the prosecutor first?"

"I'll begin with answering your first question. No, of course you haven't had time. And as an answer to your second question, I think we can start without talking to the prosecutor. Speaking of prosecutors, I just found out Åke Baum has been selected for the case, which means we should be free to do whatever we feel is necessary," Sara said confidently.

"Come on, Torsten," Rita said, and grabbed his arm.

Torsten brought the case file with him to the conference room and spread all the documents out across the table. He walked up to the whiteboard and wrote down all the names and places that were relevant to the case, just like they always did. While he wrote, he told Rita about the case and did his absolute best to give her all the details.

Rita took notes and snapped a couple of photos of the whiteboard when Torsten was done.

"I find it interesting that you never found the boy," Rita said.

"If anything, I think it's bloody strange," Torsten said.

3

Torsten flicked through the documents in front of him for a while before pushing them away. He picked up his mobile phone and tried calling Molly Altenius and Staffan Ehn. Neither of them picked up. *Typical*, he thought. He turned his focus back to the documents and started going through the interrogation transcripts from the old investigation. After a while, he leaned back and noticed the emotions the old case had roused within him.

He remembered how the young Molly Altenius had looked at him with something accusing in her eyes. "I don't understand. Who would take someone else's child?" she had asked him with tears streaming down her face. He had felt horrible. But back then he had been sure he would find her son. Eventually, they had closed the case to free up some resources and Torsten remembered how hard it had been to tell Molly that it was over. That all his work had been meaningless.

He returned to his desk. After all these years, he could still remember Molly Altenius's and Staffan Ehn's voices. But nothing felt different when he looked at the case this time. The couple had no enemies. They hadn't been warned, and they hadn't noticed anything out of the ordinary. Staffan Ehn studied to become an engineer at the time of the boy's disappearance. Nothing strange there. Molly was a med student, and the baby's biological father was a man who died when the boy was still a baby and who had never been part of his son's life. His sister and mother lived in the States, but the little boy had no passport and there was no reason to believe he had been taken out of the country. They had investigated every aspect of the boy's family's past, but everything seemed normal. Maybe the fact that the boy's parents were both so perfect, ambitious, and loving was what had felt like a shadow all this time? Torsten didn't know.

He sighed and called his colleagues in Falun, but they were still looking into who the Nazi family could be. They promised to get back to him the following day. Torsten let out another sigh and tried calling the boy's parents again. They still didn't pick up.

He decided to go home. It was late and Rita had left the office, so there was no point in him staying. When he stopped by Sara's office to say goodbye, she was busy reading something. She didn't turn around but asked him if he had heard anything from Falun. When he told her they had nothing to tell them yet, she muttered something and kept reading.

"See you tomorrow with new energy," she said.

Torsten hummed but didn't say anything.

Three minutes later, he stepped into the train station. He was hungry and stopped by Asian Express. He ordered and sat down at a table.

It was March and the days were getting longer. It was election year and the social climate in Sweden was tougher than ever. People seemed to have adapted a more aggressive approach to things, and the growing polarisation in society made him sad. Tolerance and solidarity seemed to be concepts of the past. Now people wanted harsher punishments and deportations, and many claimed all rapes were committed by foreigners. Times had become tougher for those who were already in a tough spot and the borders were closed a while back. He didn't know how to act in the harsh social climate. He worried about the normalisation of hate, threats, and violence against anyone who spoke Swedish with a foreign accent, as well as the constant debate of who and what was "Swedish." The sense of unity was lost, and although he knew most people were good, it worried him that they stayed so quiet. What made things worse was that he knew he was one of the quiet ones. The brutal truth was that he simply didn't have the guts to stick his neck out. For every day that went by, he became more and more aware of what a coward he was. It was easy to be brave at work, but much harder in private. He had never been so bothered by it as he was now.

He ate his food but had lost his appetite. He walked with heavy steps through the tunnel and up the stairs to the platform. The train to Malmö took ten minutes. He stared out the window the whole way.

He remembered how he started to suspect the child had been murdered a month or so into the investigation. But he had pushed his negative thoughts aside and continued acting professionally. Staying professional was his refuge when things turned ugly. It protected him—protected his soul from breaking.

When he got home, he tried calling Molly and Staffan again without any luck. He wondered if they had been able to move on. If they could ever live normal lives again.

He decided to stop thinking about the case and sat down in an armchair with one of his favourite books—*King Salomon*, written under the pseudonym Émile Ajar. It made him laugh.

When he finally went to bed, he fell asleep and dreamed about little children tumbling around in his field of vision. They were all winged.

4

Sara sat down by the kitchen table. She was exhausted. It was late. She hadn't eaten all day. She had forgotten. Her children weren't home. Johannes was probably out with his friends or his girlfriend, and she was pretty sure Klara and Bella were busy with their studies. Or was tonight the night when they were helping a group of unaccompanied refugee youths with their homework? She was proud of them for doing something to help with inte gration.

In a way, she liked being home alone, but it felt empty as well. *Luxury problems*, she thought, and walked over to the fridge to assess her options.

"Should I cook some food or take the lazy way out?" she asked herself, and opened the fridge. She saw a couple of cheeses on one of the shelves. Anders had brought them over. Then she spotted an open bottle of wine. Well, why not? She took out the cheese, an olive jar, and the wine. She thought about what a fantastic experience it had been to meet Anders in the way she did. He entered her life in a time of crisis, during a summer when everything was turned upside down—again. She had really been forced to reassess herself after falling in love with Peter Matsson. *Peter Matsson, who turned out to be married to a woman he forgot to mention,* Sara thought sarcastically. Peter Matsson, who turned out to be a wife-beater and a liar who beat Sara up so badly she could barely move when he was done with her. She had walked right into his trap and allowed him to get close to her although she had seen the red flags. Even after she had figured out who he really was, she hadn't been able to walk away from the destructive relationship. She was having a hard time forgiving herself. But from her own experience from working similar cases over the years, she knew walking away was actually a really hard thing to do. She knew very well that any woman could end up a victim of domestic abuse and that it didn't matter how educated, smart, or strong she was.

The worst part was that Sara had allowed it to happen to her despite knowing all that. She thought about when she was young and her father, who was a diplomat, was kidnapped during a time in her life when she was also raped. The two events and the horrible years that followed had haunted her ever since. What her father had been through made him mentally ill and at the time, she felt like he was letting her down. Much later in life, she realised that he didn't let her down because he wanted to, but because he was sick.

She *did* have a present mother. But Sara's relationships with men had always been tumultuous. She didn't trust them. Even when she married Göran and had children with him, she let her past experiences affect her. She couldn't love him with her whole heart. There was something holding her back. She would probably have left him anyway though, as they were simply not a great match for each other. At least it made her feel better to think that way.

Sara cut some bread, arranged the cheese on a beautiful platter, lit some candles, and poured the wine. Then she sat down again. Enjoyed the silence. She let her mind race and left her past in the past. Instead, she thought about Anders again. Anders, who was such a loving person and who put up with her strange approach to love and relationships. Anders, whom she hurt sometimes but who always took a step back when she did. He never blamed her. It was so wonderful and it made her feel free in a way she had never experienced before. But she couldn't quite shake her past. It wasn't an ideal situation, especially not for Anders.

Despite her complicated emotions, she had never been anything but devoted to her children though, and she had always been a loving and present mother. Today, she was strong and healthy. She thought about her own mother and felt grateful. Her mother had always been the family's rock who had never given up and always loved her. Sara relaxed.

Suddenly, she heard her phone ringing in the hallway. She had forgotten it in her jacket pocket. She got up and went to take the call. It was Klara.

"Hi, sweetie," she said.

"Hi, Mum! We just wanted to make sure you were home. We'll be back in a minute and we really need to talk to you," Klara said. She sounded upset.

"Is something wrong?"

"Yes, I would definitely say so," her daughter said, "but let's talk about it when we get home."

"Okay, but—" Sara said, but didn't get to finish the sentence before Klara ended the call.

Sara sat down again, but changed her mind and stood up. She was anxious and couldn't relax. *It's bloody impossible to get a peaceful moment around here*, she thought. There was always something going on.

Ten minutes later, she heard Klara and Bella outside. They sounded angry and very upset.

The door opened and the girls stormed in. Sara sighed and went to meet them in the hallway. They were both talking at the same time.

"Calm down, I can't hear what you're saying. Take off your jackets and come sit in the kitchen."

They both started talking again.

"No, stop it! One at the time," Sara ordered, and slammed both her hands into the table.

The girls fell silent. Klara nodded at Bella, who took a deep breath.

"Mum, we're upset! That's why we're both talking," she said.

"Yes, I understand. But I can't hear what you're saying. Now, tell me what happened."

"Tonight we helped a group of unaccompanied refugee youths with their homework at uni," Bella said, and took another deep breath. When Sara realised she was holding back tears, she stroked her hand gently.

"A group of guys showed up and told us they were nationalists. They threatened our students and scared the shit out of all of us." Bella's chin started to tremble.

Sara got up and sat down next to Bella instead, stroking her hair.

"In what way did they threaten you?" she asked with a serious look on her face as Bella's tears fell onto the table.

"They attacked the refugee students and told them they weren't welcome here. Then they said they would make their lives a living hell," Klara said. "And then they approached Bella. They stood super close to her and told her she was a traitor to the nation. And then they turned around and pointed at the other Swedish students who were there to tutor these kids. I mean, it felt like they were threatening us. Then they left," Klara told her mother with her blue-green eyes wide open.

"How many were they?"

"Five. They were all blond and you know . . . super Swedish. They wore black trousers and white shirts. They looked strangely proper, if you know what I mean?" Bella said after calming down slightly.

Sara was furious. "And what happened to your students?"

"One of the younger guys was so scared. He called his foster family and they came and picked him up. I don't think we'll see him again. Reza, another one of our students, stood up and tried to say something, but they ignored him and turned to the refugee girls instead. There wasn't much more Reza could do, but he was very brave," Klara said, and looked down at the table. "It was horrible. But they all stayed until those idiots were gone. And Bella and I and the rest of us walked the students home. That's why we're late." Klara looked devastated, which made Sara sad and furious at the same time.

"What were their names, these nationalists?" she asked, and clenched her jaws. She wasn't tired anymore and her whole body tensed up.

"No idea," Klara answered "But I thought I recognised one of them. He's also in law school so I've seen him around Juridicum."

"Is he the same age as you? And what about the others?"

"I'm not sure if all of them are law students, but I know that if they are, they're not my age. I think I would have recognised them if they were. I only recognised one of them. He's tall with almost white hair. He's pretty recognisable. I have no idea if the others are students."

"Then I'll have to find out," Sara said.

"Maybe we can do it ourselves?" Bella suggested. "We could at least try."

Sara nodded, but she had already decided she was going to find out more about the nationalist group.

"At this point I would say what they did was harassment, but it gets more serious because of the hate motive," she said. "I'll talk to the prefect of Juridicum."

"Yes, that would be great, Mum. Thanks. We'll try to find out who they are and if they study law. Teamwork," Bella said with a smile.

"You're the best, Mum," Klara said, and hugged her mother.

"Do you guys want something to eat?" Sara asked, and stroked her daughters' backs.

"Yes, please. We're starving," answered Klara.

Sara grabbed a couple of eggs, a jar of mayonnaise, a cucumber, and some tomatoes from the fridge. Then she found a bag of frozen shrimp in the freezer.

"*Starving*, Mum," Klara repeated.

5

It took a while before someone picked up the phone.

"Daniel Vasquez, Lund University," a deep voice finally answered.

"Hello. My name is Sara Vallén and I'm working with the Lund Police Department. I have a daughter named Klara Vallén and she's a first-semester law student here in Lund."

"Hi there, Sara. Has something happened?"

"Yes, I would say so," Sara said, and twisted a lock of hair between her fingers to stay calm.

"Please, tell me."

"My daughters, Klara and Bella Vallén, have started a student association that helps unaccompanied refugee youths with their homework. They've been given permission to borrow a room at Juridicum to host these meetings. I assume this means you support this type of activity?"

"Yes, your daughters' initiative is truly fantastic and creative. And there has been a lot of interest to join the association from what I've heard."

"Yesterday, they were upset and scared when they came home," Sara said, and paused for a second before she told the prefect what had happened.

"Oh my God, who are these people?" Daniel exclaimed, and Sara heard him swallow a couple of times.

"Are you saying you're not aware of all the associations that operate within the walls of Juridicum?" she asked sceptically.

"Well, I'm aware of all official associations, but I had no idea there was a nationalistic one," he answered quickly. "Unfortunately, I can't tell you who these guys are as I've never heard about this group."

"Then I suggest you find out, because I really want to know. It's a safety precaution. My daughters, their friends in the association, and the young people they're helping shouldn't have to deal with this."

"Of course not. I'll look into it straight away. They're probably aware of what they can and can't do according to the law though. Unfortunately, we can't stop nationalistic associations from existing. But there is a huge difference between a political association and an association that takes part in criminal activities. We do *not* tolerate any criminal activity, obviously."

Sara left her name and number with Vasquez, and he promised to get in touch with Klara.

As soon as they had ended the call, Sara called the girls to tell them what the prefect had said. She also asked Klara to be careful.

"Maybe it's better if you host the next class at my house?" she suggested.

"Mum, you know we can't be there. We need access to computers and books and stuff. We have to be at Juridicum. We have no other choice."

"Okay, but be very careful and don't let your students walk home alone. Their situation is tough enough as it is."

"I promise. But the next class isn't today, it's on Thursday. Two days from now."

"The thing is, I might have to travel up to Falun this week. I want you to stay with your father when I'm away. And I want you to tell him about this."

"Oh, but you know how he is. He'll forbid us from going and then he'll probably lock us up," Klara laughed.

"No, he can't. You're adults, you know."

"I do. But still.. . . . You know how he is."

"Yes. He just cares about you girls, that's all. You have to tell him, or I will. Tonight."

"Sure, we'll tell him tonight. I promise."

Sara wasn't sure if she could trust her daughters, so she decided to tell Johannes as well. That way, their father would definitely hear about what had happened. She smiled at her plan.

She sat down to go through the case file from 1998. How would she have survived if she had lost a son like that? She looked at the greyish-brown landscape outside the window. If she could skip a couple of months every year, she would pick January, February, and March without hesitation. She could barely stand them. When she caught a glimpse of her own reflection in the window, she didn't like what she saw. She pinched her cheeks to give them some colour. *Jesus*. She had to start working out. It had been a long time since she practiced judo, and she hadn't gone for a run since October. She felt like a sack of potatoes. But she also knew it was up to her to make the change. Nobody else would make it for her. She rubbed her face again. For some reason, it suddenly made her feel more alert. And more determined.

6

Torsten walked past Sara's office when he came to work. She was on the phone with a glum expression on her face. She looked up and aimed a dismissive wave his way. He noticed one of her eyelids was drooping slightly, which meant she was unhappy or upset. Or both.

He took off his jacket and hung it on a hook next to the door to his office. Then he sat down in the armchair and thought about the dream he'd had. Was it an omen? *Maybe*, he thought, but decided to let it go. He didn't believe in anything that wasn't supported by science.

He began reading through the case file connected to the missing boy. He found it hard to focus. A thousand thoughts raced through his mind. Although his wife had left him years ago, he missed her more than ever. She had been his best friend. His beloved wife. And it had taken him by surprise that she had slowly slipped away from him. Or perhaps it had been the opposite. He flicked through the documents and found the transcript of an interrogation with Molly Altenius from 1998.

Interrogating Officer: Could you tell me about Staffan's past?
Molly Altenius: Why?

Torsten closed his eyes and remembered how Molly had twisted a piece of tissue paper between her fingers after blowing her nose with it.

IO: We're not suspecting him of anything. But we have to look at this from all angles to find something that might help us find your son.

MA: He moved a lot. His father is in the military and they move all the time. Last time he lived with his parents, they lived in Falun. Staffan moved out in 1995 and began studying mechanical engineering in the autumn. We met a year later. At a party.

Torsten sat up straight. Staffan. Falun. Of course. The shadow suddenly felt less elusive, as if Torsten could see its outline. The tip could very well be more than a long shot. He kept reading.

IO: Have you met his family?
MA: No, not yet.
IO: How come?
MA: They live up north so we haven't had the chance to meet. They came to visit once, but Karl-Axel and I ended up staying home with the flu.

Torsten remembered how her chin had trembled and how she had cried silently. And how he had put his big hand on top of hers in an attempt to comfort her.

7

Rita was still upset when she came to work. The night before, she and Linda had had their first real argument. The whole thing had ended with Linda crying and Rita being pissed off. Very pissed off. Linda had rushed out the door and slammed it so hard behind her that it echoed throughout the whole building, which had then made Rita even more furious. She hadn't been able to sleep afterwards. She had twisted and turned in bed for what felt like an eternity before finally glancing at her watch and realising it was just before 4 a.m. At that point, she had decided to go for a run instead of sleeping. The run had helped her clear her mind and she had cried in the shower afterwards. Angry tears.

Linda had accused her of not caring enough about her, being married to her job, and not being able to step out of her role as a police officer. Rita knew she had a point. But she was equally passionate about her love for Linda. She was a passionate person overall. She was definitely passionate about work. And about working out. And running. And her home. But still, Linda had made her furious. Because if there was one thing she hated, it was people acting like martyrs.

"I can't believe you're lying there crying and feeling sorry for yourself," she had said to Linda—to the person she loved. When she thought about it now, she realised how mocking her tone must have sounded. *Smart? Not so much.*

"What do you mean?" Linda had asked, her usually soft face looking stern. The light from the lamp in the corner had made her red hair look like fire.

What *did* she mean? Rita remembered thinking about it for a while before finally answering.

"I think you're acting like a martyr," she had said, not quite sure if that was what she actually meant.

As a response, Linda had got out of bed and aimed a murderous look Rita's way. Then she had reached for her clothes, thrown them on, and slammed the door shut behind her.

Jesus, how dramatic, Rita remembered thinking after Linda's emotional exit, and now when she sat in her office waiting for Molly Altenius, she felt bad about it. And she realised something. She wasn't innocent. She pictured herself sitting there with a grin on her face, acting like an absolute arsehole.

Should I call her? No, yes, no, yes. No, I won't call her. Maybe later.

She forced herself to stop thinking about Linda and her own guilty conscience. Instead, she made some notes about what to ask the woman she was about to interview. She was quite sure Molly had another child born after Karl-Axel. She looked through the documents on her desk. Yes, Molly had a daughter too. Molly and that man . . . Staffan Ehn.

She looked up and saw Torsten's face in the doorway. He smiled at her and told her that Staffan used to live in Falun.

"Don't you think it could be connected to the tip?" he asked.

"Sounds pretty likely," Rita said.

Rita looked at the woman in front of her. She looked tired. And grey. *A mother who never recovered,* Rita thought. Molly's blonde hair was tied back in a loose bun. She was still beautiful.

"Have a seat," Rita said, and pointed at the chair across from her own.

The woman sat down on the edge of the chair. She was obviously suspicious. Rita tried to look relaxed, as if their conversation wasn't that big of a deal.

"What is it? Do you have any new leads?" Molly Altenius asked. "Why else would you ask me to come here after twenty years?"

"We received an anonymous tip," Rita answered honestly. "A tip that *might* have something to do with Karl-Axel's disappearance twenty years ago."

The woman sat up straight and Rita noticed the spark in her eye. Rita realised she had never given up hope.

"Is he alive?"

"We don't know. There are still some uncertainties about the tip, but he could be."

"Why aren't you doing something, then?"

"We're working on it as we speak, but we need to talk to you and Staffan again to see if we can contextualise this tip before we move on."

The woman nodded slowly and her eyes filled with hope. She wanted to know and she wanted to help, which was always a good starting point when questioning someone. Her sceptical attitude disappeared in a heartbeat, and it was clear that she knew Rita and her colleagues weren't suspecting her of anything. She knew—because she had nothing to do with what happened to her son.

The investigation twenty years ago had been long and meticulous, and they had found nothing to suggest Molly or her husband were guilty of anything.

"How old were you when you had Karl-Axel?"

"I was twenty. He was born in May, and I started my first year in med school that autumn," the woman answered.

"Right. And when did you meet Staffan?"

"In September that year. He was twenty-three, and I fell in love with him instantly."

"Did he live in Lund then?"

"Yes, he did. But before that he lived in Kristianstad. He couldn't find a student flat in Lund in the beginning. If I remember things correctly, he moved to Lund in January 1996."

Rita studied the woman. When she leaned forwards, so did Rita. Torsten had taught her to always mirror the body language of the person you're interviewing. According to him, it was a great way to show respect and create trust.

"What happened to Karl-Axel's father?"

"We were never really together. And he died quite soon after Karl-Axel was born."

"I see," Rita said, and aimed a friendly smile Molly's way.

"It was sad, but I don't think he was mature enough to care for a child. Staffan was an amazing father."

Rita nodded.

"Do you know for how long Staffan lived in Falun?"

"His father was in the military so they moved around quite a bit. But they stayed in Falun for a long time. He moved into his own flat when he was nineteen. And then he moved to Kristianstad three years later."

"Did you ever consider that something in Staffan's past might be connected to Karl-Axel's disappearance?"

The woman stared at Rita as if she couldn't believe what she was hearing.

"Staffan's past? The police asked me about that back then too. No, not at all. He comes from a good family and had a wonderful childhood. Everything he touches turns to gold," she answered, and looked proud.

"Gold?" Rita wasn't sure she followed. She had never been much of a philosopher.

"Yes. I mean, everything he does turns out great—perfect, even. He's an amazing father to our daughter. She turns sixteen this year. They have such a beautiful relationship. He's an intelligent man with high morals and good values. I couldn't wish for a better man. That's why your question confuses me."

"I understand," Rita said, and felt slightly stupid. "But can you think of anything that might be of interest when it comes to his life before he met you? Was there anything that stood out about where he used to live or who his friends were for example?" Rita heard how difficult she made things sound. But the woman across from her was bright.

"Not that I can think of, and I think I would've known," she said.

"How does a normal day look for you guys?" Rita asked.

"Well, I work a lot and so does Staffan. He travels quite a bit for work. But not too much. He plays chess and golf. I run. That's all I have time for. I only travel on rare occasions when I have to attend a conference related to my research."

"I see. So nothing out of the ordinary, then?" Rita said, and couldn't stop a sarcastic smirk from playing on her lips. Luckily, Molly didn't seem to pick up on it. She nodded.

"As I said, his father was in the military and they moved a lot when he was young."

Rita decided it was time to tell Molly where the tip had come from. "The tip came from a caller in Falun. And we know Staffan used to lived there. Did you live there too? Or do you have any ties to the city?"

"Why do you think this has something to do with Karl-Axel?" The woman opened her eyes so wide that it looked like they were about to pop out of their sockets. Rita wasn't sure if she was scared, hopeful, shocked, or excited. Either way, she avoided giving her a straight answer.

"We're still not sure if the tip will actually lead to anything. But we have to follow every lead. Maybe you can tell us something more about Staffan's past and his time in Falun? Is he still in contact with anyone there? Maybe a golf buddy?" Rita had no idea if they had any golf courses in Falun, but she assumed they did.

Suddenly, it looked like the woman across from her was about to start crying. But she bit her lip and managed to control her emotions. *Years of practice*, Rita thought.

"I honestly don't know. We don't speak much about the past. It hurts too much. I don't think he's ever mentioned staying in touch with any-one back in Falun. I mean, he hasn't lived there in ages. But you'll have to ask Staffan. And I've never been there. But what are you going to do now?" Molly asked, and straightened her back.

"Yes, we're going to talk to Staffan too," Rita said. "And we're going to work together with our colleagues in Falun to investigate the tip we received yesterday," she added to make sure the woman across from her understood how seriously they took the new lead.

Molly Altenius looked very serious. "What can I do? Or what *should* I do?"

"Nothing, right now. We'll get back to you as soon as we know more," Rita said, and locked eyes with the woman.

"It'll be difficult doing nothing," the woman said laconically. "I assume you'll call me the moment you have something new to tell me?"

That's exactly what I just said, Rita thought to herself, and nodded.

The interview went on for a little while longer, but nothing new came out of what Molly told Rita—or possibly didn't tell her. Rita ended the interrogation and thanked Molly for her time.

"Promise you'll keep me updated?" Molly asked again before she left.

"Of course," Rita said. "Hopefully, it won't be too long."

"I'll talk to you later, then."

* * *

Rita wanted to talk to Sara, but she was on the phone. Rita didn't want to disturb her so she wrote her a note and left her office.

It was time to call Linda. It was time to apologise. If a woman who had lost her son forever could keep living with her husband despite how hard the loss must have been on their relationship, Rita should be able to apologise to the woman she loved. When she thought about it, her fight with Linda felt so silly in comparison. She picked up her phone and dialled Linda's number. For some reason Rita felt reluctant, but she suspected it was mostly about her hating to apologise for her way of life. *Just talk to her!* she thought.

8

Staffan Ehn had agreed to come to the station for an interview with Torsten at 12:15 p.m.

Torsten found it strange that Sara hadn't mentioned Ehn's connection to Falun. He thought she had read all the interrogation transcripts.

Sara looked up. She was still holding her mobile phone. Torsten noticed how worried she looked but decided to leave it for now.

"Falun," he said instead.

"What about Falun?"

"Staffan Ehn lived there for quite a while."

"He did?" Sara looked surprised. "I didn't know."

"I thought you read through the case file."

"I read the reports and all that, but I didn't go through all the interrogation transcripts. I thought *you* had read them. And I'm surprised you didn't remember this." She gave him a crooked smile.

"Well, it's quite a lot to go through. And I had forgotten all about it. I got reminded of it a moment ago as I was studying one of the interrogation transcripts. By the way, Staffan Ehn will be here soon. I have no idea what he was doing in Falun, but he was young when he lived there. Could be something there anyway though."

"Exciting. Let me know what you find out. And what about Molly Altenius?"

"Rita questioned her."

Sara nodded and looked at her phone again. Torsten took it as a sign that she wanted him to leave.

Torsten kept looking for something interesting in the case file but couldn't find anything he hadn't seen before. Time moved slowly. A while later, the receptionist called to tell him Staffan Ehn had arrived. Torsten ran his fingers through his hair and shook his head in an attempt to wake up a little. He needed a cup of coffee and decided to get one in the break room after picking Staffan Ehn up from reception. Maybe he wanted a cup too. Torsten smiled to himself as he walked through the station to receive his guest.

"Torsten Venngren," he said, and shook the hand of a man who was ten years younger.

"Staffan Ehn, but you already know that," the man said, and looked at Torsten. "We've met before. Twenty years ago. I remember you."

"Not bad," Torsten said, and asked Staffan Ehn to follow him to the interrogation room.

They both helped themselves to a cup of coffee from the machine on the way. Torsten quickly emptied his cup. He needed to wake up.

Torsten noticed that Staffan wasn't drinking his coffee. He just sat there, waiting. Torsten had seen something that he couldn't quite put his finger on in Staffan's gaze twenty years ago, but whatever it was, it was no longer there. Staffan Ehn was slender and tall, and judging by his clothes and shoes, he was wealthy. He radiated confidence.

"Okay, so what's going on here?" Staffan Ehn said, taking control of the situation.

Torsten decided to take it back right away. It had been twenty years, but he was still slightly suspicious of the man facing him.

"Sometimes we stumble across a new lead that makes us pick up an old case again."

The man across from him looked calm, but Torsten noticed a movement in his face. It was a tiny twitch underneath his right eye. It was over in an instant, and Torsten wondered if Ehn had even felt it. He probably hadn't.

"Okay, and I assume this is about Karl-Axel's disappearance?"

Torsten realised it was more of a statement than a question.

"Yes, that's correct," he answered anyway.

Staffan Ehn crossed his right leg over his left. Torsten paid close attention to his body language.

"How do you feel about that?"

"If you find him alive, I would be overjoyed, of course," Staffan said, and gave Torsten a serious look.

"Well, we're definitely not there yet. But we need to talk to you as the tip we received is tied to Falun," Torsten said, and studied the man on the other side of the table.

Staffan Ehn frowned. Torsten waited patiently. He noticed the man's hands were big and looked rougher than one might expect from someone who works in an office all day. But he still looked very much like a businessman, or maybe even a CEO. Torsten always had a hard time figuring out men like him. They had an attitude that he just didn't get, and they compared themselves to each other in a completely different way than Torsten and his male police colleagues.

"Let me think," he said.

"As you lived in Falun for quite a while, you probably got to know some people in the area. Especially considering you went to school there," Torsten suggested after a while.

"Yes, I had a couple of friends in school. I'll write you a list of the names I can remember."

Torsten pushed a notebook and a pen across the table.

"Did you have any enemies in Falun? Maybe someone even threatened you?"

"You asked me the same thing twenty years ago," Staffan Ehn said.

"Yes, and now I'm asking you again."

"I guess I'll give you the same answer again, then," Staffan said, and smiled faintly. "No."

"Any girlfriends?" Torsten looked right at him.

"Not really. I was too young."

"As I said, we received a tip from Falun. The tip is connected to the Nazi community. Does that mean anything to you?"

Staffan Ehn looked shocked and was lost for words, at least for a second.

"What the hell are you insinuating?" His blue eyes turned dark.

"Me asking you about Nazis doesn't insinuate anything at all. Let me rephrase. Does this bring any new memories to mind from your time in Falun?" Torsten refused to give up.

"No," Staffan Ehn answered.

"Could anyone you know have Nazi sympathies without your knowing about it?"

Staffan Ehn stood up and slammed his fist onto the table. "Are you suggesting I have Nazi friends?"

"So you do still have friends in Falun?"

"I *had* friends in Falun. I don't anymore," Staffan Ehn said curtly. He was still standing up.

"I think we'll end the interview here," Torsten said, and turned off the recording device. He realised he wouldn't get any further.

Staffan walked ahead of Torsten through the corridor. When they got to reception, Torsten reached out his hand. Staffan shook it a bit too hard and was clearly upset.

Torsten passed by Sara's office on his way back. She was on the phone again and waved him away.

9

Sara asked them all to come to her office. When Torsten, Rita, and Jonny entered the room, she asked them to have a seat. It was crowded, but there were enough chairs for them all.

"Jörgen has had a stroke. He's been admitted to hospital and his wife, Angela, said they're still not sure if he's going to make it. He's been sick for a couple of days and Angela thought it might be connected to the flu somehow. Apparently, he suddenly got a lot worse and then he collapsed. She called an ambulance. They're not sure what triggered the stroke."

You could cut the tension with a knife. The silence was deafening.

"We can't go to see him yet," she told the pale faces in front of her. "But at least his condition is stable, so I'm sure he'll be fine," she continued.

"What can we do to support Angela?" Rita asked.

"Right now, she's sitting next to him twenty-four seven, so I don't think there is much we can do. But I'll talk to her again tomorrow and let you know how we can help."

Sara was a lot more worried than she showed. She knew there was no way of knowing how things would go.

"Jonny, are you working on something at the moment?"

"Yes, I'm swamped."

"Me too," Rita said. "At least for now. But I'll help you guys if you need me, of course."

"It's okay, we'll be fine for now," Sara said, and stretched out her back. They would eventually need more brains to solve this case but she and Torsten would be enough for now.

Jonny sauntered out of the office, but Sara noticed his posture had improved. His new workout routine and diet had done him good and turned him into a much happier and easier person to deal with. *I guess the lemon has finally become sweet*, she thought.

"Our friends in Falun are expecting us," she said, and turned to Torsten. "Let's go there as soon as we can."

Torsten stood next to her with his head in the clouds. Sara nudged him with her elbow.

"Wake up."

"Yes, sorry."

"We're in a less than ideal position here and we have a twenty-year-old case with a bunch of loose ends. If this boy is alive, he's twenty-two years old. In other words, he's not a little boy anymore. Things like that can really mess with your mind."

Torsten looked defeated and Sara looked at him.

"It's not your fault, Torsten. You did what you could. This is not the first time a child has gone missing. You know that, right?" She fought an impulse to hug him. He looked lonely somehow, and she realised he had probably always looked that way. But it had become more and more noticeable since his wife left. The divorce had been rough on him.

"I know. But it's one of those cases I've always been ashamed of. I can't shake it," he said. "But I promise I'll try. Maybe we have a chance to resolve this once and for all." He straightened his back and smiled, but the smile didn't reach his eyes.

"Unfortunately, I've got something I need to deal with first," Sara said. She decided not to tell Torsten about what was happening to her daughters. "Tell me as soon as you know if our guys up in Falun have tracked down those Nazis."

10

Sara got up early the next morning. She hadn't spoken to Anders for days. She felt happy when she thought about how lucky she had been to end up with him after all these years. Just when she had needed him the most, after her short but violent relationship with Peter Matsson. There he was—the man she had been in love with as a young woman. At first, he had been her lawyer, but when they fell in love, he withdrew from the case. She was ashamed of how much she had hurt him. All those times when she had tried to push him away. She had done it because of her fear of being abandoned. *My poor baby*, she thought, *I've put him through so much*. But he stayed. Patient and strong in his love for her. It was beautiful.

She giggled to herself when she thought about how crazy she had acted. Her behaviour had felt strangely logical to her at the time though. She had her reasons. But still.

She picked up her phone.

"Hi, baby," she said, and heard Anders sigh on the other end of the line. Maybe it was a sigh of relief.

"Hi, honey," he said. "I haven't talked to you in ages."

Sara listened for something accusing in the tone of his voice, but it wasn't there. She knew that. She wanted to laugh again. At herself.

"Well, I'm not sure if I would call it ages. Three days, maybe?" she said before telling him she had missed him too.

"That's way too long if you ask me. Enough to make me worry. I know you're busy though, so I didn't want to bother you. And it feels like I've been in court twenty-four seven lately."

"But now I'm calling. Isn't that great?" Now she was really laughing.

"Yes!" he exclaimed, and started laughing too. "Do you want to meet up with me tonight?"

"I don't know if I can. I think I have to go to Falun today or first thing tomorrow."

"Oh, why?"

Sara told him about the case. Anders understood but still insisted on seeing her later that day if possible.

"Let's talk later and see if I can make it work. Something pretty serious has happened to Bella and Klara as well."

"What?" Anders said, sounding worried.

Sara told him what had happened to the girls. It made him upset and he wanted to come talk to them. He had worked a lot of cases centred around similar types of crimes.

"These acts are normally committed by young men like the ones you've just told me about. I'm not saying the extreme right is more violent than other extreme groups, but these guys sound like Nazis or fascists to me, and that's something completely different."

"That's what I'm worried about too. The girls are planning another class for tomorrow. I'm not sure if I should allow it."

"I think you should. You must never give in to this type of threat," Anders said resolutely.

"No, you're right. I'm just scared they'll get hurt."

"I guess I'll have to be there with them tomorrow, then," Anders said.

"I mean, you're wonderful," Sara said, and kissed him through the phone. "But I think Göran will be there."

"It wouldn't hurt if both of us were there," Anders insisted.

"No, I guess you're right. I have to go. I need to head to the station to figure out if we're going to Falun today or tomorrow. I call you this afternoon. I should know by then."

"I love you," Anders sighed.

"I love you too," Sara giggled. "Bye."

Sara got dressed and then went into Bella's room and kissed her forehead.

"Be careful today," she said, and stroked her daughter's cheek gently. "Call me if anything happens. Okay? I love you."

"Love you too, Mum. And I will. I promise." Her daughter yawned and stretched out like a cat.

Next, Sara went to Klara's room and repeated the whole process.

"Mum, can we continue with our classes or not?" Klara yawned.

"Your father will come with you tomorrow. Anders might come as well. That way, you can feel safe," Sara said, and kissed her daughter's forehead. "I love you."

Sara's bike stood next to the stairs in the garden and she walked it out to the sidewalk. She was worried about her daughters—and about the little boy who had gone missing without a trace. She decided to call Vasquez again first thing in the morning as he hadn't called her back.

When Sara arrived at the station, it was quiet and empty. She glanced at her watch. It was only 7:30 a.m. That explained it. There was a note on her desk from Karin Augustinsson.

The report is done and I put it on your desk. I've spoken to the local surveillance unit and they'll see what they can find out about these clowns. —Sergeant Karin A.

Thank God for my colleagues, Sara thought, and had a seat behind her desk. She spun her chair around a couple of times while she made up a plan for the day.

First, she would call Falun. Then she would call Daniel Vasquez. And then she would call Anders and Göran to talk to them about her daughters' study group.

She found the list of names that Ehn had given them and called Falun.

"Sergeant Sam Svensk," a man with a northern accent answered.

"Hi. This is Sara Vallén, chief inspector and lead investigator with the Major Crimes Department in Lund."

"Hello there! What can I do for you?"

Sara told Sam about Staffan Ehn. Then she asked him to check if any of Staffan's old friends belonged to the Nordic Resistance Movement or were known to have Nazi sympathies. He promised to look into it as soon as possible. Before they ended the call, he told her what they had already found. She heard his fingers fly across the keyboard as he looked for the right documents.

What if, she thought, and leaned back in her chair.

At that very moment, Torsten popped his head into Sara's office.

"We need to recruit someone to replace Jörgen," he said. "I don't think he'll be back for a while, poor guy. And poor Angela."

Sara stretched her neck, tilting her head to the right and then to the left. Then she straightened her back.

"I know. I've been thinking about asking Ali Saunier to cover for him until he gets back. What do you say? I've heard he's really good at what he does."

"I don't know Ali very well. But I'm sure it's a great idea. He seems like a nice guy. But I heard he had a hard time while working in Malmö. That's why he decided to relocate to Lund."

"All right. Could you go get Rita and meet me in the conference room? I have some news from Falun."

Torsten left the room.

"See you in five minutes. Try to get Jonny to come too," Sara shouted after him.

"Yes, Captain!" he shouted back.

11

Sara was just about to unlock the front door to her house when she heard upset voices out on the street. It was Klara and Bella, and a couple of deep, male voices. She heard the girls shouting, but couldn't make out what they were saying.

She ran towards the gate, where she was met by her daughters. They looked furious. She couldn't see anyone else around.

"Fucking idiots!" Bella exclaimed. "Do you know what they did, Mum?"

Sara shook her head and kept her distance while she waited patiently for Bella to tell her what had happened. She knew it was never a good idea to touch someone who was as upset as Bella. Not even when that person was your daughter.

"They followed us all the way home and I think they know where we live because they left just before you came out. They mocked us and said we looked like PC whores who . . . . I can barely say it . . ." Bella fell silent.

Sara waited.

"They said we like fucking little immigrant boys with beards," Klara said calmly.

Sara held back a laugh at the same time as she felt outrage.

She had to take a deep breath before she was able to talk. It took her a while to calm down and the girls stared at her.

"This is terrible. I'll call Vasquez again. Did they do anything else? Did they threaten you or attack you physically?"

"No, they're smarter than that," Klara said, and looked furious. "Are people allowed to behave like this? Huh?"

"No, of course not," Sara said.

Bella walked towards the front door. She turned around and stared at her mother.

"You almost laughed before," she said, and did something that Sara had never seen her beautiful daughter do before. She stuck her tongue out.

"Yes, sorry. I was just so upset that I didn't know how to react."

"Oh, so we're supposed to laugh when we're upset? Don't you think that's a bit stupid?"

"Yes, of course. I was just shocked."

"I know. So were we," Bella snapped.

Sara started the kettle and put bread, butter, and cheese on the table. She sliced some cucumber and picked a couple of leaves from the potted lettuce on the kitchen counter.

"We have to talk about this," she said, and turned to her daughters, who were whispering to each other by the kitchen table.

Klara gave her mother the thumbs-up. Bella was still annoyed and stared down at the table.

"Bella, don't be upset with me. I know laughing was stupid. But I couldn't help it."

"Okay," Bella said, and looked up. Her eyes were filled with tears. "I'm just so angry, sad, and scared."

"I understand, honey. But let's try to think of a way to handle this. Let's talk it out."

"Today we didn't have a class scheduled with the students so I met up with Bella outside Åhléns department store on Stora Södergatan . . ." Klara started.

Sara gave the girls an encouraging nod.

"Suddenly, they showed up and approached us. They walked right up to our faces and whispered that we were whores and traitors." Klara stopped to take a breath.

"And when we left, they followed us. It was super scary," Bella added.

"They followed us all the way home," Klara continued, "and they must know we live here because they left right when we approached the gate. Can you imagine how scary it was?" Klara held her hands out in front of her and looked so deflated that Sara wanted to scream.

"And they kept telling us we were whores who liked sleeping with little immigrant boys with beards. So bloody disgusting. I wanted to punch them in their stupid faces but couldn't work up enough courage," Bella said.

"Let's report this right away," Sara said, "I'll contact the sergeant and ask her to take a statement."

Sara pulled out her work phone and and placed a call.

"Sergeant Karin Augustinsson," a husky female voice said on the other end of the line.

"Hi, this is Sara Vallén speaking."

"Hi, what's on your mind, sweetheart?" the friendly sergeant asked.

"My daughters have been harassed by a group of nationalists. A least one of them studies at Juridicum, but I don't know any of their names. I've asked the prefect to find out who they are. He has promised to get back to me."

"I actually have a moment to take your statement and file a report right away if you want," the sergeant said calmly.

"Thanks! But no need to file a new report. You can just add this to the report I filed earlier."

Sara gave the sergeant the reference number to the existing police report and then she described what had happened.

"Thanks for making this so easy for me," Sara said, glancing at her daughters. They seemed a bit happier now but still looked scared.

"I'll take care of this first thing in the morning. These guys probably won't bother you again today. But now you have a job to do. You know what I'm talking about, right?"

"Yes, we need to call Dad," the girls said in unison. They sighed and got up.

"And I want to talk to him once you're done, so don't hang up," Sara shouted as her daughters left the kitchen.

12

The police in Falun had zeroed in on a couple of families with Nazi ties and a son at the right age. When it came to Staffan Ehn's old friends, they had found nothing of interest. Some of them were still living in Falun while some had moved. As far as they could tell, none of them had any ties to the known Nazis in Falun or the Nordic Resistance Movement. *That's a shame*, Sara thought.

As Sara and Torsten were driving towards Sturup Airport, they received a call from a colleague in Falun, who told them they were pretty sure they had found the family they were looking for. Tom and Carola Karlsson. They lived in an area not far from the city centre.

"Jackpot! They think they've found the right family," Sara told Torsten after hanging up.

"We can't know for sure that this is the right family though," Torsten said sceptically.

"No, of course not. But it sounds pretty likely, don't you think?"

"I don't know. I'm not an expert in probability," Torsten said, and laughed.

"It's all so strange," Sara said once they had boarded the airplane.

Torsten lifted his gaze from the in-flight magazine.

"What did you say?"

"I think it's strange because apparently, Carola and Tom Karlsson have *one* son. His name is Wilhelm Karlsson and he's almost twenty-two.

If they only have one son, then what have they done with Karl-Axel Altenius?"

"True . . . If they took Karl-Axel, shouldn't there be records of them suddenly having two sons? But then again, the caller said the woman had called her husband a murderer . . ."

Sara wasn't sure what to think and she worried they were looking in the wrong direction. Then she thought of something.

"What if Tom and Carola's biological son was murdered by his father? What if the mother kidnapped Karl-Axel to replace him? Maybe they hid in the house to hide their son's death and maybe they left town to cover up the fact that they had kidnapped the Altenius boy? The caller mentioned suitcases."

"Yes, but shouldn't there be a record of their son's death in that case?" Torsten asked, and snapped his fingers in front of Sara's nose. *What a strange thing to do*, Sara thought before she answered.

"But what if he was murdered and they covered it up? Maybe they buried him? Or maybe they're storing his body in a freezer somewhere?"

"Well, that's completely bizarre. It sounds like something from a crime novel," Torsten said, laughing.

"Yes, but it would explain a lot," Sara said without smiling.

"Hmm," Torsten hummed. "We'll see. A DNA test will tell us who Wilhelm's father is—if we can find the boy."

"Another question is how the couple even knew Karl-Axel existed," Sara said.

"Yes, that's the strangest thing if you ask me. There has to be some kind of connection that Staffan hasn't thought about. He gave me a list of the friends he could remember, which means there are probably more. Anyway, we'll see how things go." Torsten ran his fingers through his hair.

"Did you ever talk to Staffan's parents?"

"Sure. They had no idea what could've happened. I remember they weren't very chatty. But I think I should talk to them again. Maybe I can help them remember."

Sara nodded and felt slightly preoccupied. She was still worried about Klara and Bella. Göran and Anders had agreed to both attend the girls' study group later that night. It felt good, but it didn't make her less worried. And she hadn't been able to get ahold of the prefect again, despite several calls to his secretary, the school's receptionist, and the vice principal. They had all told her the prefect was attending a conference. When Sara lost her patience, the vice principal finally promised to look into it himself, but she wasn't sure she trusted him to do so. A surveillance unit was trying to identify the boys, and Sara had told Jonny and Rita about the girls' situation. They had promised to keep an eye out too.

Torsten had fallen asleep with his chin resting against his chest. Sara leaned her head back and tried to get some rest. The airplane was headed towards Borlänge, where they were supposed to rent a car and then drive up to Falun. She needed some rest to prepare for the long day ahead. The very long day ahead.

She was awakened by Torsten grabbing her arm gently.

"We've landed," he said.

Sara shook her head to wake up.

The rental car was waiting for them outside the airport and Torsten took the wheel.

"You rest some more," he said.

"I'm happy to let you drive, but I don't need more rest. I'll call Rita to see how things are going with the Nazis—or, the nationalists."

But Rita didn't pick up. It was only 8:30 a.m, so probably nothing new had happened. She tried calling Anders instead to tell him they were on the road. He sounded calm, which made her feel calmer too.

"Don't worry. Göran and I will make sure nothing happens to the girls. I love you. Talk to you tonight," he said, and blew her a kiss through the phone. Sara felt reassured and told herself it would all be okay. Maybe the nationalists weren't dangerous. Maybe they were just being cocky.

After driving for about an hour, they arrived at the police station in Falun. They both agreed that the roads up north were in worse condition than the roads down south. The speed limits had kept changing during the drive and it had made Torsten curse silently to himself. The police station was a big, brown, curved building that looked reasonably modern. There was plenty of room to park, which was something Sara and Torsten weren't used to. They left their bags in the car, walked into the building, and approached one of the windows in reception.

"They're expecting us," Sara said professionally, and flashed her badge.

"One moment," the receptionist said, and picked up the phone. "Sara Vallén and Torsten Venngren from Lund are here to see you," she said before thanking the person on the other end of the line and ending the call.

"Kabhat Celali will be right with you," she said, and pointed to a row of chairs. "Please, have a seat. Unfortunately, we don't have any coffee to offer you."

"Don't worry about it. We'll be fine," Torsten said, and smiled.

The woman smiled back at him.

13

Chief Inspector Kabhat Celali was a round and alert woman with brown eyes and red lips. She spoke with a thick northern accent.

Kabhat walked up to the whiteboard in her office and quickly scribbled down the information they had found so far.

"Carola and Tom Karlsson live in Hälsinggård. Tom is a Nazi. He joined the Sweden Democrats and became a member of the city council, but after about six months, he stepped down and became independent. Now he's representing the Nordic Resistance Movement. They have a son named Wilhelm Karlsson—or Will. He's twenty-two and pretty well-known around here. He joined the Moderate Youth League and made a name for himself as quite the provocateur. But we haven't seen him in about a year, so I looked him up. He studies law down in Lund now."

"In Lund?" Sara exclaimed, and raised her eyebrows. "Do you know if he has Nazi sympathies?"

"All we know about his political views is his membership in the Moderate Youth League. As far as I'm aware, they're not known for supporting the Nazis," Kabhat said, and smiled.

"No, but aren't there people in the Moderate Youth League who sympathise with the extreme right?" Sara wondered.

"Well, not that I know of," Kabhat answered.

Sara let it go and decided to look into it later.

Torsten and Sara were both impressed with how swiftly Kabhat moved in front of the whiteboard. Neither of them said anything while waiting for her to take charge.

"We've worked hard to find out the identity of the caller who phoned in with the anonymous tip. It was obviously a neighbour, so we started looking at the people living in the houses closest to Tom and Carola's house. It was quite easy to single out a family who had lived abroad for years and rented out their house. So now we know who the caller is."

Sara and Torsten nodded, but didn't say anything as they didn't want to interrupt Kabhat.

"Tom and Carola have *one* son though. Not two. If Wilhelm Karlsson isn't their biological son, the question is—and I'm sure you've already asked yourselves the same thing—where is their biological son? The caller wasn't completely sure he'd heard the woman call her husband a murderer. We've looked in every record and have confirmed they only have one son. The woman's husband accused her of stealing someone else's child and if that's true, they should have two children now, right?" Kabhat stopped talking and looked at them.

Sara squirmed in her seat and decided to share her theory, discussed on the flight, with Kabhat.

"Well, either they've kept one child hidden all these years, which doesn't sound very likely —or possible. Or their own son is dead and they kidnapped Karl-Axel Altenius to replace him. Can we check the paediatrician's records somehow?"

"Yes, we thought about that too," Kabhat said, "and there is actually one period during which they didn't show up to their appointments with the paediatrician. According to the paediatrician's notes, the family were abroad at the time and couldn't come. This should clearly have raised a red flag, but nobody reacted. If your theory is correct, I have a lot of questions. What did they do with their dead son? Because I think it's fair to assume he must have died before he was replaced by Altenius's son. But why was he murdered? And, more importantly, how come we're not aware of this murder? If a murder had been committed, that is."

"Right," Sara said, and nodded.

Torsten stayed silent and Sara suspected his mind was racing. His hands rested peacefully on his knees, but she knew it didn't mean the rest of him was at peace.

"What I don't understand," Sara continued, "is why nobody has reacted until now."

Torsten hummed. He looked pale, and Sara nudged him with her elbow to make him focus.

"It's probably good to keep our minds open here. There could be plenty of different ways to explain this. Wilhelm could be Wilhelm, and nobody else. This could all be a misunderstanding," Chief Inspector Kabhat Celali said, and threw her head back in what could be described as a backward nod. Sara had seen it many times in Greece and knew it meant roughly the same thing as shrugging your shoulders.

The silence spoke for itself. The three of them thought about it for a while. Suddenly, Torsten stood up and grabbed a pen. He turned to Kabhat to give her a chance to grab her mobile phone and take a photo of her notes. Then he erased everything from the whiteboard.

"So, where do we start? How should we approach this?"

The three of them started a lively discussion, and Torsten made notes on the whiteboard as they spoke. Now and again, he took a step back and scratched his head with strong and slender hands.

"Okay," he said, "it seems as if the first thing we need to do is call Lund. We need to get a DNA sample from Wilhelm Karlsson. We know he's down there, as long as he hasn't moved."

"No, we looked it up yesterday. He lives in Lund. And he should still be there as it's the middle of the semester," Kabhat said. "I'll reach out to a couple of colleagues. We need to find out more about the Karlsson family. Especially as Tom Karlsson is a known Nazi."

Sara thought about what would happen if Wilhelm turned out to be Molly Altenius's son. Would they ever be able to repair their relationship? She decided that it wasn't a good time for speculation and pushed her thoughts to the side. After lunch, Sara called Beatrice to tell her what they had found out so far during their visit in Falun. Then she called Rita and asked that she and Jonny contact Wilhelm Karlsson. She also said she didn't have an address for him, but that he was a student at Juridicum.

"You could try calling the prefect. If you do, please remind him that he never called me back about the nationalists and their association. And can you ask Jonny to talk to Staffan Ehn and ask him if he knew Carola or Tom Karlsson when he lived in Falun. I think it's best if Jonny talks to him in person so he can pay attention to his reactions."

Rita sounded tired but happy and took on her new tasks without complaining.

It was 2 p.m. when the chief inspector in Falun had finally put together a team to help with the case.

Sara and Torsten stood in front of a whiteboard in the conference room and it was their job to brief the team about the case.

"Most important now is to gather more information about the Karlsson family. Check if anyone in the family is a blood donor or if they have given blood samples in any other context. If they have, we can use the already existing samples to run our tests. We're incredibly grateful for all the help we can get," Sara said after introducing herself and Torsten.

A tall, gangly man stood up.

"I'll check with the hospital and the blood bank. It might be difficult to get them to tell us anything. If a prosecutor was assigned to the case, it would be a lot easier."

"You're right," Sara said, and smiled at him. "In fact, we do have a prosecutor assigned to the case and direct orders to collect every journal or other document that could be relevant to the investigation. We're talking about major crime here, after all."

A woman raised her hand and waved.

"I'll check online to see what I can find out about Tom Karlsson. He's a bit of a celebrity around here. I wonder in what way Tom and Carola have raised their son, by the way—or the boy they call their son, maybe?"

"It's a relevant question, but we don't need to answer it at this time," Torsten said calmly. The woman didn't seem bothered by his thick southern accent and didn't add anything more to the conversation.

"If Wilhelm is in fact the Altenius boy, we'll have to investigate what happened to their biological son. But we'll leave that to you," Sara said, and smiled. She enjoyed the positive vibe in the conference room and felt grateful for all her knowledgeable and helpful colleagues. It made her feel at ease.

Two women and a man were asked to see the neighbour who they assumed was the man who called in with the tip. Kabhat gave quick orders and spared the details. Probably because she knew her staff well.

"Come talk to me the second you have anything that might interest our colleagues from the south. We'll meet again when we have more to go on," she said, and ended the meeting.

Everyone hurried out of the conference room—except for the tall, gangly man, who didn't look like he was in a rush at all. *A thinker*, Sara thought.

"Okay, it's already 3:30 p.m. Let's grab a bite to eat and get some rest. I'll contact you when I have something to tell you. We probably won't know anything more until tomorrow morning," Kabhat said with a quick smile. "I must say, this whole thing is quite exciting," she added.

Sara and Torsten made their way back to the hotel. They decided to meet up again at 5:30 p.m. Sara's plan was to make a couple of phone calls and then get some rest—or at least try to.

14

Klara and Bella paced back and forth in the classroom, waiting for their father and Anders, as well as the rest of the volunteers and the students.

People would start arriving half an hour later, and the girls wanted to make sure no uninvited guests showed up. The prefect had contacted Klara earlier that day. He hadn't been able to figure out who the young men were, but he promised that he would do everything he could to find out and asked her to take their photo if they returned.

The whole thing felt scary, but Klara and Bella had talked about it a lot and agreed they would never give in to the nationalists' threats. They had also had a conversation with their students. All but one wanted to go on with their meetings, which settled things.

"Let's continue, then," Klara had said. "And for the record . . . whatever these guys call themselves, they're Nazis, if you ask me."

One after the other, the other volunteers started to show up. It was obvious they were all anxious, but they did their best to act like everything was normal.

When Anders and Göran arrived, the mood lightened up a bit and people seemed to relax.

"This is our father, Göran Vallén," Bella said. Göran said hello to everyone in the room. "And this is Anders Magnusson. He's a lawyer."

Anders walked around the room and shook everyone's hand.

"It's admirable that you started this study group, and I'm impressed with the work you do to help these young people with their schoolwork. And you're very courageous," Anders said. Göran nodded to show that he agreed.

"We'll have to find a different solution eventually, but as long as we don't have a better plan, we'll be taking turns to make sure one of us can always be here," Göran said, and smiled.

A couple of minutes later, the students showed up. They were all there, except the younger boy who had been picked up by his foster family and the guy who had stood up to the Nazis—Reza.

"Have you guys seen Reza?" Bella asked the students.

"No, not today," one of them answered. The others shook their heads. Reza was the only one of them who lived in his own flat. He was an ambitious young man, and just like the rest of the students, he spent most of his free time studying. The first time the group met, Reza told them his goal was to continue his studies at the university after finishing high school.

"If they let me stay," he had said, and Klara saw the anxiety in his eyes. The way she looked at him made him stare down at his shoes.

Neither of the girls thought more about Reza during the class. Anders and Göran also sat down to help the youths with their studies, but it was impossible to ignore the anxious energy in the room. It made it hard for the students to focus. But the nationalists didn't show up.

When the study session was over, the volunteers walked the youths to their bus stops and homes. Klara and Bella were going to their father's house, so they said goodbye to Anders at the car park.

"I wonder why they didn't show up today," Klara said as they were driving home.

"Yes, maybe they got scared?" Göran suggested.

"No, I'm sure we'll see them again. But maybe they realised we had brought support this time," Bella said. "Those guys are seriously creepy. You know, Dad . . . they looked so put-together and proper that it's hard to imagine them harbouring so much hatred."

Göran nodded.

"Yes, I know the type."

Once they got to the house they saw their father's new girlfriend, Laura, waiting for them by the window. The girls waved at her and smiled. They liked her and were happy their father didn't have to be alone.

"She's cool," Bella told her father.

"I'm glad you like her," he answered, and put his arms around his daughters.

"She's cool *and* kind," Klara said. "She makes it easy to like her."

Laura met them in the hallway. She was tall and her eyes were green. Her hair was grey and she wore it in a loose bun at the back of her neck. She was calm and balanced and very beautiful.

"Call Sara now," she told the girls, who nodded. "She's probably very worried. I know I would be if I was her." She gave the girls an encouraging nod and turned to Göran. "All good?"

"Yes, they didn't show up. But you could tell everyone was nervous. In a way, I'm disappointed they didn't show up. I could've talked to them and made sure they stayed away."

"Two adult men won't be enough to scare those guys," Laura said calmly, but with a worried expression on her face. "And you can't always be there."

"I know. But at least we could be there today. We'll see what happens next."

Klara and Bella listened and agreed. Then they went to their room to call their mother.

"Hi, how did things go tonight? Did they show up again?" Sara asked, and she did indeed sound worried.

"No, they didn't. The young guy who got so scared last time didn't come. And neither did Reza, a guy from Afghanistan," Bella said. "Do you think we should be worried? He's very ambitious and it feels odd that he would miss today's class without telling us he wasn't planning to come."

"No, I don't think you should worry. Maybe he's sick, or just busy?"

"Yeah, you're probably right."

"How's your father? And Laura?"

The girls picked up a somewhat sharp tone when their mother mentioned Laura.

"Good. And it felt great to have Dad and Anders there tonight. Even if we were still a bit anxious," Klara answered quickly, and hoped her mother would let it go at that.

"And what about Laura? How is she?"

"Great. She's so sweet." This time it was Bella's turn to answer quickly. Both girls thought their mother's question felt a bit forced.

"How are you doing up in Falun?" Bella asked to change the topic.

"I'm doing all right. So far, we've mostly been going through the case file and we haven't really made any progress yet. But we're getting to know the team that is helping us and tomorrow we'll try to make something happen," Sara said.

The girls heard her yawn on the other end of the line and it sounded as if she were sitting next to them. They both giggled.

"Tired," their mother said. "I should really go to sleep. I have a long day ahead of me tomorrow, but I'll call you when I can. Give Johannes a hug from me."

"We will," the girls said in unison.

15

They sat down across from each other at lunch. Bella had walked all the way from the Faculty of Engineering so they could eat together.

"We should go to Reza's flat. Mohammed called today to tell me Reza wasn't in school yesterday or today. I'm worried." Klara picked nervously at her cuticles. Then she started spinning the silver ring she wore on her right ring finger.

Bella tried to be rational, but Klara's nervousness rubbed off on her.

"Okay, so let's go," she said. "Right away."

They got up. Neither of them had an appetite anyway.

They walked briskly to Botulfsplatsen and took the number four bus to Gunnesbo, where Reza had been assigned a transition flat. They got off the bus across from Alfa Laval and started walking towards Gunnebo. Bella stared at the map on her phone. It wasn't easy to find Reza's flat, but at least they knew they were in the right area.

Everything felt so ominous.

"What if they've killed him?" Klara said, and swallowed.

"You're so morbid," Bella teased her sister. "I'm sure he's fine. He's probably just busy with something." She took her sister's hand in an attempt to reassure her.

They found Reza's building and Klara looked at the note in her pocket. Third floor. She walked up to the entrance door and pushed the door handle. The door wasn't locked.

"I thought all entrance doors were supposed to be locked," she said to Bella, who nodded and shrugged her shoulders.

They ran up the stairs. There was no lift in the building, but they didn't need one.

They got up to the third floor and saw Reza's name on a little note next to one of the doors. They rang the doorbell. At first, it didn't sound as if anyone was home. Then, finally, they heard footsteps in the hallway. Bella and Klara realised that the person inside the flat was watching them through the peephole. They both felt relieved. He was okay. But when the door opened, they were met by a young man who wasn't Reza. His hair was a mess and he looked confused.

"What do you want?" he asked, and rubbed his eyes.

Bella and Klara were so surprised that someone other than Reza opened the door that neither of them knew what to say.

"We're looking for Reza," Klara said after a couple of seconds. "We thought he lived here."

"He does," the young man said, "but I haven't seen him since yesterday morning."

"But, but . . ." Bella shook her head. "Aren't you supposed to have adult supervision?" was all she could think of saying.

"Yes, someone comes to check on us three times a week," he answered.

"When was the last time you saw Reza?" Klara asked.

"Yesterday morning, like I said. I wasn't home last night. But why do you want to see Reza?"

"We're helping him with his studies. He didn't show up to class yesterday, which is strange as he's always there," Klara said, and felt her heart beat in her chest. She looked at her sister. "Where do you think he is?"

"Don't know," Reza's flatmate said, sounding hesitant. "Maybe he's been in an accident?"

"We don't know. But do you know anyone else who might know where he is?" Bella asked, looking at him.

"Yes, he knows a lot of people in your study group," the guy said.

"Okay, we'll ask them. Thanks. Could you please call us if he comes home?"

"I will."

Klara gave him both their numbers.

"Maybe he moved?" the guy suggested.

"No, I'm sure he would've told us if he had. Thanks for your help," Bella said, and dragged her sister down the stairs.

"I'll call some of the other students," Bella said once they had left the building. "If we can't get ahold of him, I think we should file a missing person's report."

Klara nodded. A million thoughts raced through her mind. What were they supposed to do now?

"Let's call Mum as well," she said to her sister.

"No, she's busy in Falun. We can take care of this on our own," Bella said, and hugged her sister. To her surprise, she realised they weren't the same height.

"Did you measure your height lately?" she asked.

"What?" Klara looked confused. "Why?"

"When I hugged you, I noticed you're taller than me." Bella flipped her hair back and her eyes sparkled with laughter.

"I am?" Klara opened her eyes wider and copied her sister's body language while she laughed too.

"Maybe a centimetre," Bella said. "It's true, I promise."

They both looked down at their feet, and as they were both wearing boots, they couldn't blame the difference on their shoes. They wore their hair the same way, so it couldn't be that.

"How strange," Klara laughed. "I've never noticed that before. Last time I measured my height was before going to Kenya. Then I was five-nine."

"Shit, I'm five-eight," Bella said, looking slightly disappointed. "But my legs must be longer than yours because your trousers are always a bit too short for me."

They laughed again and started walking towards the bus stop.

On the bus, they started calling all of Reza's friends. None of them had seen him. The girls feared that something terrible had happened to him and decided to stop by the police station, hoping that Rita would be able to help. But instead, they were asked to wait in reception.

Their visit to the police station turned out to be a disappointment. The officer who they got to talk to leaned back in his chair and his stomach was so huge that it hung out underneath his uniform. He kept yawning while he took their statement. Bella and Klara grew more and more upset as the conversation went on.

"Don't you get it? He might have been murdered," Klara exclaimed. Her hands moved passionately as she spoke.

"Most people choose to disappear. We can't waste resources on these things," the officer said, yawning.

Bella's face was pale. Klara's face was red. Identical twins weren't always completely identical after all. The girls stared at the police officer, and although their faces had taken on different colours, they looked equally upset.

When they finally left the station and stepped out into the cold again, they took a moment to gather themselves.

"We'll put together a search party to look for Reza," Klara said. "But let's wait for tomorrow. He might still show up."

"Fine. But I have a feeling he's in trouble. What if the Nazis did something to him?" Bella gasped.

"Yes, what if . . ." Klara said, looking worried.

Bella was going back to the Faculty of Engineering, so the sisters said goodbye to each other outside Juridicum.

16

Although the woman didn't really like walking in the area after dark, she decided to take a shortcut along the dams that worked like a sewage treatment plant. She was going to Klostervallen and the shortcut would save her loads of time compared to taking the road from Värpinge towards town. She knew she was being irrational anyway. Why would anybody attack her there of all places? What would a maniac be doing at a sewage treatment plant?

She considered turning on the flashlight on her phone but decided it was probably smarter to stay hidden in the dark—just in case a maniac was roaming around the area after all.

She took the path to the right of the dams. The bushes next to the path were dense. Although it had been a mild winter almost without snow, it was an unusually cold night. And it was humid.

Suddenly, she heard something. Whispering voices. She saw four people emerge from the bushes a little further ahead. They looked young. She stopped and stepped into the bushes next to the path. She felt relieved when she saw the youths walking away from her. They clearly hadn't seen her. They took the path towards the industrial park. It was the same path she had planned to take. She waited for a while.

When the youths were gone and she felt safe again, she walked slowly in the same direction as they had gone.

When she passed the spot where they had popped out of the bushes, she couldn't help wondering where they had come from. What had they been doing in there? Suddenly, she felt brave. Or maybe just curious. It didn't matter. She stopped and turned on the flashlight on her mobile phone. She couldn't see very far in the dark, and she aimed the flashlight at the thicket that grew along the river.

Suddenly, she saw what she thought looked like drag marks through the brush. The bushes had been pressed to the ground.

She wasn't sure if she should keep going, or if she should turn around.

"I have to," she said to herself to work up the courage to go have a look. She had a feeling something wasn't right.

She took a deep breath and started walking through the bushes with her flashlight in front of her. The light was too strong and she couldn't see much. She lowered the brightness slightly.

17

It was in the middle of the night and the usually peaceful area was full of police officers, a K-9 unit, and forensics. Rita and Jonny were also there, as was Ali, who was covering for Jörgen. Rita talked to the woman who had found the dead body.

The young man had been found lying face down in the water. They had turned him over to see if he was still alive, but he was dead. Now he was lying on his back with a canvas as a blanket. Someone had carved a swastika into his forehead. Strong lights lit up the young man's face and body.

"He looks like he could be from Afghanistan," Ali said.

Rita believed Ali knew what he was talking about. If anyone should know, it was him. He was of Afghan descent too.

"Hazar," he added. "Probably unaccompanied."

Ali spoke like a true professional, but Rita saw the sadness in his beautiful, almond-shaped eyes. Rita felt sad too.

She thought about what had happened to Sara's daughters and their study group for unaccompanied refugee youths and wondered if it could be connected to the dead boy somehow.

The woman who had found the body shuddered.

"So you saw four men step out of the bushes right next to the spot where you found this young man in the water. Can you tell us anything more?" Rita wished Torsten and Sara were there. Messy situations like the one she found herself in weren't her strong suit. She was better at handling the action in the middle of an investigation than conducting interviews during the critical first steps of one.

The woman trembled enough to make Rita worry about her physically breaking. She knew shock was something that needed to be taken seriously, and she asked one of her colleagues to go get a blanket. He ran over to the police car and returned with a dusty covering.

"Sorry, this was the only one I could find," he whispered apologetically.

Rita shook her head.

"It's fine," she said, and draped the blanket over the woman's shoulders. It was cold enough for them to see their breath in front of them as they spoke.

"I saw four men—or, youngsters—step out from there," the woman said, and pointed to the bushes.

"What makes you think they were youngsters?" Rita asked.

"Something about how they moved. I don't know, but I'm pretty sure I'm right. Young people move differently than adults."

Rita nodded.

"Can you tell us anything more about what they looked like?"

"They were all gangly. Two of them were taller than the others. One of the shorter guys was shorter than average. I think they wore dark clothes, but the only light source out here was the moon so . . ." The woman looked up at the sky. The moon was hiding behind a cloud.

"Did you see what colour their hair was, or maybe even their faces?"

"No, they were wearing hats or hoodies. It was too dark and I was too far away to see. I heard them talking, but I couldn't hear what they were saying."

"I understand. Did you happen to hear what language they were speaking?" Rita asked.

"It's hard to be sure as I couldn't hear what they were saying, but the intonation told me it was Swedish," the woman said. "I'm a linguist," she added.

Rita nodded again.

"And where did they go?"

"They walked towards Åkerlund and Rausings Väg."

Rita quickly sent a unit in that direction and turned to the woman again.

"You'll be asked to come to the station for an interview, but right now we're going to give you a ride home. Do you have anyone there who can look after you?" she asked.

"No, but I can call my boyfriend."

"That sounds like a good idea," Rita said, and waved at the young officer who had just given her the blanket. She asked him to take the woman home.

Once the woman had left, Rita walked over to Jonny and Ali, who were talking to the uniformed sergeant.

"We've cordoned off the area and forensics have arrived. We've got a K-9 unit on the case and I've sent some of my people to Åkerlund and Rausings Väg. The witness told me the group of guys was heading in that direction. But it isn't hard to disappear without anyone seeing you at this hour," she said.

"I don't think he died tonight. I think the body has been here since yesterday, at least," one of the forensic technicians told them.

"How strange. Why would these guys be here tonight, then?" Jonny wanted to know.

"Maybe to check if someone had found the body? What do I know? But he must have been murdered by them, right?" Rita said, and clenched her jaws.

18

Rita had worked all day and barely slept at all because of the murder. Still, she had agreed to go to Linda's to talk about their fight. She got on the train towards Eslöv, where Linda lived. They had been a couple for almost six months, but hadn't talked about moving in together yet. Rita wasn't sure if she wanted to live with someone else in her two-bedroom flat. And she knew she didn't want to move to Eslöv. She preferred living in a bigger city. Linda loved her garden and thought her house was the perfect size. *Oh well, we'll cross that bridge when we get to it,* Rita thought as she sat on the train.

She started thinking about the dead boy instead. It was so incredibly sad.

For once, her train arrived on time. Linda was waiting for her on the platform. Rita wasn't sure what to do but decided to hug her girlfriend. When she did, she couldn't help noticing how stiff Linda felt when she hugged her back.

As they drove towards Linda's house, Rita didn't know what to say. It wasn't something that happened to her very often, but what could she do? She sighed. Linda didn't even look at her.

When they stepped out of the car, the vibe between them felt as frosty as the grass in the garden. Grey and boring. She stopped and took Linda's hand, but Linda pulled it away.

"Hey, I love you. Don't let our love die, not because of this. Let's talk about it."

At first, Linda didn't answer. She stood there, staring at the ground with her red hair glistening in the sun that had decided to peek out for a second. But then it looked like she'd made up her mind about something. She looked up. Her freckles always made her look curious, but the look in her eyes sent another message.

"I love you more than anything. But we need to talk about this. I agree," she said, and she took Rita's hand again, squeezing it. Rita felt love flow between them. After all.

They walked into the house and turned towards each other. Rita placed her hands on Linda's face and leaned over her much shorter girl-friend to give her a gentle but passionate kiss. Linda walked backwards towards the living room with Rita's lips still pressed against hers. She turned and guided Rita into the bedroom. Their clothes fell to the floor and suddenly, they were standing completely naked in front of each other. Rita was amazed by how beautiful and overwhelmingly feminine Linda was. She kneeled in front of her. *Make-up sex*, she thought before she was overcome by lust.

"You're incredible," Linda said, laughing, as they lay in bed next to each other after making love, "but I'm hungry."

"You might be hungry," Rita answered, "but I'm starving."

Linda jumped out of bed. She looked like a child who had just finished her last day in school before summer break. *Naked and happy*, Rita thought.

"Now, let's talk," Linda said. They sat at the kitchen table, eating mush-room soup accompanied by slices of sourdough bread and a delicious cheese. "Would you like a glass of wine?"

"Yes, I would love one."

Linda stood up—just as naked and happy as before. Then she put two glasses on the table and got the wine from the refrigerator.

"Not too much," Rita said. "We actually need to talk too."

"Of course," Linda said, and poured the wine almost all the way to the top of Rita's glass.

Rita laughed.

"Isn't it a great idea to talk about these things when we're both feeling happy, relaxed, and slightly drunk?" Linda asked with a grin on her face.

"You're crazy," Rita said, and formed her hands into a heart.

Linda threw her head back in a sudden movement that made her hair dance around her head.

"It looks like you've got a halo." Rita felt intoxicated.

Suddenly, Linda turned serious.

"I don't know what came over me the other day," she said while her freckles turned pale.

"Same here," Rita said. "What came over *me*, I mean. But it's natural to fight now and again. We can't always agree with each other."

Linda shook her head slightly.

"I know, but it was so silly. I felt jealous. Jealous of your job and your boss, Sara. And jealous of everything that I'm not allowed to be a part of."

"I see. I think we need to talk about who I am and what my life looks like."

Linda nodded.

"First of all, my job means that I could be called in at any time and that there are periods when I have to work constantly. Secondly, I'm not married to my job, but I find it fun and challenging. A while back I was thinking of quitting, but I realised it was a bad idea. What other job would be as challenging and offer me the same chance to experience everything I get to experience? I'm pretty sure I wouldn't find it any-where else."

"I understand. And I know all this. I was being stupid and irrational." Linda's eyes had taken on a blue colour that was almost as pale as her freckles.

"I know you know, but I still want to talk about it. I want to talk about it once and for all. Thirdly—although I should probably have said this first of all—I love you. I might not always agree with you, but I always love you."

Linda's eyes regained their colour, just as her freckles did.

"And finally, I want to know why your eyes and freckles lose their colour when you're upset—or when you feel guilty?" Rita asked without really looking for an answer. She leaned over the table to kiss Linda. But Linda didn't pick up on her body language.

"I guess the problem is that we expect different things from each other and this relationship," she said instead.

"Yes, and that's okay. But it's probably good if we clarify our expectations," Rita said, and heard how authoritative she sounded. Just like a police officer.

When Rita fell asleep a while later, she was buzzing from love and wine. She knew she would have to pay for the wine in the morning. But she decided it was worth it. She slept like a baby and to her surprise, she woke up feeling well rested and ready for a new day.

<h1 style="text-align:center">19</h1>

Rita, Ali, and Jonny were about to make a plan for how to move forwards with the investigation, but Rita felt uncomfortable. The whole team wasn't there and she wasn't used to that level of responsibility. But she kept telling herself that she should have no problem completing the task Beatrice had given her as she had helped solve a number of major cases. The commissioner had turned to Rita for a reason. She trusted her competence. *If that's not enough, I don't know what is,* Rita thought, and decided to believe in herself.

"I talked to the prefect at Juridicum, and he confirms that he received a request about this group that call themselves nationalists. He doesn't know who they are, but he's told Klara and Bella to contact him if they see them again. First of all, we need the medical examiner to confirm the time of death, as well as the cause of death. We also need to find out if we've secured any DNA." Rita looked at her colleagues. "What more do we need?"

"We need to find these nationalists. At least that would be a starting point," Jonny said. "But it might be a good idea to have a little bit more to go on before we bring them in—once we've found them, of course."

"*If* we find them, you mean. And I'm not even sure nationalists and Nazis are the same thing. I'll check online to see if someone might have uploaded something relevant. I know Nazis like to share what they're up to. It's like they want to show off what they've done," Ali said, and looked up. He tilted his head slightly.

Wow, so beautiful, Rita thought, and flinched when she realised she was smiling. She quickly wiped the smile off her face.

Ali aimed an amused glance her way and winked.

"Those law students might have nothing to do with this. They might be all talk and no business," she said after a couple of seconds. "But let's start there. It feels natural. But let's keep an open mind. Jonny, I want you to contact the medical examiner. And I'll do my best to find those students." She fell silent again. She wanted to say something to Ali but felt too awkward about it. Instead, she walked up to the whiteboard and scribbled down a list of things to do and assigned each chore to a name. Rita, Jonny, and Ali.

"There we go," she said, and avoided looking at her colleagues. "Ali, I want you to work the investigation from the station for now. When necessary, you'll come with me or Jonny. I'll let you know." They had no idea she was blushing.

"Okay, I'm on it," Ali said with a smile on his face.

Rita turned to her colleagues again. This time, she didn't blush. Instead, she laughed a little and put a hand on her forehead. Jonny stared at her as if she had lost her mind, which made her laugh even harder. He rolled his eyes, shook his head, and smiled. Rita couldn't tell if he was mocking her or not. It didn't matter.

20

Sara woke up early. She felt worried. Or anxious. As she stood in front of the mirror and brushed her perfect teeth, she realised she was struggling with a bunch of different things at once.

She felt anxious for not being at home with her daughters in case things took a turn for the worse. But she knew their father was there. And she knew he would have their backs. She felt a pinch of jealousy. Laura. Beautiful Laura. She probably wouldn't be able to handle the girls if something happened.

Sara immediately became aware of what direction her thoughts were taking. She recognised it. The consuming frustration about being a woman.

"You're being silly, Sara Vallén," she said loudly to herself. "You've been divorced for years and you have a wonderful man in your life. Why do you even care about your ex and his new girlfriend?"

But she couldn't shake the feeling.

"What's wrong with you?" she asked herself, and sighed. "You can't have your cake and eat it too." She shook her fist at her own reflection and decided to let it go. But she knew that when she finally met Göran's new girlfriend, it would be hard for her to hide her feelings.

She started worrying about what it would be like to meet the Karlsson family instead. The family with a son who might not be their son at all. And what if he was their son? What if the tip was useless?

She finished brushing her teeth and pulled her hair back into a ponytail that she removed right away. *Not my style*, she thought, and decided to leave her hair loose. She cursed at herself for not getting up an hour earlier to go for a run.

Then another wave of anxiety washed over her. What if? What if her girls were harassed again? Or—what if the nationalists attacked them? She grabbed her mobile phone and called Göran.

"Göran's phone, Laura speaking."

"Hi, it's Sara."

"Yes, I saw. Hi, how are you?"

"Good. But I have to speak to Göran." Sara didn't bother being polite.

"Here he comes," Laura said on the other end of the line.

"Göran," Sara's ex said without saying hello first.

"Sorry I'm calling like this, but I worry about the girls. How did it go at the meeting with the study group?" Sara heard how forced she sounded and how quickly she spoke.

"Nobody showed up. Maybe they lost interest," Göran said, and seemed to think about something. He took a couple of deep breaths. "The girls are all grown up. They have to take responsibility." Göran breathed in and out a couple of times as if he were in labour.

Sara couldn't hold back a giggle.

"I know, I've had the same thought myself a couple of times. But it never lasts."

Göran let out a short, dry laugh.

"It's bloody hard being a parent," he said, and Sara couldn't help thinking that he hadn't endured half of what she had. She didn't say anything about it though.

"Well, I'm glad to hear the nationalists didn't show up again. Thanks. Have a good day. Bye," she said quickly, ending the call.

She put on her jacket and hat and put her gloves in her pocket. The hotel was warm and there was no point getting fully dressed before she went outside. It would only make her sweaty. She threw a glance in the mirror in the hallway and smiled at her reflection to thank herself for handling the phone call so well. Then she noticed a couple of new lines around her mouth and wiped the smile off her face. The lines were still there. *I can't believe I haven't seen these lines before*, she thought, and touched her cheek. Winter skin. She opened the door and left the room.

* * *

Torsten was waiting for Sara in the hallway, but it looked like he was miles away. He didn't even see her until she was right in front of him. They walked with brisk steps to the station, where Chief Inspector Kabhat Celali was waiting for them.

"Great, let's go to Hälsinggården," the chief inspector said, and jumped into the driver's seat. "The Karlsson family have lived in the house since they were young. They bought it when they met. The father owns a plumbing company that's been in business for years."

Kabhat Celali spoke without a foreign accent. Sara hadn't thought about that until now.

"Where are you from?" Sara asked without thinking. She normally would never ask such an inconsiderate question. She knew there was only one possible answer.

"I'm from Falun." Kabhat smiled. "But I assume you're wondering where my parents are from . . ."

Sara felt embarrassed and nodded awkwardly.

"It's okay," Kabhat said as if she wanted to help Sara out of the stiff situation. "They're from Iraqi Kurdistan. But I was born here. They came to Sweden in the beginning of the 1970s." Kabhat smiled again. Her smile was crooked and Sara caught a glimpse of one of her canine teeth. It was pointy. *Like a vampire*, Sara thought, and scoffed at how silly she was.

"It was a silly question," Sara said. "I'm sorry. I didn't mean to be rude. I'm just curious."

"Really, don't worry about it. I'm used to it. And I'm not offended." Kabhat turned towards Sara, who could see a sparkle of something in the chief inspector's eye. Was it mischief?

The drive to Hälsinggården was short. The sky was just as grey as back in Lund during the winter, but Sara thought about how much lighter everything seemed because of the snow. And the green fir trees helped too. Kabhat parked the car next to the Thuja hedge that surrounded the house. Sara had always hated Thuja trees. She found the plant ugly and it bothered her that homeowners often let them grow way too tall. They were so dense and by the looks of it, they wouldn't let a single ray of sunshine through to the garden.

Kabhat took the lead and walked up to the front door ahead of Sara and Torsten. The grass was covered with snow, but the garden looked neat and tidy. Almost a bit too neat and tidy. It didn't match the appalling hedge. The family's name was engraved on a wooden sign next to the door. Underneath their name, there was a sticker that said, "Nordic Resistance Movement." It made the three police officers feel uneasy. Sara felt a wave of anger wash over her. Kabhat scoffed loudly and her eyes turned a shade darker. But when she rang the doorbell, her face turned neutral again.

The door was opened by a woman with perfectly bleached hair. She stared at Kabhat, and then at Sara and Torsten. She gasped as if she had been caught in the middle of something, but Sara suspected seeing the dark-haired police officer on her stairs had simply spooked her. Sara imagined the woman could just as happily have put up a "No blacks welcome" sign on her front door. But that would have been a crime, which was possibly the only reason she didn't own a sign like that. Besides, if you were rude enough to people who weren't welcome, it was normally easy to keep them out without breaking any laws.

Kabhat reached her hand out, but the woman didn't take it.

"I'm Chief Inspector Kabhat Celali. This is Chief Inspector Sara Vallén," she said, and gestured. "And this is Inspector Torsten Venngren. Can we come in?" It was more of an order than a question.

The woman took an unsteady step to the side. Kabhat entered and wiped her shoes on the doormat but didn't take them off. Sara and Torsten glanced at each other and did the same.

"What . . . What do you want?"

"I think it's better if we talk about it inside," Sara said before Kabhat had time to answer the woman. Kabhat threw an amused glance Sara's way. *I'm looking forward to this*, her eyes said. A tiny smile played on her lips. Sara felt the same way. If there was one thing she detested it was racists and all other extremists, including Nazis—whatever they chose to call themselves. She had raised her children to be respectful and empathetic people, and they kept showing her she had done a great job. As they stood outside Carola Karlsson's door, she felt extra grateful for that.

"I don't speak to foreigners," the woman said suddenly.

"Oh," Kabhat answered her quickly, "lucky for you then that none of us are foreigners."

Once again, Sara saw the amused sparkle in her colleague's eye.

"Well, *you* are," the woman said, and nodded towards Kabhat.

"Nope, I'm Swedish," Kabhat snapped.

The woman looked confused and glanced at Sara's brown eyes and dark curls as if she couldn't make her mind up about her either.

Sara shook her head. Then the woman looked at Torsten, who kept a neutral expression on his face and didn't say a word. Sara knew he felt like it was beneath him to talk to her. The woman stood there silent for a while, wringing her hands.

"You can sit in the kitchen," she said finally, giving in. "What do you want?"

21

The murdered Afghan boy was most likely Reza Mahmoudi—the boy Sara's daughters had reported missing. His age and appearance matched their description. Rita was on her way to the group home for unaccompanied children where Reza had lived before he was assigned the transition flat in Gunnesbo. She needed to ask someone there to identify Reza, as the team had decided it was inappropriate to ask Sara's daughters to do it.

Despite the dreary weather, Rita rode her bike like she always did. The group home was situated outside of Lund, close to Vallkärra. The area looked quite dull in the winter, but Rita knew it would look nicer in the summer.

Rita often missed the beautiful lakes and forests back home in Värmland, but she was pretty good at accepting things as they were without getting too nostalgic. In other words, she was pretty good at choosing to see things in a positive light. And she knew the south of Sweden offered things you couldn't get back in Värmland.

She knocked on the door and waited. A pale young woman who looked like she was about twenty-five opened the door. She looked sad. Rita realised she was the woman she had spoken to over the phone. Rita reached her hand out and felt the woman's cool, young hand in hers.

"Hi, I'm Rita Anker from the police. You must be Annika."

"Yes, hello. Come in." She opened the door and let Rita in. The inside of the house looked like an institution, not like a home. Rita thought about how it would feel for a young person who had just arrived in a new country all by themselves to move into the house. It was a bleak place to live, to say the least.

The young woman showed Rita into a spacious kitchen. A couple of the youths who lived there were cooking together.

"Shouldn't they be in school?" Rita asked.

"Yes, but they've all had tonsillitis so I'm keeping them home for a couple more days."

The young woman walked up to one of the boys and gave him a motherly hug. It made Rita feel better. Then the two women walked into a small office where they could talk.

"Could you please tell me about Reza? Then I'll ask you to come with me to the hospital. I know it's horrible, but I need you to identify him. We're almost one hundred percent sure it's him, but we still need to confirm it like this." Rita gave the woman a friendly smile. The whole situation made her strong police-heart ache.

"Reza was one of our kindest and most confident guys. He's eighteen years old. That's why he was allowed to move into the transition flat . . ." the woman said as her eyes welled up.

"I see," Rita said, and nodded to encourage the woman to go on.

"He was a great student and an athlete. Very ambitious. His dream was to become a pilot. I think he'll be able to . . . he *would've* been able to accomplish his dream. He was super intelligent. And he was so sweet to the other boys who were younger than him and had been through a lot. I think he talked to his mother often. Will you let her know, by the way?" the woman asked, staring at Rita.

"Yes, we'll get in touch with her via the embassy. Can you tell me anything else? Did he have a lot of friends?"

"Well, he did attend a study group at the university with a bunch of other refugee kids."

"What do you think he was doing by the dams?" Rita asked, and realised she hadn't told the woman where Reza's body had been found yet. "That's where we found him," she added.

"Well, he was quite often sad and struggled with anxiety. He didn't have anyone here. None of them do." A tear broke away from her eyelashes and trickled down her cheek. She wiped it away with the back of her hand. "Well, anyway . . . When he felt anxious, he would go for long runs. There aren't that many nice parks to run in around here."

"Okay, so you think that's what he was doing by the dams? Running?"

Annika nodded.

"Do you know if he had a best friend or someone who was closer to him than others?"

"Not really. Maybe someone from the study group . . . I think he talked quite a bit with one guy who lived in another group home. I don't think Reza was close to his flatmate, who also used to live here. He's a good guy too, but quite uninterested in others. Or maybe he just stopped caring. It's quite common. I mean, these kids have to cope with a lot. They're lonely and a lot of them have problems with anxiety and mental illness. Not all of them have enough energy left to care about others. But Reza was special. Mature and courageous."

"Don't these kids get to talk to a therapist?" Rita asked. Hearing about how bad things were for the young men and women who looked for a refuge in Sweden felt like a punch in the gut.

"Yes, of course. But I must say the quality of the therapy isn't the best. I'm a psychology student myself and very sceptical about how these young people are treated. They come all the way here only to be told that things will get better with time. Sometimes they're even accused of faking it. It's sick. I mean, why fake it? And fake what?" The woman pulled a face and clenched her fists.

Rita had a hard time believing what she was hearing. Could it really be that bad?

"Do you have it in you to come with me to the hospital?"

"Yes," she said. "I have to, right? But I can't go now. There is nobody else here. Someone will relieve me in an hour. Then I can drive over there."

"Perfect. I'll cycle back to the station now, but call me when you're on your way to the hospital and I'll meet you there. We'll talk more then."

Rita got on her bike. She was furious.

22

The woman held her head high and let her furious gaze wander between Sara and Kabhat. Now and again, she looked at Torsten with a somewhat kinder look in her eyes. She was so full of hate they could almost touch it. You could cut the atmosphere in the kitchen with a knife.

But she reluctantly answered their questions about her beauty salon and her husband's business. She was less interested in talking about his political activities though.

"I'm not interested in politics," she said, and crossed her arms. "He knows a lot about politics, but not me. I do know one thing though. Immigrants are ruining this country."

The woman's statement made Sara very uncomfortable but she noticed that Kabhat didn't even flinch. *Impressive poker face*, she thought.

"What party does he belong to?" Torsten asked, and straightened his back. Carola Karlsson was petite, but as she was sitting on a bar stool, she was a head taller than Torsten.

"He's a political independent," she answered. "But I can tell you he's definitely not a member of the Swedish Democrats. They're weak. That's what Tom always says. And I agree."

"Do you find ideology important?" Torsten went on.

"I don't know. I think it's important that only Swedish people live in Sweden."

"And who would you say is a Swedish person?" Kabhat asked, and flashed her pointy canine tooth again in a smile that looked more like a wolfish grin. Sara realised Kabhat's question was meant to provoke. *Good*, Sara thought, *we can't just accept this*. She studied the woman on the bar stool. Her hands were dry and red as if they had been washed far too often over the years—which was most likely the case. Her nails were long, like claws, and painted in hot pink. It looked horrible.

"Well, not you," the woman said, and stared at Kabhat. "And not you," she said, and turned to Sara. Sara laughed. She couldn't help it. There was something pathetic about the forty-five-year-old woman and her bleached hair, hot pink and claw-like nails, equally hot pink lips, and bright blue eye shadow to top it all off. Sara found her very off-putting and had a hard time separating her appearance from her political ideas. Somehow, the two aspects of Carola's persona seemed intertwined. Sara took great care not to show what she felt though. She took great care not to show any feelings whatsoever. But still, she would be lying if she said she didn't feel like punching Carola right in the face.

Sara decided to change the direction of the interview and asked Carola Karlsson to tell them more about her husband's political career.

She was obviously proud of her husband. She told them about how he joined the Swedish Democrats and became a city council member, only to step down a while later to become an independent. Talking about him brought a big smile to her lips. It surprised Sara how cute it made her look. *Love does something to people*, she thought as Carola kept talking.

"He's representing the Nordic Resistance Movement at the moment," she said before she could stop herself.

"Do you share their beliefs?" Sara wasn't sure if her question was justified. People had the right to their opinions, as long as they weren't expressed in an illegal manner. But the question had to be asked. Although she already knew the answer.

"Yes, of course," the woman answered. "Anyone who isn't Swedish or born into the Aryan race should leave Sweden. I think everyone is responsible for their own lives. And we want a pure Sweden," she said, sounding like a child.

It was such a dumb thing to say, but it made the hair on Sara's arms stand up. Something about the woman scared her, and she felt like telling her about where the Aryans came from and how the term had come about. But she decided not to.

"Are you Swedish?" Carola asked Sara abruptly. "You don't look Swedish."

"I'm Swedish," Sara answered, and resisted the urge to raise her eyebrows.

"But you're not Swedish," Carola said again, and pointed a finger at Kabhat.

"Yes, I am," Kabhat said again, without an ounce of emotion in her voice.

Carola laughed and waved her index in front of Kabhat's face. "You naughty girl," she laughed. "Don't you know it's bad to lie?"

Sara decided to change the direction of the conversation again as they weren't getting anywhere.

"You have a son," Sara said, and paused.

Carola looked proud, but Sara saw something else in her eyes too. *Worry*, she thought.

"Will is a law student," Carola said, and smiled.

"Why did he choose that path?" Sara wanted to know.

"He's a very intelligent boy. Just like his father."

"Sure, but why do you think he chose law?"

"He's interested in the law and how it can be interpreted. That's what he told me."

"How old is Wilhelm?" asked Torsten, who had been unusually silent.

Carola clearly liked Torsten more than the other two and turned to him. The coldness disappeared from her eyes, but Sara could see that she was still worried. Carola wasn't sure what the police officers wanted from her.

"Twenty-two. It's his birthday in September. And he's already finished his first year down in Lund."

"Ambitious," Torsten said with that soft, warm voice that was always so effective during interrogations.

"Oh yes. He's such a good boy, our Will."

"Do you or your husband know a man called Staffan Ehn?" Torsten smiled at her.

She froze for a second, but gathered herself quickly.

"No."

"Are you sure?"

"Yes, I am," she said with a short tone.

"Does your husband know him?"

She stared at Torsten.

"If I don't know this Staffan, how would I know if my husband does?"

Maybe she's smarter than she looks, Sara thought.

"Well, my question can be interpreted in a number of ways. Maybe you know *about* him, even if you don't know him?"

"I don't know about him either. You'll have to talk to my husband," the woman said, and looked away.

Torsten shook his head but decided to let it go. It took Sara by surprise, but she assumed he had a plan.

"The thing is we got a call yesterday," Torsten said. "The caller told us he heard you and your husband having a loud argument. And he heard your husband say something about you stealing someone else's child from Skåne. Would you like to tell me about this?"

Carola's gaze wandered across the room and she looked nervous for a second before she composed herself and looked at them again.

"No, he never said that. Who told you this?"

Torsten ignored her question.

"So, what did he say, then?" Torsten said, and looked right at her.

"Nothing," was all she could think of saying.

"How is the relationship between Wilhelm and Tom?" Torsten asked, switching focus.

"Good."

"Why did you move abroad twenty years ago?"

Carola squinted her eyes, and the blue eye shadow made her blue eyes look even bluer.

She was as tense as a violin string.

"We lived abroad from May until"—she thought for a second—"until August or September." She stared at Torsten.

"Where did you live, and what did you do?" Torsten kept his tone friendly.

"We lived in Thailand. Tom had to go there for work." Carola looked like an upset child again. She crossed her arms in front of her chest.

"Oh. How strange. There is no record of this." Torsten was lying as they hadn't actually checked if there was a record of the family living abroad. They would have to look it up later.

"Oh, okay. But that's what we did, so . . ."

"Yes, I see . . ." Torsten said, and it seemed as if he was about to let it go. But Sara knew it was all an act.

"And when you were in Thailand, did you make sure Wilhelm got all his vaccination shots?"

Carola looked offended.

"We are fully capable of taking care of our child."

"Hmm," Kabhat said.

"You have no idea. You're just a disgusting Muslim," Carola said, turning to Kabhat.

Kabhat looked straight at Carola without flinching.

"What you just said is a crime," Sara said, feeling a jolt of anger spread throughout her body.

"I don't give a shit."

Torsten signalled to Sara to stay out of it, so she stayed silent.

"I must say it's pretty strange that we can't find any records of you living abroad. We suspect something isn't right with your family," Torsten tried. "Why do you think we would get that idea?"

"No idea," she answered. "What do you want?"

"We want you to tell us about the fight you had with Tom in the garden." Torsten sounded sterner now.

"We couldn't agree on what to do with the hedge," she said, and had clearly decided to change tactics.

"You see, I don't believe you," Torsten said, shrugging his shoulders.

"Oh, I'm not sure what I can do about that. Believe what you want."

"So why do you think a person passing by your house would make up a story about Tom accusing you of stealing a baby? It's a strange thing to lie about, don't you think?"

"I think what's strange here is you suggesting that I don't know what we were fighting about," Carola said, and pursed her lips.

Torsten asked a few more questions about the argument and finally asked if it was true that she had called Tom a murderer, but Carola stubbornly kept claiming she hadn't said anything like that. And just as stubbornly, she kept repeating that she and her husband were capable of taking care of their own child every time Torsten mentioned their stay abroad. Torsten decided to leave it for now. He was convinced he would get the opportunity to approach the subject from a different angle at a later time.

"What happened in November 1997?"

"Why don't *you* tell *me* what happened in November 1997?" Carola Karlsson retorted.

"Why did you pull all your blinds, and why did you stop leaving your house during this period?" Torsten asked.

"Who told you this?"

"It doesn't matter. Just answer the questions." A red spot appeared on Torsten's neck.

"We never pulled our blinds. I was out with Will all the time," Carola answered, but she suddenly looked pale. She was lying.

"Do you have any photos from or before 1998?" Sara asked. The good thing about changing the subject abruptly was that it created confusion. Torsten gave her an appreciative smile.

"No," Carola answered way too quickly.

"I think you do," Torsten asked, sounding friendly again.

"No."

"Let's have a look, just in case," he insisted, and brought his thumb and index finger to his nose as if he was thinking about saying something else.

Torsten gave Sara a nod. She stood up.

"You can't go through our things," the woman shouted. "You need a warrant!"

"You've watched too many American TV shows," Torsten said, and stood up at the same time as Kabhat.

Carola grabbed Torsten's shirt and pulled at it. He grabbed her hand and this time, there was nothing kind about the way he looked at her.

Sara, who was standing next to them, suddenly spotted something on Carola's neck as the collar of her turtleneck was pulled down.

She walked up to her and gently pushed her to the side—away from Torsten.

"What's that around your neck?"

"A turtleneck?"

"And underneath the shirt?"

The woman quickly brought a hand up to her neck and looked surprised for a second, before composing herself again.

"Well, my necklace got stuck when I was taking my shirt off. And I guess it left a mark."

Sara decided to let it go, but she was convinced what she had seen was a strangulation mark.

"Here," Torsten said fifteen minutes later, and held up a photo album. *"My First Year."*

He looked happy with himself as he brought the book over to his colleagues. Carola had locked herself in the bathroom. The earliest photos were taken in September 1996. The first one was of a smiling mother holding a newly delivered baby. The baby looked like most other infants. Then there were a couple of photos of a baby in a bathtub. Nothing out of the ordinary. But then, suddenly, the next photo was from 1998. It was a photo of a boy sitting on a toy car. And then a couple of pictures of a child on a beach, surrounded by palm trees. It looked like the family's trip to Thailand wasn't made up after all. The photos didn't really tell them much.

"Let's bring her in regardless. It's obvious we need to interrogate her further," Kabhat said. "And we need a DNA sample."

Sara and Torsten nodded. If she was planning to refuse to come with them, they were sure they would be able to get the prosecutor to issue a warrant for her arrest.

Torsten knocked on the bathroom door. No answer.

"Hello, come out now," he shouted through the door.

Still nothing. Then, out of the blue, they heard a car speed off.

"What on earth!" he exclaimed, and ran towards the front door and stepped out on the stairs. Sara and Kabhat followed him.

Kabhat picked up her phone and called dispatch.

23

It was cold out. Jonny shuddered when he stepped into the pathology department. He had decided to go see the medical examiner in person. He wasn't sure if the medical examiner appreciated his visit, but he didn't really care.

He lingered for a while in the warm air that was aimed at the entrance to stop cool air from entering the building when the doors were opened. Jonny didn't really see the point with keeping the cold out as the examination room was always kept so cool anyway. But the warm breeze felt great.

When he saw the new medical examiner, he flinched. He was tall. *Probably over two metres*, Jonny thought as he leaned his head back slightly to look him in the eye.

"Hey," the medical examiner said. It sounded like he came from the capital.

Jonny had to stop himself from laughing at his accent. It was a lot more noticeable than Sara's accent.

"Hello," Jonny said. and followed the medical examiner, who guided him into the examination room.

The Afghan boy was lying naked on a table. He had contusions on his head, on the temples. His face was swollen and his body was covered in bruises.

"He was alive when he was left face down in the water," the medical examiner said, seemingly unaffected by the situation. "He was kicked a lot before that though," he continued, pointing at the shoe marks that were clearly visible on the boy's skin.

"He looks like hell," Jonny said. Seeing and smelling the dead body made him feel nauseated. "Did he have water in his lungs?"

"Yep, he did. And clay. My guess is it came from the bottom of the stream. There wasn't a lot of water where he was found."

"He has no family in Sweden," Jonny said, starting to feel anxious. Death always made him feel that way.

"No, but I'm assuming you'll contact his family abroad," the medical examiner said, and raised his eyebrows.

"Of course, as long as we can find them. I'm not in charge of that though."

"The cause of death is technically drowning. But he would've died anyway, judging by the extent of his injuries. This boy has been seriously beaten and the injuries to his internal organs and head are severe enough to be fatal in themselves."

"The people who beat this kid up must have been full of hate."

The medical examiner nodded.

"I'll send you my report at soon as I can. It'll be a day or two. But I can tell you one thing right now. This guy put up a fight. There are a lot of defensive wounds. Also, we found DNA underneath his fingernails and fibres from clothes on his back. It could mean that someone was sitting on top of him at one point, either to keep him still during the abuse or to drown him."

"Did you send everything off to the NFC?"

"Of course," the medical examiner said, looking slightly offended.

"Yes, of course," Jonny repeated. "How long do you think he's been dead for?"

"I would say fifteen to twenty-four hours. I can't tell you more than that at this point."

"Okay, thanks," Jonny said. "I'll head back, then."

"Okay, talk to you soon." The medical examiner reached his hand out, and Jonny shook it.

* * *

Jonny stepped outside. He took a couple of deep breaths to get rid of the smell of death and shake his anxiety. It was a cool and clear day in March. He got on his bike and cycled through the hospital area and past the old university buildings. He got off his bike by Lund Cathedral and walked across Kyrkogatan. He was hungry and parked his bike outside Patisseriet on Klostergatan. It was nice and warm inside the café. He wasn't going to order any sweets, just a coffee and a panini.

"And a lemon tart," he heard himself say to the young woman behind the counter. He just couldn't stop himself. The girl looked at him in a way that told him she didn't think he needed a lemon tart at all.

He had a bite of the lemon tart and instantly felt guilty. *Whatever*, he told himself, and had another bite. Before he knew it, the whole tart was gone.

When he left Patisseriet, his whole body screamed for more. More sweets. *Idiot*, he thought.

The construction on Bantorget made it difficult to cycle across the square. The city had decided to renovate it—maybe in an attempt to make it match the impressive Grand Hotel. He decided to navigate towards Stortorget instead. In the summer, it was bustling with activity and students who were sunbathing either outside the restaurants and cafés or on the benches in the square. Across the street from Stortorget, on the corner of Stora Södergatan and Lilla Fiskaregatan, there was a famous bookshop. Most of the other shops around were department stores. In the grey March light, nothing looked particularly cheerful and people kept their heads down to escape he wind. It was hard to imagine the sound of laughter and chit-chat. Jonny changed his mind again and turned onto Lilla Fiskaregatan. The fastest way to get back to the station was to bike across Bantorget after all. There would be ways to get past the construction. He pedalled as fast as he could, avoiding pedestrians and other cyclists.

When he got to the police station, he decided to take the stairs to make up for the lemon tart. He remembered a psychologist he had dated once. Her name was Helena. Or Helen. He couldn't remember exactly. Either way, she had told him there were people with weight issues who could gain weight just by looking at sweets. He wasn't sure if he believed her.

In the corridor he bumped into Ali, who grabbed his arm and guided him into the conference room. The lights were turned off in the room and a video was projected onto the whiteboard. Jonny froze. Rita rushed up to him and put an arm around him to make sure he wouldn't fall over.

"What the hell is this? Is that Reza? Is it the murder? Holy shit," Jonny said, and felt a shiver down his spine.

The video showed a group of four men kicking and beating a guy on the ground. The young man's head was thrown from side to side depending on what direction the kicks came from. It was hard to watch. It was too real.

Jonny's face turned red.

"I'm sorry," Ali said, "but we have to see this. Because, yes, this is the murder of Reza Mahmoudi."

"But you can't see the perps' faces," Jonny said. Then he gasped. He had just seen something. "Stop the video. Stop it."

Ali did as he was told. Jonny approached the whiteboard and pointed to one of the men's wrists.

"A swastika," he exclaimed, and jumped up and down a couple of times. "Zoom in on it."

"I can't zoom in more. We'll have to send it off to Forensics," Ali explained.

Rita moved closer to the whiteboard and wanted to have a closer look at the tattoo.

"Good eye," she said happily.

Jonny smiled, enjoying the compliment.

"How did you find this video?" Jonny asked.

"I was searching the internet and stumbled across this on a Nazi web-site. I almost fell off my chair when I saw it. These guys are absolutely ruthless. And you should see the comments. It's sickening." Ali looked as sad as he looked angry.

"I guess it's good for the investigation though, in a way," Jonny said in an attempt to comfort the others.

24

Sara and Torsten stayed up late together with Kabhat and her co-workers. They went through photos and waited to see if the search for Tom and Carola Karlsson had yielded any results.

"You know what?" Kabhat said, and looked at them. Her eyes were slightly red. "I have a feeling we'll find the Karlssons at their house. Not many people are prepared to go on the run. I think we should go over there right away. What do you guys say?"

Both Sara and Torsten gave her a thumbs-up.

When they came to the house, they noticed all the lights were switched off. One of their cars was parked in the driveway though, and Kabhat drove past the house and parked a bit further down the street—just in case the Karlssons were home.

They walked along the hedge and approached the house as discreetly as possible. The last thing they needed was two suspects on the run.

It was a cold night and Sara was bothered by how loud their shoes were as they walked through the snow. But as nobody else seemed to care, she decided to let it go.

When they saw that all the blinds were closed, they glanced at each other. Kabhat nodded.

Torsten walked up to the front entrance and pressed his ear against the door. Not a sound was heard from inside the house.

He turned to Kabhat for further instructions.

"If they've been home the door should be locked, and if they haven't been home, it should be open. Right?" she said, and raised her eyebrows.

Torsten put his hand on the door handle and pushed it down. The door opened. So they hadn't been home.

They all looked at each other. Something didn't feel right.

They stayed silent and Sara pulled her weapon out of its holster—just in case. Torsten and Kabhat did the same. They walked towards the kitchen in formation to make sure they wouldn't shoot each other should a situation arise in which they were forced to use their weapons.

Torsten entered the kitchen first and stopped when he saw a woman on the floor. He pointed to her and Kabhat squatted next to the body while Sara and Torsten kept an eye out for any surprises. It was possible someone else was still in the house. Kabhat shook her head and pointed at the woman. She was dead.

Torsten and Sara continued into the house. It was completely silent. Sara walked into the living room first and jumped when she saw a man sitting in the armchair. He wasn't moving and she quickly understood that he was dead. Sara had a closer look and saw a bullet hole in his forehead. Torsten nodded to her as a sign that he wanted her to go examine the man as he kept moving further into the house.

Sara squatted next to the man while Torsten turned on the ceiling light so she could see better.

"There is nobody here except for the two dead people," Torsten said when he returned a moment later.

The man in the armchair was Tom Karlsson. Next to the bullet hole, someone had carved a swastika into his skin. Kabhat entered the room. She held a paper napkin in her gloved hand.

"I found this in the hallway, right by the front door. The perp must have used it to wipe down the crime scene. I'll give it to the dog handler and let the dog sniff it."

Kabhat stopped for a second and looked at the man in the armchair. Sara thought she looked unaffected, but knew from experience that most officers were good at hiding their feelings when they were at a crime scene. It took a lot of energy, but it was necessary to be able to do the job as efficiently as possible.

"There is a bullet hole in Carola's forehead and a swastika carved into her skin next to it," Kabhat said. "The same goes for him. And they're definitely dead, but her body is still warm. So this couldn't have happened too long ago."

"But how is it even possible?" Sara looked at her colleagues. "We were here this morning. And now they're both dead."

"I have no idea," Kabhat said, and shook her head. "But it's creepy as hell."

"Did you make the call?" Torsten asked.

"Yup. Forensics and a K-9 unit are on their way," Kabhat answered.

They took great care not to touch anything and stepped out of the warm house into the cold, dark night. Torsten went back to the door to turn the outdoor lighting on. There wasn't much more they could do, but they would have to wait for both backup and Forensics to arrive at the scene.

"Why would anyone murder them? And what's up with the swastikas?" Sara asked, frowning. She felt her eyelid starting to droop and shook her head to make it stop.

"No idea," Torsten said. "But it all has to be connected. Somehow."

Fifteen minutes later, more officers arrived at the scene. The Karlsson family's house was cordoned off and curious neighbours exited their houses to see what was going on. The police asked them to step inside again. Half an hour later, two forensic technicians showed up. A man and a woman dressed in white protective suits. Finally, the coroner arrived to declare both of the victims dead. It felt a bit unnecessary, but it had to be done. The medical examiner would perform the autopsies and determine the cause of death later.

Kabhat stayed at the house while Sara and Torsten headed back to the station. They had been told they wouldn't be part of the murder investigation, so now all that was left for them to do was to wait for the analysis of the photos and see if there was a child's body to be found somewhere on the Karlsson family's property. It would take a while to get the results back from the DNA tests, so there was no point waiting for them. They already had a pretty good idea of what they would show anyway. Now they had to focus on finding Wilhelm Karlsson and get a sample of his DNA. They also needed to tell him about his parents' death. Because to him, Tom and Carola were still his parents, regardless of whether they shared DNA or not.

As they were walking up to their car, a man approached them. He wore a down jacket over his striped pyjamas and it looked like he was more than seventy years old. Sara looked at the fur hat on his head. *Good choice*, she thought.

Torsten stepped between Sara and the approaching man. Just in case.

"Sorry to bother you," the man said with a thick northern accent.

Torsten didn't say anything and waited for the man to continue.

"I was contacted by the police today and I know you know I was the one who called earlier," he said, and smiled. "I couldn't tell them anything more than what I've already told you. But what's going on now?"

Sara took a step towards him.

"We appreciate you calling us. Maybe you have something more to tell us about what happened here tonight?" She gave the man a stern look.

"No. I haven't seen or heard a thing. I just noticed all the police activity and came out." His eyes were smiling at her. "That's why I asked you what's going on," he said, and pulled his hat down over his ears. It was freezing.

"At least you told us about the argument and pointed us towards this family, so thanks for that. We might need to talk to you again later," she explained to the friendly man.

"No problem."

Sara liked the sound of his accent. It sounded beautiful.

"Thanks, we'll talk again soon."

Sara looked over at Kabhat, who was talking to a group of uniformed officers. She pointed at the neighbouring houses and at the old man who was walking back towards his own house. She was clearly giving her team instructions to question everyone in the neighbourhood. She waved at Sara, who walked over to her.

"Take the car. I'll ride with someone else back to the station. We must act swiftly here. The dog is trying to pick up a scent, but my guess is he won't find anything. You never know though."

Sara nodded and then she and Torsten got into the freezing car and drove back to the station.

The next morning, they met up with Kabhat, who hadn't slept at all. Sara and Torsten had barely slept either. They had stayed up late reading interrogation transcripts and searching their records for something that could possibly explain the murders.

Although they knew Kabhat was probably just as tired as they were, she looked happy and satisfied in a way only someone who'd had success could look.

"We've found a child's skeleton buried at the back of the house. Most likely, it belongs to their biological son, Wilhelm. Other than that, this case is full of question marks. But I think you should go home. We'll handle these murders on our own. I promise we'll send you the DNA results as soon as they're back from the lab. And can I ask you to tell Tom and Carola's son down in Lund about their death? I mean, even if it turns out he's not their biological son, they were the ones who raised him and taught him everything he knows, prejudice and all," Kabhat said, not being able to hide the sour tone in her voice.

"Holy crap." Torsten looked surprised.

"Yup. And"—Kabhat paused for a second—"the dog picked up a scent and guided the dog handler to a hat that the perp must have dropped."

"Wow," Sara said, "that's great."

"Yes, great! We found a lot of hair in the hat, so we should be able to get DNA from it," Kabhat said, looking very pleased.

25

Sara and Torsten were on their way back to the hotel to eat a late breakfast. Sara was exhausted. She felt like she hadn't slept for days. But they were finally going home, which made her feel relieved. She couldn't wait to get back to her children. And she looked forward to seeing Anders and catching up on some rest. After their date, she would have to turn her focus to the murdered Afghan boy. Judging by what Rita had told her over the phone, the case was far from solved, although they had made some progress. Apparently, someone had carved a swastika into the boy's forehead.

"What? Really?" Sara had exclaimed when Rita told her about it and she hadn't been able to hide how surprised she was.

When she told Kabhat, she frowned.

"Call me the moment you have more to tell me about this," she said, and hugged both Sara and Torsten. "It's been great working with you."

"Right back at you," Sara said, and meant it.

Sara wondered why some people radiated so much warmth while others didn't. Tom and Carola Karlsson seemed to completely lack empathy, while Kabhat, Torsten, Rita, Anders, and everyone else in her circle of friends and family were more empathetic than most. Sara figured Tom and Carola were probably both full of insecurities and a tad—or completely—out of their minds. The boy had been caught up in it all—forced to spend twenty years of his life being fed with hateful ideas and his parents' suffocating and desperate love. Maybe their version of love was better than no love at all, but still.

Just as they were leaving the police station, Kabhat came running.

"I forgot to tell you that I spoke to Edvin Nordlund last night. The witness. Or, the caller. We already questioned him once, but I held a second interview with him, forcing him to repeat his story all over again. It was basically in the middle of the night, poor guy. He told me he'd been suspicious of the Karlsson family for a long time. As you know, Tom moved abroad with his family for a couple of years and didn't think much about his neighbours. But then when they came back to Sweden, the Karlsson family moved into the same house next door and Nordlund started noticing a bunch of strange things about them. Apparently, they didn't have a lot of friends and never socialised with their neighbours, for example. I asked him why he hadn't called us until now and do you know what he said?" Kabhat asked, letting out a little laugh. "He told me he didn't want to meddle in other people's business. Anyway, I'll add the interrogation transcript to the case file digitally so you can read it too. We have the skeleton now, of course, but the neighbour's story supports our timeline."

Sara gave her a thumbs-up. Then she walked over to Torsten.

They walked into the breakfast restaurant just as it was about to close.

"I'm glad we're not working the case with the dead child in the garden, even if it might be connected to our swastika murder," Torsten said with his mouth full.

"Yes, I agree," Sara said. "I doubt they'll be able to prove a crime has been committed when it comes to the child though. And besides, it doesn't really matter as the child's parents are dead. Both of them. But I'm worried there might be a connection between the murders of Tom and Carola Karlsson and the murder of that Afghan boy. I just can't figure out why they all had swastikas carved into their foreheads. Something about it doesn't make sense."

"Yeah, it sure seems strange. But you never know how things are connected. Let's focus on one thing at a time." Torsten kept eating and smiled at her with a piece of cheese stuck between his teeth.

"If the skeleton turns out to be Wilhelm Karlsson and the Wilhelm who is still alive turns out to be Karl-Axel, how do you think he'll take it when he finds out? And how is the meeting going to go between him and Molly—his real mother?"

"We don't actually know anything yet so there is no point worrying about these things now. If it turns out to be that way, there is nothing we can do about it. We'll cross that bridge when we get there."

"You're right. But isn't it strange that something like this can even happen? Shouldn't it have been picked up by social services or the paediatricians? I mean, I can't believe something like this could have slipped between the cracks for all these years."

"It's unbelievable to say the least," Torsten said after swallowing another mouthful. He grabbed a napkin and wiped his face. "Man, I love hotel breakfasts."

Sara laughed and felt relieved to be reminded there was a normal life and everyday things to be amused by as a contrast to all the darkness she was forced to face at work.

Sara packed up her things and brushed her teeth before heading down to the lobby, where Torsten was waiting for her. She felt impatient and wanted to get going. A quick stop at the police station, a drive to Borlänge, and then they would get on the plane.

"What's on your mind?" Torsten asked, and put an arm around her shoulders.

"Well, I'm thinking about how tragic it is that a boy had to grow up in a home characterized by hatred and racism with a mother who might not even be his real mother and parents who don't believe in democratic values. It's a strange world we live in."

"Did Jonny talk to Staffan Ehn, by the way?" Torsten asked abruptly.

"No, apparently he's on a business trip. He should be home the day after tomorrow," Sara said.

Torsten nodded. Kabhat had left them.

They drove out of Falun and arrived in Borlänge an hour later. Torsten had driven as fast as the speed limit allowed. He was also anxious to get home.

"The murder of this young Afghan man . . . I think it'll be a tough case," Torsten said once they'd returned the rental car. The slushy snow made their feet wet, and they were both cold. There was a bit of a walk between the car park and the airport. They didn't mind as they weren't in a rush and there was plenty of time before their departure.

"Yes, I'm sure you're right. They've found a video online. A video of the murder. It's disgusting. One of the perps has a swastika tattooed on his wrist."

"I hope we can solve this," Torsten said, and stopped walking. "This is our gate."

Sara walked ahead of him. The gate was quiet and calm, with few people. They sat down on the uncomfortable plastic armchairs and stared out the window. Sara glanced at her watch to calculate when they would land.

"This weather is horrible, by the way."

Torsten looked as gloomy as Sara felt. He ran his fingers through his hair and as always, one of his fingers got tangled up in a knot.

"Maybe it's time for me to cut my hair," he said while he tried to free his finger.

"No, don't. Your curls are so beautiful. Don't cut them," Sara said, and realised her face was hot.

"Why are you blushing?"

Sara squirmed in her chair.

"I don't know. I guess I got a bit too personal there. I don't want you to take it the wrong way." The redness spread down Sara's neck. She could feel it and pulled her scarf up to hide it.

Torsten laughed again. It was a friendly laugh.

"I think it's nice. I seldom get complimented by women."

"Oh, come on," Sara said, and squirmed even more.

"And I find it amusing how embarrassed you are." He laughed again.

"I'm glad my awkwardness amuses you," Sara said, glaring at him.

Torsten reached for her cheek and stroked it.

"Except for Veronica and my beloved ex-wife, you're my favourite person," he said.

"Wow, what a compliment. Thanks," Sara said, blushing even more.

26

Anders met them outside the airport terminal. It was a lot warmer in Skåne than in Falun.

When Sara saw Anders, she ran towards him and threw herself into his arms.

She buried her nose in his neck and inhaled his scent.

"Hi, my darling," he said, and hugged her.

Torsten walked up to Anders and shook his hand.

"Torsten Venngren," he said.

"Nice to meet you. Anders Mårtensson."

Sara stepped away from Anders and without thinking, she hugged Torsten too.

Anders drove to Malmö, where he dropped off Torsten, who patted Sara's cheek and thanked them for the ride. Sara sat silently in the passenger seat with her hand resting on Anders's thigh. It made her feel safe somehow. Anders focused on the road ahead. The traffic on highway E22 was light. It was a smooth drive, and he didn't say anything either. Sara fell asleep, as usual. Driving always relaxed her.

"We're here," Anders said, and stroked her hair. He had stopped the car in front of the house to open the gate. Sara's old Saab stood in the driveway. She loved that car.

"It was nice to close my eyes for a second," Sara said, and yawned.

She grabbed her big purse while Anders went to get her suitcase from the back of his Mercedes.

The sun peeked out from behind a cloud and made his car glisten. When Sara stepped out of the car, she almost thought she could smell spring in the air. March wasn't her favourite month, but spring definitely felt closer down south than up north. There was no snow left on the grass. But then again, it had barely snowed all winter. The ground wasn't even frozen, even if was still cold.

They walked into the house, and it felt warm and cosy although it was empty. Anders embraced her in the hallway and kissed her. His kisses were steamy and passionate one second only to turn soft and gentle the next. She welcomed his kisses and snuggled up in his embrace. But she couldn't stop thinking about how hesitant she had felt the previous night. Where did her feelings come from? How could she even doubt what she felt for Anders for a second? She had never been in a relationship with someone as good as him.

She sighed loudly and Anders took a step back.

"What was that sigh about?" He placed his hands on her face and kissed her again.

She laughed and pulled away from him to answer. "Oh, I'm just being silly. I'm worrying about things I shouldn't worry about. I'm driving myself nuts." And then she kissed him again.

She walked backwards towards the bedroom, and he followed her with his lips pressed against hers. All she could think was that she must have found the meaning of life. Nothing else felt important.

Just as they stepped out of the shower a while later, the front door opened and Sara's three children stormed into the house. She heard them call out for her and answered them as she threw on some clothes.

She walked into the hallway as they were taking off their coats and they all hugged her.

"It's so nice to have you home again. I mean, I don't understand why this family keeps running into murdered people," Johannes said.

Sara knew he was referring to Reza and the girl he had found in Lund City Park, but his joke was a bit too morbid for her to appreciate it.

"A bit insensitive, don't you think?" Klara said, and aimed a punch at her brother's shoulder.

"But it's true."

"I know, but still," his sister said.

They sat in the kitchen, eating sandwiches and drinking tea. The flickering candle was reflected in the dark window. They ate in silence. Sara enjoyed having all her children home. As they sat there together, she forgot about everything she would have to do when she arrived at work the next day and didn't ask her children a single question. It would have to wait.

Later in bed, Sara stared at Anders. He was lying on his back, fast asleep. She loved him, but couldn't help feeling hesitant. It was as if her soul was full of rage—an uncontrollable rage that threatened to surface at any moment. She thought about it all the time she had spent talking to Louise Malmberg, her therapist, about it. Talking about the rage. And about how scared she was that it would cause everyone she loved to leave her.

"Sometimes fear of being abandoned can be so powerful that it might cause you to act as if you want to be abandoned. It's contradictory, but quite natural. Imagine a child whose parents never believe in her although she tries her hardest to do good. After a while, the child will stop trying and start acting like her parents expect her to anyway," Louise had explained.

"I recognise that," Sara had answered. "As my dad left me in a way, I could never trust my relationship with him fully. Especially not after he was kidnapped and held hostage. I guess my inner child is still making herself known. Her insecurity is always there. But that's not all. I can't stand being pushed around. Especially by men."

"I understand. But do you think you might tell yourself you're being pushed around by men because you don't trust them?" Louise had asked her and given her a curious look.

"Hmm . . . Are you trying to tell me I'm reading things into certain situations that only exist in my head?" Sara had asked, but Louise had raised her eyebrows and shrugged her shoulders to show she wasn't trying to tell Sara anything at all.

Sara remembered every word of their conversation and she had thought about it a bunch of times without being able to determine what it meant to her. Now she understood. The constant mistrust, suspicion, and misinterpretations suddenly made sense. She didn't trust Anders's love for her to be real—at least not completely. And instead of asking him about it, she became angry. Instead of asking, she pushed him away.

When she finally managed to fall asleep, she was determined to change her behaviour. And she fell asleep with a smile on her face.

27

When Sara woke up, she felt well rested and jumped out of bed. The determination and clarity from the night before was still there. She had a quick shower and stepped into the kitchen to make breakfast.

The girls and Johannes were already up, and to her surprise, breakfast was on the table.

"Wow, you guys are so sweet," she said, and kissed her children's foreheads, one after the other. She loved their scent more than anything else.

"What's going to happen now?" Klara asked.

"I'm not completely sure how far they've come at this point."

"Okay, did you know we were interrogated? They asked us to describe two of the nationalists to a composite-sketch artist." Klara looked unhappy.

"Do you know what the saddest part is?" Bella asked.

Sara shook her head.

"That nobody is missing him." A tear trickled down Bella's cheek.

Sara wiped the tear off her daughter's face.

"We're doing everything we can to find his parents or relatives and let them know. We always do," she said after a while in an attempt to comfort Bella.

"We *did* report Reza missing the day before he was found. We mentioned that we were harassed too. And that Reza had spoken up against the guys who harassed us. Do you know what the police officer we talked to said?" Klara stared at her mother.

"No, what did he say?"

"He told us they wouldn't do anything about it as most people who are reported missing disappear because they want to disappear." Klara squinted. "I don't even think he wrote down a word we said. But I'm not sure. I haven't heard anything back from him though."

"He said that?" Sara was furious. "I'll look into it as soon as I get to work. Did you mention this during the interrogation?"

The girls shook their heads.

"We forgot," Bella said, looking ashamed.

"I don't blame you," Sara said, and felt overcome by anger. "It's not your job to act like police officers and solve this case."

She decided to let go of her anger.

At that very moment, Anders walked into the kitchen. He looked tired, and although he hadn't even turned fifty yet, he looked old. The fine lines around his mouth and eyes looked deeper than usual.

"How are you?" Sara asked, and stroked his back as he walked past her to get a cup of coffee.

"Tired. Easter is coming up soon, right?" he asked, and smiled faintly.

"Yes, soon enough. Are you taking any time off work?"

"Yes and no. I'm swamped with work, but I guess I could use a couple of days off like anybody else."

She put her teacup down on the table and walked over to the kitchen counter to make herself a sandwich.

"I'm off but will probably have to work a little anyway, because of the murder," Sara said with a glum look on her face. "Hopefully I can take Good Friday off. We'll see. Rita is in charge of the investigation at the moment, and I'm thinking about leaving it that way."

"Sounds wise," Anders said as he leaned across the table to steal a kiss from Sara.

Sara and Anders said goodbye to each other at the gate. The weather was horrible, but Sara decided to cycle to the station anyway.

She arrived at the police station at the same time as Torsten and Jonny, who had obviously taken the train together.

"Hi!" she said with a smile on her face.

They both hugged her. She felt equally surprised, embarrassed, and happy every time Jonny showed her affection.

"Good to have you back," he said. "We've had some help here, but it's always better when we work together. That's how things get done."

"Of course," Sara said.

She took off her coat and threw it across the back of her chair before heading over to Beatrice's office to tell her about the officer who had ignored her daughters' concern for Reza. Beatrice promised to handle it.

"My guess is he didn't care because the person missing was a refugee," Sara said, and scoffed. "Or he's just really bad at his job."

Beatrice didn't answer her, but Sara thought she could see a little smile play on her lips. *Probably just my imagination*, she thought, and left her boss's office.

Ali, Rita, and a group of young officers had already taken their seats in the conference room. Sara noticed the sandwiches and the coffee on the table.

Rita walked in and gave her a big hug. The powerful arms of her tall and strong friend completely overwhelmed her. She coughed.

"Oh, sorry! Did I hurt you?" Rita laughed.

"Don't worry," Sara said. She was used to Rita's powerful embrace. Since she started working with Rita, she wore high heels much more often. Or boots. It made her feel taller.

Sara was short, but she knew she came across as powerful anyway. And energetic.

"I need a proper update."

Rita nodded and asked Ali to go over what they had so far. Sara glanced at Rita and instantly sensed the strange chemistry between them. Ali was beautiful, just as Rita was. They were both tall and athletic. Sara thought they would make a great couple but realised how inappropriate it would be.

"Reza Mohammad was eighteen years old and lived in a so-called transition flat. He was ambitious and part of the study group led by your daughters and their friends. According to the staff at the group home where he lived before moving into the flat, he was an ambitious student who hoped to stay in Sweden. He used to go for runs around the dams and along Höje River almost every day. He played football as well. The staff tells us he was intelligent and very competent." Ali walked over to the whiteboard. "Here you can see how things are connected. At least based on what we know so far. Reza was part of Sara's daughters' study group together with a number of other ambitious students. There are ten boys and three girls in the group. All of them arrived in Sweden as unaccompanied minors. Eight of the boys are from Afghanistan, one is from Somalia, and one from Syria. Two of the girls are from Somalia and the third one is from Afghanistan. Most of the volunteers have Swedish origin, except for one, whose parents are from Iraq, and one with Kurdish origin. Not that it matters, but I want to tell you everything we know."

"I see," Sara said while Torsten nodded.

"Then there is this group of young men. *Allegedly*, they're students at Juridicum."

"Why 'allegedly'?"

"I don't think that's the case. I think one or a couple of them might be law students. The rest of them probably study something else, or nothing at all. If they were all students in Lund, we would've been able to find out who they are by now, don't you think?"

"I guess."

"Also, I have a feeling these guys are real Nazis and not connected to Juridicum at all. Except for that guy they call Will—who is possibly Wilhelm Karlsson."

"We have to interrogate everyone who was there when the harassment took place. We need to ask more about what these guys looked like and if anyone remembers seeing a swastika tattoo," Rita said to Sara.

"Well, go ahead and interrogate," Sara said.

"But aren't you taking over from here?" Rita asked.

"No, I want you to lead this investigation." Sara smiled and nodded. "It'll be great practice. If you're not planning to leave the force any time soon, of course." Now she was grinning.

"Leave?" Rita said, then muttered something. "I know I've said that a bunch of times, but I mean . . . This is all I know. What would I do if I wasn't a police officer?"

"Study?" Sara suggested.

Torsten nodded, and to Sara's surprise, so did Jonny. The only one who didn't look happy about the suggestion was Ali.

Aha, Sara thought, *I was right*. She couldn't stop herself from winking at Rita.

28

They simply couldn't figure out who the nationalists were. Daniel Vasquez called Rita to let her know he was afraid he couldn't help them. The nationalists they were looking for probably weren't students. And the description of the tall young man who they thought was a law student was too unspecific to single anyone out. For some reason, Rita felt relieved to hear none of the nationalists—except maybe for one—were students. Maybe she was relieved that her assumptions about academics had been confirmed, and not based on prejudice alone? She shrugged her shoulders and decided to leave it.

She called Klara and Bella to ask them to come to the station. Then she asked Jonny to help her prepare the second round of interrogations. Torsten had taken the day off as he had a doctor's appointment. Sara sat in her office. She was on the phone with Kabhat from Falun and didn't want to be disturbed. Also, it would have been highly inappropriate to ask her to interrogate her own daughters.

Rita had reached out to some of their colleagues and asked them to question the rest of the students in the study group. None of them knew what to expect from the interrogations.

Rita and Jonny went to pick up Bella and Klara. They had to be questioned separately.

Rita talked to Klara while Jonny talked to Bella. They showed the girls a couple of still pictures from the video of Reza's murder. The swastika tattoo on one of the men's wrists was visible in one of the photos. None of the pictures showed the men's faces, but at least they showed their different body types. The violent kicks and punches had been blurred out.

"No need for them to see this," Ali had said. And he was right.

"If you could tell me everything you can remember about the men who came into your classroom, that would be great," Rita said with a smile after officially starting the interrogation of Klara.

"They were . . . I don't know how to describe them . . . polished. Blond. One of them was a lot taller than the others. He's the one I recognise from Juridicum. I've seen him many times, but not lately. I didn't recognise the others. They were all well dressed and looked tidy if you know what I mean?"

"Yes, I understand. But do you think you could try to explain it anyway?"

"Well, they wore fancy black trousers, clean white shirts, black coats, and shiny shoes. It was quite noticeable. The clothes looked new. But if you ask me, there was something else about them too. Something that didn't match their outfits and hairstyles. They threatened us and were very confrontational. They got right up in our faces. It was extremely uncomfortable. But their behaviour can't be called an unlawful threat. I've looked it up. Mum told me it can be considered hate-motivated harassment. The only one who spoke up against them was Reza, but they walked right past him and treated him like air."

"What does the word 'swastika' mean to you?" Rita decided to try a new angle.

"Well, that's the symbol the Nazis use," Klara said, "but wait. I remember something . . ." Rita waited patiently and avoided staring at Klara. During her interrogation training, she had learnt that staring could create stress.

"Now I remember! I couldn't see all of it, but I think there was a swastika on one of their wrists."

"Why do you think that?"

"I mean, I didn't really think about it much then. But I noticed the tattoo and remember feeling uneasy when I saw it. But then I forgot about it as everything else was even scarier. But I'm pretty sure it was a swastika." Klara looked proud.

"Thank you," Rita said, and kept a neutral expression on her face. "And what did the man with the tattoo look like?"

"They all looked so much alike. But the guy who studies at Juridicum looked different. Not only because of how tall he was, but he was fitter than the rest too. The others were smaller than him. I would describe them as super cocky and creepy in general."

Rita nodded.

"I'll show you a couple of photos. They are still images taken from a video. What do you see?"

She showed the young woman the photos, one by one.

"That's the swastika," Klara said. "And he looks to be about the same height as the guy I remember. He was shorter than me. I remember that. That's him. Definitely."

"But he's not a law student?"

"No, I would've recognised him if he was. I'm sure."

Rita showed her the next photo.

Klara shook her head at all the other photos.

"Would you say that any of these other men could've been part of the group that came to your class?"

"I guess. But the tall one isn't in these photos. I don't know what his name is, but I'm pretty sure they called him Will."

"Will," Rita repeated. "Is that what they called him?"

"Yes, at least I think so."

Rita nodded. Thoughts were racing through her head.

Will, as in Wilhelm Karlsson?

Rita thanked Klara and told her she was free to leave. Bella was waiting for her in reception. Rita couldn't see any of the other students who had been called in for questioning. Hopefully, they were being interrogated by her colleagues.

Rita said goodbye to Klara and Bella and bumped into Jonny, who was on his way out.

"She recognised the swastika," Rita said.

"Bella did too," Jonny said. "And what did Klara say about the rest of the photos?"

"Not much, except that one of the guys who harassed them wasn't in the photos. She called him 'the tall one' but told me his buddies called him Will. He's a law student. And the rest of them aren't." Rita gave Jonny a curious look.

"Bella also told me Klara didn't think they were law students," he said, and looked surprisingly proud.

They kept talking as their colleagues returned one by one from their interrogations with the rest of the students, who had told the same story as the twins. None of the others had mentioned the name Will though.

"At least now we know the guy with the swastika tattoo was one of the men who harassed the study group. And we know the guy called Will might actually be Wilhelm Karlsson."

"Excellent."

They headed up to Ali's office. He was busy searching for information online.

"I'll call Vasquez again," Rita said. "Will is a student there so we should be able to find him. Especially now, when we have his full name. As long as he is who we think he is, of course. There might be more tall law students called Will, but we have a better chance finding him if we ask Vasquez to look for a Wilhelm Karlsson. We also need to show Bella and Klara a picture of Wilhelm."

"No problem," Sara said. "I'll take care of that."

"Great! I'll be right back," Rita said, and left.

29

Rita and Ali sat at La Cucina, enjoying a late lunch. It was almost 5 p.m., but they hadn't had time to eat yet. So lunch had turned into dinner. Ali had asked her if she was hungry while he was sitting on a chair, stretching. He was tall and strong and she had noticed his well-defined pectoral muscles underneath his T-shirt. Their workday had started with interrogations. Then they had contacted their colleagues to make sure they showed the rest of the students in the study group a picture of Wilhelm Karlsson. They were hoping Wilhelm Karlsson and Will would turn out to be the same person. At least then they would know the identity of one of the nationalists. After that, Rita and Ali had spent hours in the office, watching the video of Reza's murder over and over again. Forensics had managed to zoom in some more, but still all they could see was a man being beaten to death. It was difficult to watch the violence, of course, but it had to be done.

"How come you moved from Malmö to Lund?" Rita asked just as the thought crossed her mind.

"I was sick of the attitude," he answered.

His reply made her instantly curious.

"What attitude?"

"People back in Malmö kept making jokes about my background, my name, and about me being an immigrant in general."

"I get it," Rita said in a slightly thoughtless manner.

"No, I don't think you do," he smiled.

"Sorry, you're right. I don't. But I understand why you moved."

"I think a lot of people want a simple explanation when it comes to criminality. Nobody seems interested in the fact that criminality is normally extremely complex," Ali continued.

"You're probably right. Simple solutions normally don't solve complex problems," Rita answered.

Out of the blue, Ali took her hand.

"Maybe you see things most people don't," he said, and kept holding her hand gently.

Rita wasn't sure how to act. Something told her she should pull her hand away, but a part of her wanted to leave it right where it was. She thought about it and realised she was feeling immoral. And guilty. But she didn't move her hand.

"I doubt it," was all she could say.

"This is how it is," he said. "People talk about immigrants as if they're trash. If I ever point out that I'm an immigrant too, they say something like: 'but we know *you*—you're great.' It's hard to take. One day I got so fed up with it that I threw a paper cup full of water at a colleague. Then I asked my boss for a transfer."

"Wow, that's a pretty strong thing to do.

"I needed to take responsibility for my actions. I crossed the line. I was aware of that."

"And how did it affect your friendship with the colleague?" Rita had a hard time imagining not being friends with her colleagues. Even if she'd had a couple of arguments with them, it felt more natural being friends.

"Well, we were never friends. We just worked together. I apologised, and he accepted my apology. I guess that's all you can ask in a situation like that."

"And what about your boss?"

"I don't think he could've cared less. All he told me was that nobody is irreplaceable. I find it quite sad, really. The workplace culture, I mean."

Ali appeared to be deep in thought, so Rita stayed silent and waited for him to continue.

"Many of my colleagues were great. But I got sick and tired of trying to talk to the guys who kept acting like arseholes."

"Did you hear about that Facebook group that's protesting against the sexist jargon, objectifying comments, harassment, and physical abuse within the police force?" Rita was curious to hear Ali's answer.

"Yes, and I support it. I think it's awful that men are allowed to act like dicks. It makes the whole police force look bad."

Rita listened to him as he spoke and absorbed his words like a sponge. *Damn, what a man*, she thought.

In her imagination, she leaned over the table and kissed him—full of passion and greed.

What are you doing? Have you lost it completely? she thought, and forced herself to snap out of it. The waitress who had just walked past them smiled and winked at her. Rita felt as if she'd been caught with her hand in the cookie jar and looked away.

They ate without speaking for a while.

"I'm sorry if I'm coming on a bit too strong. I'm just really interested in you," Ali said, locking eyes with her. Confident and unwavering.

"No need to apologise, but I'm in a relationship. With a woman. But I'm responsible for that, not you. And also, nothing has happened. You held my hand, that's all."

He leaned forwards and stroked her cheek. His hand was warm and strong.

"You know what? I think it's best if we pay and head back to work," she said.

"Yes, of course," Ali said.

Rita felt confused.

30

Jonny couldn't find Wilhelm Karlsson. Vasquez had given him a phone number, but it was out of service. None of the people in Wilhelm's class had seen him lately and nobody seemed to be able to give Jonny a straight answer about him. Judging by what he was told, it seemed like Wilhelm kept to himself and didn't spend much time with anyone else. The professors seemed more or less uninterested in their students.

Jonny decided to pay Wilhelm's dorm room a visit. He lived in the huge student accommodation complex called Sparta.

Just as Jonny exited Juridicum, his phone rang.

"Hi, it's me," Ali said.

"What do you want?"

"I wanted to tell you that I stumbled across an interesting group online. It seems to be a breakaway group from the Nordic Resistance Movement. You better come back here so that we can look at it together—the whole team."

"I'm on my way to Wilhelm Karlsson's dorm room. Can this wait?"

"No, Sara asked me to call you. She wants us to look at this together. We can visit Wilhelm after we're done."

"Fine, I'll be right there," Jonny said.

When he walked into the conference room, Sara, Torsten, Rita, and Ali were waiting for him. He felt warm and took off his sweatshirt.

"That's better," he said, and wondered why everyone was staring at him. "What?"

"Look at your shirt," Torsten said with a crooked smile on his face. "Your armpits," he clarified.

Jonny lifted his arms up and realised his sweat stains reached all the way down to his waist—if he'd had one.

"This is actually your fault. I biked incredibly fast to get here as soon as possible," he said as he laughed and wiped the sweat off his forehead.

The others turned to the whiteboard, and so did he.

Ali pointed to a long row of photos from what looked like a campsite in the forest. Young men dressed in white shirts, black trousers, and shiny shoes. Their faces were covered. One of them was holding a book.

"That's *For My Legionaries* written by the Romanian author Corneliu Zelea Codreanu," Ali pointed out. "He supported Hitler and is considered a legend in these circles."

"I've never heard of him," Jonny said, and looked at the others.

"Me neither," Rita and Torsten said in unison.

Sara squirmed in her chair.

"I've heard about him. A little."

"That's good. Then you know what he's about," Torsten said, and smiled.

"I don't know about that," Sara answered.

"If you pay attention to the photo, you can see most of the men are young. You can tell by looking at their posture, body types, and hands," Ali said. "But the man holding the book is definitely older. I've talked to one of my contacts today. He tells me Nazis look different today than they did in the past. They've left the leather jackets and jackboots behind and adopted a more polished appearance. But their violent ideology stays the same."

"Jesus," Jonny said.

"I've dealt with these guys before," Ali said. "In Malmö."

"Good," Sara said. "Then you can tell us more about them."

"They are taught to study, speak properly, and stop behaving like thugs. There are also splinter groups that have broken away from the Nordic Resistance Movement. My guess is we're talking about one of these groups in this case. I've asked a couple of experts to look at the surroundings in these photos. A biologist I talked to said he was convinced the photos had been taken in Torna Hällestad." Ali fell silent and looked at the rest of the team, waiting for a reaction.

"How could he tell?" Sara asked.

"The twisted beech. It only grows there." Ali pointed at a couple of trees in one of the photos.

"Oh," Sara said, "I've walked there a lot of times. The twisted beech only grows in a few other places in the world, including the Netherlands, if I remember correctly. I guess that means the group is based here in Lund? Or at least close to here?" Sara suggested.

"Sounds likely. And look at this . . ." Ali showed them another photo. "Do you see it?"

Jonny leaned forwards and squinted his eyes.

"Isn't the tattoo on that guy's wrist the same tattoo as the one in the footage of Reza's murder?" He was baffled and quite impressed with how much material Ali had managed to gather up.

"Exactly. I've studied it carefully and it's the same one. We still need to let Forensics give us their expert opinion, of course. But I'm pretty sure it's the same wrist."

"Great. Now we just need to figure out who the man with the tattooed wrist is," Rita said.

"Exactly," Ali answered.

"Do you think your contact could give us more information about these different groups?" Sara asked.

"I think so," Ali answered. "I'm sure he's willing to help us."

"What's important here is that we're dealing with an extremist group. This means we shouldn't be looking among the nationalists at the university but at more extreme groups. I bet this particular group isn't very big either."

"The question is if Wilhelm Karlsson is a member of this group," Jonny said. His stomach hurt. He found the whole situation very uncomfortable.

"Given his father's political affiliation with the Nordic Resistance Movement, it doesn't sound entirely unlikely that he would be a member of a group like this one," said Sara. "There is also a chance he's not a member at all but that he's simply friends with these guys—or at least the dude with the tattooed wrist—without knowing they belong to a breakaway group from the Nordic Resistance Movement. But let's start here. I want you and Rita to take care of Wilhelm Karlsson. We still need a DNA sample from him. And I have to speak to Baum. If Will is Wilhelm and involved in Reza's murder, we need to arrest him straight away. And if that's the case, he's the only named suspect we have."

Jonny glanced at Rita to see if she was offended. He was glad to see she looked happy and maybe even relieved. Sara had taken charge of the situation again.

31

Rita and Jonny drove to Sparta to try to find Wilhelm Karlsson.

Sara called Kabhat Celali. She wanted to ask how things were going with the double murder.

When her colleague picked up the phone, she sounded stressed.

"Hi, it's Sara."

"Oh, hi! How nice to hear from you," the voice on the other end said.

"How are you?" Sara asked.

"I'm under a lot of pressure, but it'll be okay. We haven't made much progress when it comes to the murdered couple. The damage to the child's skeleton indicates a fall from a fair height. There is massive damage to the skull and several injuries to other parts of the skeleton. We have no idea where or how he fell. And it doesn't really matter as both of his parents are dead. The DNA results came back from the lab and they confirm the dead child is the son of Carola and Tom Karlsson. Did you find Wilhelm?"

Kabhat shared the news about the dead child as if it were a subordinate clause, which surprised Sara.

"My God. So now we know for sure. And no, we haven't found Wilhelm yet. We're out looking for him and we've called him, of course. But we haven't been able to reach him. Also, we're working on something else that might concern him."

Sara told Kabhat about the murdered Afghan boy, Reza. Kabhat listened in silence, but judging by how fast she was breathing, Sara could hear how much the case upset her.

"Do you think this is connected to the murder of Tom and Carola?" she asked finally.

"The murders resemble each other as all victims had swastikas carved into their faces. But it could also be a red herring, so we should probably keep an open mind. It's happened before that we've been proven wrong after coming to hasty conclusions because things looked obvious from the beginning. So we'll see. I'll let you know when I know more. And thanks for telling me about the DNA results. As soon as we've found Wilhelm, we'll question him about Reza's murder. We'll also tell him his parents have been murdered."

Sara was taken aback with how cold and professional her own voice sounded. To tell a boy about his parents being murdered was sad and difficult and shouldn't be taken lightly. There was something especially raw about the murders they were working on, and it reminded Sara about the hardening of the social climate in Sweden. It felt as if society was in a state of dissolution. She knew the vast majority out there were ordinary and friendly people, but the power of those who had crawled out of their burrows was concerning. Thinking about it sent a shiver down her spine.

"I also wanted to tell you we've found a fingerprint. Other than that, the house was basically spotless. The murderer must have cleaned everything, probably with the napkin we found. But he or she forgot to wipe down the door to Wilhelm's room. That's why I suspect the prints might belong to Wilhelm. We'll see if we can match the DNA with the hat and the napkin. We should know by tomorrow. I'm not sure if we can get any DNA from the napkin though, but we might. The guys at the NFC are busy, but they'll make this a priority," Kabhat said.

"Exciting. And now the question is, what would it mean if the DNA *does* belong to Wilhelm, right?" Sara didn't wait for an answer. "As I said, we're doing everything we can to find him and I'll let you know the moment we do. He might actually be involved in the murder of the Afghan boy. We don't know yet."

"Hmm," Kabhat said. "We'll see what happens next. But I'll talk to you soon."

* * *

Sara got a cup of coffee from the coffee machine and sighed at how poor the quality of it was. It tasted bland and nasty and the milk wasn't real milk but something called *white*, whatever that was.

She stood by the coffee machine for a while, thinking. Ali took his job seriously and was both innovative and interested. He wasn't overworked or disillusioned and he had great pathos. Jörgen was a good officer, but he had seemed less and less interested with work lately. And now he was sick. She realised she hadn't spoken to Jörgen's wife for days and decided to call her.

"Angela," a tired voice said on the other end of the line.

"Hi, it's Sara. Sorry for not calling until now. I've been out of town. How's Jörgen?"

"He's much better but still hospitalized. We've been lucky as it could've been much worse."

"Great news," Sara said, and realised she had forgotten to breathe. Now she felt relieved. "And how are you doing? You sound tired. Are you getting any rest?"

"I'm very tired and on sick leave. There is so much to deal with and I'm all alone now. I need to care for the children and our home, deal with the tax office, and visit the hospital several times a day. But at least now I don't have to be with him all the time. The most critical part seems to be over."

"Poor thing. But I'm glad to hear Jörgen is doing better. Can we visit him?"

The woman on the other end of the line paused for a moment before she answered the question.

"Yes, but don't come all at once and spread out the visits," she said. "He's exhausted and sleeps a lot. But I'm sure he would love to see you. Especially you and Torsten."

Jörgen's wife suddenly sounded slightly less miserable.

Sara thought Angela was probably relieved to hear that she and Torsten were planning to pay Jörgen a visit so that she could let her guard down for a second.

"Should I call Jörgen?" she asked.

"No, I'll talk to him tomorrow and let you know what he says. Is that okay?"

"Sounds great," Sara answered. "Take care."

"Thanks. Easier said than done, but I'll do my best," Angela said, and by the sound of it, she was smiling.

Sara leaned against the doorpost leading into Ali's office.

"Any news?" she asked her colleague.

"No, but I'm not a quitter," he said, and took his eyes off the screen.

"I know you're not," Sara said.

"I've asked my contact to get back to me with a list of names of the members of this group. They call themselves Action Now! with an exclamation mark."

"Let me know when you hear from him."

He nodded.

In the corridor, she bumped into Torsten, who stopped in front of her and waved a bunch of documents in the air to get her attention.

"Here," he said, "are some old notes about the missing boy. I found them in a folder in the case file. Maybe it'll enlighten us."

Sara smiled and took the documents from him.

"I'll look at this later," she said. "But first I have to check with Jonny and Rita to see if they've found Wilhelm Karlsson."

"Sure," Torsten answered.

"Also, you and I need to go visit Jörgen. Angela said he's doing better. She'll let me know when it's a good time for us to visit."

"That's great news," Torsten said, and his face relaxed slightly. Better a single piece of good news than none at all.

"Do you want to go for a walk after I've talked to Rita? The weather is horrible, but I could really use some fresh air."

Torsten nodded and placed a hand on her shoulder.

"Let me know when you're ready."

She tried calling both Rita and Jonny, but neither of them picked up the phone so she gave up. The weather was dreary but she didn't mind. She put on her grey wool coat, a scarf, and a pair of gloves and went to pick up Torsten, who smiled when he saw her.

They walked with brisk steps towards Värpinge to get to the dams, which was the closest thing to a park they could think of.

Torsten was more than a head taller than she was, but Sara walked with long strides and had no problem keeping up with him—despite her high-heeled boots.

"Why do I get the feeling it's all connected?" Sara asked her colleague.

"I don't know, but I get the same feeling. That's why I wanted you to read my notes from 1998."

"I'll read them, but why don't you tell me about them as well?"

"It's hard to tell you. It's better if you read it. But I can try," Torsten said. "I had a feeling back then—I would call it a hunch or a feeling in my gut—but I couldn't put my finger on what it was. I just couldn't wrap my head around the fact that it had been so easy for someone to walk into a preschool and walk out again with a child when two teachers were right there. How could it happen? I just couldn't work it out. At times I thought Staffan Ehn had something to do with it, but I could never prove it. It was just something about his approach and the way he looked at me . . . I tried and tried, but I couldn't find the right angle."

"Isn't it interesting that you were such a star investigator back then too," Sara said, and nudged him.

"Now I realise there must be a connection that we've missed somewhere. Why did this woman decide to replace Wilhelm with this particular child and how did she know he went to that particular preschool? She could've done her research, of course. But it wasn't easy to find this type of information back then. I'll contact Staffan Ehn again today to see if he's ever heard of Carola Karlsson. It feels like he should at least know who she is. Right?"

"Unfortunately, we'll never know why Karl-Axel was singled out as both Carola and her husband are dead. With swastikas carved into their foreheads, which obviously connects the two murder cases. It's interesting because the modus operandi differs in every other way."

Sara stopped while Torsten kept walking.

"Stop!" she shouted after him.

"What is it? Tom and Carola were Nazi sympathisers. And we believe Reza was murdered by a group of Nazis. It doesn't make sense."

"Let's go back," Sara said. "I'll read your notes, later. But as soon as Jonny and Rita get back, I want us to sit down and have a chat with the rest of the team to see what they say about all these new questions."

"New and new," Torsten said seriously. "I asked myself the same things back then too."

"Yes, but we know more now," Sara said.

32

I don't understand where he could possibly be. He hasn't been to his lectures this week. And he hasn't been at home. So where the hell can he be? Do you think he knows we're on to him?" Rita looked deflated.

So did Jonny.

"Maybe it's not that strange. If he had anything to do with the murder of Reza Mahmoudi, he's probably staying far away from here," Sara said.

Ali looked just as energetic as he always did.

"I think it's fair to assume this guy is part of an extremist group. I understand these men find each other online and that they're quite good at knowing where to find people who share their political ideas. My contact is working on trying to identify who these guys could be. He'll get back to me tomorrow."

"Wow, can't wait," Rita said, and stretched.

Sara watched her closely and still felt convinced she was right about the chemistry she could sense between her and Ali. She just found it strange that Rita hadn't said anything to her about it.

"Surveillance knows we're looking for Wilhelm—or Will, who's probably the same person—and they'll keep their eyes open. It's important that whoever finds him swabs him. Surveillance knows about this as well. And now, I think it's time for us to go home," Sara said.

Her colleagues nodded and looked relieved. Big cases like the one they were working meant they had to be available around the clock, and suffering from sleep deprivation was more a rule than an exception. Being told to go home was basically like being granted a holiday. Sara laughed at the comparison.

As she walked towards the door, she touched Torsten's shoulder gently.

"See you tomorrow. I'm grateful to have such fantastic colleagues as you and the others."

Torsten smiled and nodded.

"Thanks. And right back at you. See you tomorrow."

Sara grabbed her coat, and on her way out, she saw Ali step out of Rita's office. She smiled again. She knew she was right and it was a very satisfying feeling.

"Hello," she shouted when she stepped in through the front door.

Johannes emerged from the kitchen. She could tell straight away that he was in a bad mood.

"Bella and Klara are so annoying. They ate all the food I saved from yesterday. I'm starving." He slammed the door frame with his hand.

"But there must be something for you to eat," Sara said, and felt too tired to deal with her grumpy son. "Is there something else going on?"

"Like what?" he asked, and pouted.

"You look like an angry little child. But you're a big boy now."

"I have the right to be annoyed, don't I?" he said, and walked away from her.

"God, give me patience," Sara muttered.

"I heard that," Johannes said, and poked his head out from his room. Then he laughed. "I know I'm being a baby. I just hate when you say that."

"I know—that's why I do it," Sara said, and poked her index finger into his stomach.

"You're weird." He laughed again.

"I'll make something to eat and I'll give you some—if you're nice. And I'm not weird, I'm the best mum in the world. But I'm also the most tired mum in the world."

Johannes hugged Sara and kissed her on the forehead. He was even taller than his father and he made Sara feel tiny. But she didn't mind. She hugged him back.

"It feels strange to hug a stomach," she said, and giggled.

"I told you you're weird."

"You know it's not always a bad thing being weird, right?"

Sara made some pesto as she knew her son loved it. She made it from scratch, using fresh basil. Sometimes she even managed to impress herself. She called Anders, who didn't pick up the phone. Maybe he was disappointed at her for not calling him for a couple of days. The eternal wavering among infatuation, love, and doubt was exhausting in many ways. If she could only find a way to accept the ambivalence, maybe it would go away. She sighed as she shredded some parmesan cheese over the pasta. Then she told her son to come to the kitchen.

They sat at the kitchen table and talked about everything between heaven and earth. When Klara and Bella came home, she prepared more pasta and they all kept talking. *Just like the old days*, Sara thought, and enjoyed spending time with her family. All her children were interested in helping the people around them and very keen on defending democracy and humanitarianism. It made her proud. They would all vote in the upcoming election and she knew they would all vote with their hearts.

Johannes told them about a discussion that had arisen in his class. He had been called a communist for expressing his support for refugees. When he told his family about it, they all laughed.

"Communist," Bella said. "I'd rather be called a communist than a fascist, that's for sure."

Johannes nodded.

"But I don't want to be called a communist either," he said seriously.

"No, all I'm saying is people who say stuff like that don't know the difference between the left wing and communism. And if you ask me, I would rather be associated with the left than the extreme right. The Left Party aren't communists anymore. They even removed the word from their name," Bella said.

Her brother nodded again and everyone around the table became serious.

"How's the investigation going?" Klara asked.

"It's moving in the right direction, but there are still a lot of unanswered questions and I'm sure you understand I can't tell you anything," Sara said, and stroked her daughter's cheek. The love she felt for her children was the only thing that never changed. The only thing she really cared about.

"We know, but I really hope you find whoever killed him," Bella said, and clenched her jaws.

"We will, believe me."

When Sara and her children were finished with dinner, it was already 9:30 p.m.

Sara sat down to read Torsten's notes from 1998. There had been so many questions back then. And now they had even more questions. Why were Tom and Carola Karlsson murdered? Who murdered them? At least now they knew that their biological son, Wilhelm, had been buried in a little grave under the Thuja hedges for all these years. And most likely, their living son was in fact Karl-Axel Altenius. But where was he?

Sara kept reading all night. She had planned to call Anders, but she never got around to it. While she read, she pictured Torsten's face and imagined how he must have been pulling his curly hair, rubbing his temples, under-lining words he found interesting, and coming up with answers only to realise they weren't the right ones. And how he had finally given up.

Staffan Ehn: Is he involved? If he is—why? I see something there at the same time that I can't see anything at all—what is it? What is he hiding?

Why Karl-Axel Altenius? How did the perp know the boy would be there at that particular moment? Is there a connection between the perp and the family? That must be the case.

I've asked so many questions but none of them give me the right answers. What questions should I ask instead?

Sara read Torsten's notes over and over again only to confirm they still didn't have all the answers.

She glanced at her watch. It was 2:30 a.m. She stretched and gathered all the documents in a neat stack on her desk. Then she turned the light off in her office and walked into the bathroom.

She stared at her pale face in the mirror. Her hair looked dry and she looked exhausted. She didn't like what she saw and spotted the disap-proval in her own gaze. She looked away and reached for her toothbrush. After brushing her teeth, she went to bed and fell asleep—all alone.

<h1 style="text-align:center">33</h1>

The day started with a meeting. Ali was supposed to tell them more about the Nazi group suspected of murdering the Afghan boy. His mysterious contact had provided him with information. Sara had no idea who the contact was, but she suspected he was a scientist or journalist.

Ali started his laptop and the projector. An evidence board full of pictures and names showed up on the whiteboard. There was the woman who had found Reza's body, the Nazi group they had found online, and the man with the swastika tattoo. Klara and Bella's student association was also on the board, as well as the group of young men who had harassed them and their students.

Three arrows showed that the man with the swastika tattoo was connected to both the Nazi group from the website, the gang that terrorised Bella and Klara, and the group that was seen assaulting Reza in the video. He was the link.

Wilhelm Karlsson's name was on there too. From his name, Ali had drawn an arrow to the Nazis and another one to the man with the swastika tattoo. Then he had drawn a dotted line from Wilhelm's name to Reza's murder, and another dotted line to the Nazi group they'd found online. Next to Wilhelm's name, he had written the names Karl-Axel Altenius and Molly Altenius, as well as Tom and Carola Karlsson. There were two crosses next to Tom's and Carola's names and another cross next to Reza's. Finally, there was a list of relevant geographic locations, including the dams by the sewage treatment plant and Torna Hällestad.

"Let me tell you about these Nazis," Ali said seriously.

They all looked at him, curious to hear what he had to say.

"This group call themselves Action Now! and they're a breakaway group from the Nordic Resistance Movement. They're aggressive, young, and fearless. Their leader, however, is an older male. You can see him in photos posted online. My contact doesn't know who this man is. But he did tell me that leaders of these kinds of groups often operate in secret and don't flaunt their political opinions in public. It's not unusual for them to be considered successful and respected members of society. Apparently, most of them have a background in humanities and not in natural sciences as one might expect. But we don't know if this is true in this case, of course."

Ali looked at his colleagues. Sara could tell that he was as eager as the rest of them. The case was big and exciting, and uncharted territory for all of them.

Sara glanced at Rita to see if she looked interested in anything other than Ali's presentation. But her facial expression was neutral.

"Considering Wilhelm Karlsson's background, he might very well be part of this group. These guys normally find each other online and start their conversations on less controversial websites. Chat rooms, for example. But let's remember that Wilhelm might not have anything at all to do with these people. Also, he's still missing. Rita and Jonny have been trying to find him, but he's not at uni and not at home. There is no way of knowing what that could mean. My contact tells me these Nazi groups are specialists in finding lost, young men who are insecure and easily persuaded. Most of them show affiliations to the extreme right, though. And now I'm about to tell you something that I think might help us." Ali paused for a second.

It was almost as if he was intentionally trying to create tension in the room. Ali had a dramatic side to him that Sara liked. His personality was interesting and attracted people's attention. And just like most people with great self-insight, he knew how to act to keep people interested.

Ali's contact had managed to get them some information about the man with the swastika tattoo. He couldn't tell them his name, but he knew a tattoo artist who was known for designing tattoos like the one on his wrist. The woman he talked about—Amanda Svensson—was apparently well known in Nazi circles and also belonged to a political group on the far right. Not Action Now! though. Apparently, the tattoo was rare. Not the motif itself, but the placement of it. The problem was that Amanda Svensson was constantly on the move and had no permanent address.

Sara gasped.

"We have to interrogate her immediately," she said.

"Sure, if we can find her," Ali answered.

"Okay, let's put out a BOLO to our colleagues in Malmö and Lund to keep an eye out for her as she might be important to the investigation. Let all units know where she could possibly be. Do we know what she looks like or how old she is?"

"Yes, she's twenty-eight years old and blonde. She looks quite ordinary, but I have a photo." Ali showed them all a picture of the woman. "She's not from Lund. She's from Falun."

"Falun?" Torsten exclaimed. "What the hell? Why do all these monsters come from Falun?"

"I'll call Kabhat Celali right away," Sara said. "And we must intensify our search for Wilhelm Karlsson. I hope nothing bad has happened to him." She rushed out of the room.

"Chief Inspector Kabhat Celali, Falun Police Department."

Sara told Kabhat everything she knew and asked her to look into Amanda Svensson's background and family history.

"We still haven't found Wilhelm Karlsson. Did you get the DNA results back yet?" Sara was impatient. "I'll update the case file so it's ready if we find any of Amanda's friends or family members who we can interrogate. We should probably try to find out if she knows Tom and Carola Karlsson too."

"The DNA results came back regarding the napkin and the hat. The good news is the two items seem to belong to the same person. This person doesn't appear in our records though. The fingerprints we found don't appear in our records either. But I think we've found our perp. Now I hope you can find Wilhelm," Kabhat said. "I'll call you as soon as I know more about Amanda Svensson."

They ended the call and Sara stepped out of her office. Her team was busy putting out the BOLO and planning their next move. Sara barely had to lift a finger.

Rita approached her, but before she could speak, Sara grabbed her by the arm and pulled her into her office.

"Is something going on between you and Ali?" Sara asked after letting go of Rita's arm.

Rita's jaw dropped.

"No, why do you ask?"

"Because it's obvious you guys are interested in each other." Sara looked serious.

"Maybe, but nothing is going on between us," Rita answered honestly.

"Okay. We're all friends and work close together. But it's important that no romantic relationships exist within the team," Sara clarified.

"But what would we do if two team members fell in love with each other?"

"One of them would have to leave the team and find work elsewhere. Simple as that."

"Okay, I agree," Rita said, and looked down.

34

Ali came running into Sara's office.

"I think I've found something." He was so excited that he literally jumped up and down a couple of times.

Sara looked up.

"Found something?"

"Yes, Amanda Svensson. I think she's in Sofielund. In Malmö." Ali moved his hands and arms wildly as he spoke and stood so close to Sara that she had to lean backwards to look him in the eye.

"Excellent. Finally, we're moving forwards," she said, and felt a jolt of adrenaline. "Where is Torsten? I want him to come with me."

"He went to the bathroom. She's on Rasmusgatan with another tattoo artist called Morris Carner. He's American. Alt-right."

"Do you think we should bring backup? If things get violent?"

"No idea. None of them are suspects, so it should be okay. I found Carner in our reconnaissance register and Amanda was linked to him. He has no criminal record and neither does she. But they've been linked to a lot of criminals. *White* criminals, that is," Ali said, and grinned.

Sara laughed. She knew what he meant—that they were both far-right and would never socialise with people who weren't white.

"Well, no surprises there," she said.

* * *

Sara and Torsten drove towards Malmö and Rasmusgatan.

Although Torsten knew Malmö like the back of his hand, he wasn't sure how to find the tattoo parlour as the street was long and the house numbers didn't seem to appear in order.

"Let's park the car and walk instead," he said, and quickly found a free parking space.

They searched the street until they finally found the tattoo parlour. A discreet sign saying "Carner Tattoo" confirmed they'd found the right address. The tattoo parlour was located in the basement, and the stairs leading down to it ran along the outside of the house. Torsten and Sara made their way to the door. The sign next to it said "Open," and a little bell rang when they stepped inside.

A man was lying on a bench and a woman leaned over his back with a tattoo machine in her hand. The woman looked up at Sara and Torsten and by the appearance of it, she quickly realised they weren't there for a tattoo. The man on the bench in front of her turned around to look at them. He also seemed to understand they weren't customers. Both of them seemed suspicious.

"Hi there," Sara said as she and Torsten flashed their badges.

"What do you want?" the woman asked.

"You're Amanda Svensson, right?" Torsten said.

"Yes. Why?"

"We need to talk to you," Sara said. "Don't worry, you're not in trouble," she added.

"I know," Amanda said without looking at them. Instead, she kept working.

"I'm going to have to ask you to stop working and come with us," Torsten said decisively. When he used that tone, people normally listened. But not Amanda Svensson.

"You're disturbing me," she hissed, then stood. Something about Amanda's body language made Sara put her guard up.

"If you don't want to come with us voluntarily, that's no problem," Torsten said, and took a step forwards. Sara followed him.

"I don't have time for rubbish like this. And I don't talk to cops."

Sara realised the situation could turn ugly at any second, but to her surprise, Torsten took another step towards Amanda.

"I don't think you understand," he said, and locked eyes with her. "This is not a request. It's an order."

Amanda seemed to finally grasp the seriousness of the situation.

"Fine, but I can't just stop working in the middle of a tattoo," she said.

"Then I guess we'll talk to you while you work," Torsten said with a friendlier tone.

"Okay," she said.

The man on the table didn't say a word.

Although he stayed calm, Sara could sense the animosity.

"I know you tattooed a swastika on a guy's wrist. Why did he want a swastika?"

"Why do you want to know?"

"I'm the one asking the questions here," Torsten said firmly.

"How would I know why Greger wanted a swastika?" she answered, and scoffed. Then she gasped, as if she realised that she had just given the police officer a name.

"Greger," Torsten repeated.

"Yes, is there something wrong with the name Greger?" she asked brazenly.

"You have Nazi sympathies too, don't you?"

"You have no idea what you're talking about."

"What's Greger's surname?" Torsten continued stubbornly.

"I don't know Greger," she answered, just as stubbornly.

"I know you know Greger, and I know you're the one who gave him his swastika tattoo. You told us so yourself."

"Fine. What I mean is that I don't know Greger well enough to know his surname," Amanda said. "Greger is a brat. He wanted a swastika and I gave him one. But I'm not a Nazi. I'm a nationalist. There is a huge difference, but I guess cops don't get that," she said provocatively.

"So you don't know his surname?"

"No. I know he lives in Genarp or Staffanstorp or something like that."

Amanda clearly didn't want the police to get anywhere close to her business. That's probably why she gave them more information than they had expected her to.

"Who are Greger's friends?" Sara asked, and wondered if Amanda would be able to read between the lines.

"I don't know," Amanda said, and stared at Sara.

"I think you do," Sara continued, "and I think you should take our questions very seriously."

"I don't give a shit about you. I don't want anything to do with the police," she snapped. There was no doubt Amanda Svensson was cocky, but Sara picked up something else too—fear, maybe? Or was she mistaken?

"Are you afraid of Greger and his friends?" Torsten took a step towards Amanda.

She flinched as if someone had just slapped her.

"No way. I'm not afraid . . . of anything or anyone." Her pupils were dilated. She sure looked like she was scared, whatever she said.

"When did you see him last?" Torsten asked with a calm and friendly tone to his voice.

She flinched again.

"I mean . . . a while ago."

Sara knew it was Torsten's strategy to stay calm and friendly, even when his questions where quite the opposite. The goal was to get as much information out of Amanda as possible.

"And when was that, exactly?"

"I don't know."

"Do they come here a lot?"

"Who?"

"Greger and his friends?"

"Greger isn't the leader," she said, and flinched once more when she realised she had said too much.

Torsten and Sara gave her their business cards and told her they would be back.

"My God, that was great," Sara said once they got back to the car. "You're a master."

Torsten laughed and picked up his phone to call Ali.

Sara drove while he talked to him. She could hear how impressed Ali was with their progress. Sooner or later, everyone who worked with Torsten realised how brilliant he was.

Sara went to the library to pick up a bunch of books and magazines. Her knowledge of neo-Nazism was limited, and she really needed to learn more about it. She knew a fair bit about the rise of National Socialism in the 1930s and the Second World War, but the modern Nazis seemed to differ significantly from their more rough and violent predecessors from the 90s.

The Nordic Resistance Movement was formed in the end of the 90s. Back then, the organisation called themselves the Swedish Resistance Movement. Around the same time, another group—National Youth—was also formed.

National Youth seemed more elitist than the Swedish Resistance Movement, and their intention was to act as vanguards in the impending National Socialist revolution.

It surprised Sara that she had never heard of a Nazi revolution. She kept reading.

One of their goals was to overthrow the Nordic democracies and replace them with a united state ruled by the Nazis.

Nazis had clearly transformed from vulgar thugs to more sophisticated and well-read National Socialists. They trained and studied and were groomed to fit the new, updated image. Sara felt a shiver down her spine. The more she read, the more uneasy she felt. Before she knew it, it was late and she had to go home. She returned most of the books but decided to take one of them home. She wanted to know more.

35

Sara drove to Anders's house that night. She knew they didn't see each other as often as they should. But she also knew it was good for their relationship not to see each other too often. She needed some space, otherwise she felt suffocated. As time passed, she became more and more aware of her own behaviour and how she functioned when she was in a relationship. The feeling of being suffocated could sometimes get tangled up with her fear of being abandoned. It was incredibly contradictory and led to self-loathing. By now she was aware of the fact that she was a contradictory person and knew she would have to live with that. Just like she would have to live with her past.

She missed her father. She missed the man he was before he was kidnapped and the man he became afterwards—the one who never recovered. Although he hadn't been able to cope with his own life, he was still her father. She needed him alive, but he wasn't. It hurt.

Memories wrapped around her like a heavy blanket of sadness.

When she arrived in Malmö, she stopped by the side of the road. She needed to collect herself and shake off the melancholy. She had a look at herself in the rear-view mirror and reached for her lipstick. She painted her lips red. Then she took a couple of deep breaths, started the engine, and drove onto the road again.

A second later, she was stopped in her tracks. A truck that was just about to pass her tore up the entire side of the Saab—her dear old Saab.

The truck stopped a couple of metres in front of her and the driver stepped out. Sara was already standing next to her car, staring at her scraped-up door.

"What the hell?" she shouted, and stomped her feet.

"It wasn't my fault," the driver of the truck shouted back.

"I know, that's why I'm screaming," she answered.

The truck driver walked up to her and scratched his head while he inspected the damage.

"What were you thinking?" he asked, and punched the palm of his hand with a clenched fist. "How did you even get your licence?"

"I didn't see you," she answered quietly.

"You didn't see the truck?" The man sounded angry and was very upset.

"No, I guess I didn't," she snapped.

"The rim on the right rear tire is all scraped up. It was brand new and you'll have to pay for it."

"Sure," she said, "I guess I will."

"It was expensive, just so you know."

She wondered why he sounded so triumphant but decided to let it go.

"Okay. I guess we better get to the paperwork, then," she said, and opened the door to the driver's seat, which wasn't an easy task as the door was badly dented. She found her insurance papers and walked over to the truck to see what damage she had done. The truck driver followed her.

"That wasn't much," she said, and pointed to the barely visible scratch.

"It was a brand-new rim," he said, and avoided meeting Sara's gaze.

"Oh," she said, and felt deflated. *Bloody hell*, she thought, and shook her head.

As the truck driver drove off, she could see the smile on his lips. She called Anders and asked him to come pick her up. Then she called a tow truck. *This will cost a fortune*, she thought to herself. *It could've been worse though*, she thought immediately after.

Ten minutes later, Anders showed up. He shook his head and hugged her. It felt nice. Feeling a bit sorry for herself felt nice too. And liberating.

Once they got to his beautiful flat, he started preparing dinner. He whistled cheerfully as he cooked, set the table, and served the food.

They spent the night talking about life and she told him more about herself than she had ever told him before. She told him why she could be so difficult and why her emotions tended to be all over the place and never moderate. He told her he loved her regardless. It made her feel warm inside.

Then they had a bath together and made love in the warm water. It was healing and refreshing, but made her tired. Grief, car accident, food, a warm bath, and love. It had been an emotional day.

She fell asleep in his arms and woke up at 7 a.m., feeling rested. And happy. *Today will be a good day*, she thought as she started the coffee maker and prepared breakfast.

A couple of minutes later, Anders walked into the kitchen. His hair was an absolute mess and he looked at her with eyes full of love. She gave him a kiss.

"I have to leave in thirty minutes. Do you want to eat breakfast with me or do you want to wake up a little first?

"I'll eat with you," he said. "It sounds cosier than eating by myself later."

She pinched his stubbled cheek gently and kissed him again.

"Take my other car. It'll be quicker than public transport," Anders said, and handed her a car key while she was brushing her teeth in the bathroom.

"Aw, that's sweet of you."

As Sara drove towards Lund, there was almost no traffic. All cars seemed to be driving in the opposite direction—from Lund to Malmö.

It was great driving the Alfa Romeo instead of the Saab. It had a powerful engine and at times, it felt like she was travelling at the speed of light. She loved it.

36

Sara read the medical examiner's report and felt nauseous. There were similarities to an old case from years ago, when a fifteen-year-old boy was murdered in a similar manner by a group of Nazis. Jonny had brought her the report. Even if they all knew what had happened, it always felt more real when it was written down on a piece of paper.

Reza Mahmoudi had been severely beaten. Then he had been dumped in the water—face down. There was clay in his lungs, which meant he must have still been breathing while he was in the water. But according to the report, he would have died anyway. The violent kicks and punches had mostly been aimed at his head and torso. His ribs and sternum were crushed.

The swastika had been carved into his forehead with a sharp blade.

Sara thought about the Nazi training camps in the woods, where men like those in the video went to learn things that were useful to others but highly inappropriate for violent people such as them.

It dawned on her how cold medical examiners' reports always came across. As if they weren't actually written about a human being—or by one. She knew it was a clinical statement, but it still sent a shiver down her spine. A human's life could never be talked about in clinical terms. But still, her death could be described as if she were a machine.

Sara had seen a whole lot of death in her career and she had lost count of all the suicides, murders, and accidents she had witnessed. But she would never forget her first fatality. She remembered it clear as day, and from time to time, she still thought about the young man who had died when his girlfriend drove their car into a tree. His neck was broken and he had died immediately. When Sara arrived at the scene, he was still in the car. One of his eyes was open and it stared at her. It was strange, but his death had stayed with her more than any other she had stumbled upon. Maybe because he had been so young, or maybe because it was her first.

She decided to stop thinking about death and walked over to the coffee machine for a cup. On her way there, she bumped into a colleague who she knew voted for the Swedish Democrats. She liked the colleague, but found it hard to accept his political beliefs.

Sara worried about the upcoming election. And she knew she wasn't alone in doing so. What would happen once the votes had been counted? There was no mistaking that the ultra-right was a violent group. But the hatred they spread and the threats that came along with it scared her more than anything. She worried about what the future had in store for them all.

For years, she had worked as an emergency buddy. Her job had been to take calls from anxious and lonely young people who were desperate, aggressive, and sad—and who were often victims of violence, bullying, or other difficult circumstances. What happened during the summer made her realise that volunteering for the call centre was too much for her to handle alongside her job. Now she spent all her extra energy on her son and daughters. It was the only way for her to keep her family from falling apart.

Sometimes she missed helping the young people who reached out for someone to talk to, and she knew there were more of them out there now than ever before. But she also felt relieved it wasn't her job anymore.

Rita entered Sara's office to tell her that they still hadn't been able to find Wilhelm Karlsson and that Ali was busy investigating everyone called Greger in Genarp and Staffanstorp.

"Do you think we can trust Amanda Svensson?" she asked Sara.

"I think so, but you never know. Did Ali find Greger?"

"I'm not sure. He's still looking," Rita said with a special glow on her face.

"I'll go check on his progress. By the way, Jonny is looking for Wilhelm in every café and restaurant in town as we speak. He must be somewhere. And we don't want to wait for someone to run into him by chance."

Sara smiled and returned to the medical examiner's report.

Her mobile phone rang and she saw the name Kabhat Celali on the display.

"Hi, Kabhat," she said.

"Oh, hi there," her colleague from Falun answered.

"Do you have any news for me?" Sara was curious.

"Yes, I would say so. Amanda Svensson worked for Carola Karlsson for a year or so. It was about six years ago. She did nails at her beauty salon and was a known member of a right-wing group. They weren't Nazis, but very much on the right, if you know what I mean? I think they were even further to the right than the Swedish Democrats," Kabhat said, and sounded quite pleased with herself for delivering such important information.

"Oh wow, not bad. Would you send me a memo about this?"

"Of course. I'm not sure what this means, but it's definitely interesting. And I think we can assume she knows Wilhelm too."

"Yes, definitely. I wonder how it's all connected," Sara said, and paused. "We'll bring her in. And how's your murder case going?"

"We're stuck. We don't have any technical evidence so now we're interrogating everyone in town about the family."

"If Amanda Svensson tells me something relevant, I'll let you know right away. I'll talk to you later. Thanks a lot!"

"No problem," Kabhat said, and hung up the phone.

37

Prosecutor Baum—Sara's constant companion and partner in difficult cases—immediately gave her permission to bring Amanda Svensson in for questioning. Sara called a sergeant, who promised to send a unit right away. The surveillance unit wasn't available for the task, but Sara asked the sergeant to send an unmarked car.

"It's not necessary to make a scene," she explained.

"I'll make sure to send a couple of plainclothes officers," the sergeant said, and Sara thanked him.

Then she called Åke Baum again to discuss the situation. But she didn't get to say much before he took over the conversation. *I guess it comes naturally for someone with his job to take charge of the conversation,* she thought.

"Isn't it great that things are finally moving? Baum asked. "And Ali Saunier has really contributed to the investigation."

"Yes, it feels great and Ali is a star. We're all grateful to have him on the team."

"Do you think there is a connection between the murders in Falun and what happened here in Lund?"

"I don't know. It could be a red herring. I mean, it's not all that surprising that people know each other in these circles. But I have a feeling you might be right. The problem is that Wilhelm Karlsson is missing.

We've looked everywhere for him, and as you know, there is a warrant out for his arrest."

"Do you think he could be the link?"

"I have no idea. It feels like there is a connection between the Karlsson family and the Nazis who murdered Reza. At the same time, we still can't figure out why Tom and Carola were murdered and why someone carved swastikas into their foreheads. It feels almost too obvious somehow. Or what do you think?"

"Impossible to say. We have a lot of work to do, still." Baum sighed. "I'll be over as soon as you've brought Amanda Svensson in. I would like to sit in on her interrogation. Maybe it'll give me some clarity to hear what she has to say."

"I'll let you know when she's here."

Sara and Ali went over the case and discussed all the people and places that were relevant, the modus operandi, and everything else they had so far.

"Now we can add Amanda Svensson to the list of people of interest. She did give Greger the swastika tattoo, after all. Maybe we'll get some clarity regarding her involvement after her interview," Sara said, feeling excited that things were starting to develop in a promising direction.

"This whole thing seems very complex," Ali said. "But the Karlsson family has a connection to Lund as Wilhelm studies here. Tom's political career—if you can call it a career—also ties them here, considering the Nazi group Action Now! and the murder of Reza. If you ask me, Amanda Svensson was the piece of the puzzle that made that clear. But we'll see what she has to say."

"I've been thinking," Sara said. "Tom Karlsson was an active member of the Nordic Resistance Movement and probably knew other members all over the country. This means it's fair to assume he knew people in Lund too. His son, who isn't really his son, studies law in Lund. Maybe Tom put him in contact with the Nazis he knew down here? We still don't know if he had anything to do with Reza's murder, but we do know he's missing. Why?"

"Interesting. Continue," Ali said, and gave her an encouraging wave with his left hand while he kept his right hand on the keyboard.

"We haven't told Wilhelm about his parents' murder, and as his grandparents are dead, we basically haven't told anyone about their death. We also haven't been able to get a DNA sample from him. Why is he missing? Does he know what happened to his parents? I say 'parents' as he still has no idea they might not be his real mum and dad. We know he was one of the young men who harassed my daughters and their study group. The harassment stopped after Reza's murder, by the way. We know that at least one of the guys he was with that night—Greger—murdered Reza. We don't know who the others are yet. We're assuming they're not students at the university though. Except for Wilhelm, of course. As far as we can see, Wilhelm isn't in any of the photos from the Nazi training camp in the forest, or in the video of the murder. According to my daughters, he's a lot taller than the rest of them. Therefore, he would have been easy to spot. Unless he's the man behind the camera."

"Right, that might be it! Continue; this is interesting."

"Who killed his parents? Maybe they knew something? When we started looking into them, someone might have thought it was safest to get rid of them before they told us what they knew? Or maybe another extremist group had them murdered and carved the swastikas into their faces to throw us off? I'm not sure I buy it, but what do you think?"

"Let me think," Ali said. "To me it makes more sense that they were murdered by other Nazis. I'm thinking about how things work in motorcycle gangs, for example. There, you murder traitors—or people who you think might snitch. So my bet is on your second theory."

"I agree, but what do you think they knew?"

"Maybe they knew about Reza's murder? Maybe it was a contract kill?"

"Who knows? This feels more complex than any case I've worked before," Sara said with a frown on her face.

Torsten popped his head in through the door.

"They've brought Amanda Svensson in. Do you want me to interrogate her? Or do you think it's better if Rita talks to her?"

"What do you think?"

"I'll do it," he said decisively.

"Good luck!" Sara shouted after him as he left. She decided to go find Rita.

"If Jonny calls, I want to know right away," Sara said, and gestured by holding her hand up to her ear.

"Of course," Ali said, and kept searching the records and databases for Greger.

38

He walked and walked along the side of the road, without really knowing where to go. They would find him soon. He was sure of it. What would he say? What would he do?

He picked up his mobile phone and wrote a text message.

You have to help me, I have nowhere to go.

The answer came quickly.

You're on your own. Don't write me again. Stay away.

He was cold, so he wrapped his jacket closer around himself and pulled his hat further down over his ears. He picked up his wallet and looked inside. He was almost out of money. *Shit*, he thought. *Someone must be able to help me.*

He got an idea and wrote another short text message.

Stay with you? A couple of days.

No answer.

He realised he had no choice. He had to go to his father and his father's annoying wife's house. He sighed and turned around to walk in the opposite direction. At least he knew his way around the area. He had biked there many times as a child. To school, to friends, to the beach. His bike was stolen once, and he never got a new one.

"You didn't lock your bike and now you don't have one," his mum had said, and puffed on her cigarette. She smoked in the kitchen. He hated it.

Two hours later, he was standing outside his father's house. He hesitated for a second. What would he say if the old man asked him why he had come there. He came up with a plan and opened the gate.

A dog barked inside the house but stopped after a while.

He rang the doorbell and a few seconds later, a woman opened the door.

"What do you want?" she asked with a thick southern accent.

"Is Dad here?" he asked, and felt small. He'd had no choice but to come there.

"He's in the barn," she said, and pointed. She couldn't have made it any clearer that she wasn't happy to see him, and it made him feel very uncomfortable.

"Okay," he said, and started walking.

He stood in the barn door and watched his father as he tended to his cows. He hummed to himself as he moved among his animals. His breath turned into clouds around his head. His nose was red.

"Hi, Dad," he said.

His father flinched and turned towards his son. A warm smile spread across his face.

"Oh, look who it is," he said, and hurried over to give him a hug.

"Can I stay with you guys for a while?" the young man asked his father, who suddenly looked slightly suspicious.

"What's wrong? You never wanted to stay here before."

"No, nothing is wrong. I just thought it would be nice to get out to the countryside for a while," he lied.

"That doesn't sound much like you," his father said, looking confused for a second.

He suspects something, the son thought, but stuck to his story.

"I've lost my job. The company went bankrupt, and I had to move out of the flat in Genarp," he said. He didn't have to fake his melancholy as it was his default state of mind.

"Okay, I'm sure it's fine. We have plenty of room since all the children moved out," he said, and put his hands on his son's shoulders.

"Thanks, that's cool of you," he said, and tried to smile.

He found it hard to go to sleep. He was scared. *What if I'm next*, he thought. Every time he heard a sound, he flinched. When morning came, he was still awake. The thought of them actually killing him was so frightening that he could barely grasp it. Instead, he tried to come up with different ways to get away, only to realise there was no way out.

39

What a bastard, staying away like this, Jonny thought as he walked from café to café on his way towards Juridicum. He had lost count of all the places he had visited in his search for the boy. He needed to find someone who could point him in the right direction.

The boy had been missing for quite a while now. Jonny had started looking around Sparta, but nobody there had seen Wilhelm lately. He had talked to a girl who told him Wilhelm wasn't a very social person and that he had a hard time getting along with the other students. When Jonny asked her to at least guess where he could be, she told him she tried to stay clear of guys like him.

"What do you mean," Jonny asked.

"Strange nationalistic ideas and rubbish like that," she answered.

"Are you saying he's a racist?"

"Sure, he's a racist. But I think it's worse than that. I think he's a Nazi," she said, and pulled a face.

"Why do you think that?"

"I went into his room once and saw a bunch of Nazi flags and symbols on his walls. But that's not all. I know he's been threatening other residents—the non-Swedish ones—telling them they'll be thrown out of here soon. If I can be honest with you, he's an arsehole."

When Jonny left, he was baffled by the state of the world, and the state of people's minds. Even if he too thought there were too many immigrants in Malmö nowadays, the thought of decorating his walls with Nazi flags and swastikas would never even cross his mind.

He shook his head.

You're a bit of a racist, aren't you? he asked himself. *No more. I never would have thought it would turn to this.*

He called Ali to tell him what the girl had told him.

"We still have no idea where he could be, but at least the girl confirmed he belongs to the extreme right," Jonny said.

"We already knew that though," Ali said.

"Yes, but now it's confirmed. I still can't figure out where he is though. I'll make my way back to the station now."

When Jonny came back, Sara was waiting for him. Together, they met up with Rita and Ali.

"I've got an idea," Rita said. "Could he be in Falun?"

"Of course he could. Maybe he's even at his parents' house. I know the police took down the crime scene tape. Kabhat told me they cleaned up the house too," Sara said.

Ali logged into Skype and called Kabhat, who picked up in less than two seconds.

Kabhat promised to send a unit to the house to see if he was there.

"Sometimes the most obvious answer is the hardest one to find," she said seriously.

"Do you think he might even have something to do with the murder of his parents?" Rita asked.

"I really don't think so," Kabhat answered. "I mean, he's not known to be violent. He's mostly known for spreading a bunch of nationalistic propaganda. He's not a member of the Nordic Resistance Movement, right?"

"Right. But it might be worth looking at the possibility considering all the Nazi posters and stuff in his dorm room here in Lund," Rita said. Sara nodded.

"You never know what's hidden inside a person," Sara said. "People are full of surprises."

"Of course we'll ask him about it when we interrogate him. He's wanted and detained in his absence, so he'll be arrested right away if we find him," said Kabhat.

"Great. Call me when you know if he's at the house. By the way, there was one more thing . . . do you know if he has a girlfriend back in Falun?"

"No idea, but I can probably find out," Kabhat said. "If that's the case, he could obviously be at her place," she added.

Sara waited impatiently for Torsten's interrogation of Amanda Svensson to be over. She paced back and forth like a restless soul and called Baum to tell him Amanda was at the station.

"I know," he said. "Let's see if she has anything to do with Reza's murder. If there is no indication of it, we'll have to let her go after the interview. But I've told Torsten already."

"Didn't you want to sit in on the interrogation?"

"Yes, but I don't have time. Torsten would call me afterwards."

"Great," Sara said, and ended the call.

40

You used to live in Falun and work for a woman called Carola Karlsson. When was that?"

Amanda Svensson stayed silent and refused to answer Torsten's questions.

"I'm not sure you understand the situation," Torsten continued. "If you refuse to answer my questions, you risk being suspected of things you may not have done. If we can just get through this, you'll be free to go."

"What would I be suspected of?"

"Association with a group of Nazis who murdered a foreign young man here in Lund recently," said Torsten truthfully.

"What? I haven't murdered anyone," she said, and stared at him with contempt.

"No, I didn't say that. But there are other crimes, you know. Protecting a criminal or aiding and abetting a crime, for example. So, do you want to answer my questions now?"

The young woman looked defeated.

This probably wasn't what she signed up for, Torsten thought.

"I asked you about when you lived in Falun and when you worked for Carola Karlsson. Do you mind sharing this information?"

She leaned back in her chair and placed her hands behind her neck. Torsten felt provoked but kept a neutral expression on his face.

"It was six years ago. I worked at Carola's beauty salon for a year. I did nails."

"How did you meet Carola?"

"Falun is a tiny town. Everyone knows each other. I knew she was married to the biggest Nazi in town. I'm no Nazi though, just to be clear. I'm a nationalist, and that's a whole different thing," she said, repeating what she had told him last time they met.

Torsten didn't say a word.

"Except for that, I really like Carola," she said, and Torsten noticed she talked about her as if she were still alive.

"Did you know the whole family?"

"Not at first. But after a while I was invited to their house to meet Tom and their son, Will. I visited them quite a few times. Will is a lot younger than I am. As far as I know he's a nationalist too. He's not like his dad," she said, and Torsten noticed that she answered questions he hadn't even asked.

"Oh," he said. "Do you know Greger?"

She flinched.

"I already told you the little that I know about him. I know he comes from Genarp or Staffanstorp or some shithole like that. And I know he wanted a tattoo of a swastika on his wrist. I gave him one, even if I really didn't like it."

"Is he the only one you've met?"

Torsten could tell Amanda was hesitant. At the same time, it was obvious that she definitely didn't want to be associated with a murder.

"Nope," she finally admitted, "I've met some of his Nazi friends too. They come to me, as they know I keep moving around. They like that. They always manage to find me. I must say I find them bloody sketchy . . ."

"Sketchy how?"

"They appear so proper and kind of snobby, but they're not. To me the way they talk and act makes them seem more like hillbillies."

Torsten felt a fire within—a fire that told him they were closing in on the answer.

"Okay, and what do you think that means?"

"I think their strategy is to look like big shots," she said, "but I think they're actually losers who come from tiny shitholes around the country. They're all the same. Tom too. And Carola. And I guess I'm not too different. But Will, their son, was always a different kind."

"What kind?"

"He did well in school and was quite an athlete. He was smart, at least a lot smarter than the rest of them. I don't know how to explain it better than that."

Torsten couldn't make sense of all the contradictions and other strange occurrences that kept popping up as the investigation moved forwards. Wilhelm hung posters of Nazi symbols on his wall, had grown up with Nazis, and was there to harass Sara's daughters and her friends. He was a former member of the Moderate Youth League but didn't belong to any other political party.

"Do you know where Wilhelm is now?"

"In Falun, I assume," she said, and looked surprised.

"He's in law school here in Lund," Torsten told her.

"Oh, I had no idea. I find it strange that Carola never told me, to be honest. We talked now and again. But we haven't talked in a while, I guess."

"He's studied there for more than a year," Torsten said, and found the whole situation slightly amusing.

"He has? Well, that's even stranger. I talked to Carola three months ago or something like that."

Torsten wasn't sure if he should tell her that Tom and Carola were dead or not. He decided not to as Amanda seemed genuinely surprised.

"Do you think Wilhelm might have joined a Nazi group like the one you mentioned? The one in which Greger is a member?"

"No, I doubt it. He was always a different kind, as I said."

"The thing is, I know he's been spending time with four men who we think belong to the same Nazi group that Greger is a member of. What do you say about that?"

"But-but . . ." she stuttered, "why would he hang out with him?"

"I don't know. Do you know how these guys find each other?"

"Yes. They find each other online. And they're all part of a closed group on Facebook. You should check it out. They call themselves Action Now!"

"How do you know?"

"In my line of work, you know more than people think. These guys think I'm just a dumb blonde, but they're wrong." She smiled triumphantly.

"In your line of work?"

"Yes, in my line of work—as a tattoo artist and a nationalist. But they think I'm a Nazi, of course."

"I see." Torsten had to agree about the fact that she seemed smarter than she appeared at first. "And who are the other guys? Can you give us any names?"

"No, I can't. And even if I knew their names, I wouldn't tell you. But I really don't know. I know Greger's name as he's been in my shop a bunch of times. The last time he was there he asked me to cover up the tattoo on his wrist," she said, and looked triumphant again. She couldn't hide it.

The whole situation baffled Torsten, but was careful to hide how he felt.

"And what did you cover up his tattoo with?"

She laughed a little.

"It's kind of weird, but I designed a rose for him. It's slightly bigger than the swastika and black and red—red like blood."

"Thanks," Torsten said. "And you're still sure you don't know Greger's surname?"

"I'm sure," she insisted.

"I have one last question for you now, but I might have to talk to you again later."

She nodded. "Whatever you do you can't bring me to the station. It's better if you call. Those maniacs have eyes everywhere, and I wouldn't want them to think that I talk to you guys," she said.

"Okay. My last question is, do you think Wilhelm is capable of murder?"

She gave him a serious look.

"How would I know? Ask his parents."

"Thanks, I think we're done here." Torsten officially ended the interrogation and asked Amanda to stay put for a second. "You're free to go, but we must be able to reach you if we need to talk to you again. And you'll have to let us know if Greger, or any of the others, shows up at your shop again. Also, you'll have to let us know if you move to a new address, or if you move your operations to another location. Deal?"

"Fine, but I might not be available at all times. You have my number, so just call." Amanda put a hand on his arm and stroked it before she left. It was a strangely intimate thing to do. But Torsten didn't flinch.

41

Kabhat and her colleagues carefully approached the Karlsson family's house. One of the officers looked in through the kitchen window without seeing anyone inside. They walked around the house and from the outside, it looked empty and untouched. But then Kabhat suddenly saw something inside one of the bedrooms. She was pretty sure it was Wilhelm's bedroom.

"Is that a duffel bag?" she whispered, and pointed to the window above her head. They were all squatting underneath it.

One of her colleagues, who was taller than she was, stood up and had a look.

"Yeah, there is a duffel bag there," he said, and squatted next to his boss again.

"Let's move in," Kabhat said. She got up and the rest of her team followed.

Kabhat had a key and opened the front door.

"Hello?" she shouted into the house. "Anybody here?"

The house was completely silent, so they all went inside. Kabhat prepared herself for the worst. *What if the boy was murdered too?*

But except for the duffel bag, the house was empty. Kabhat walked back to the car to get the forensics kit.

"Let's look for fingerprints," she said. "If he's been here I'm sure he left his prints somewhere. If we find them, we can try to match them with the prints we found after the murders."

They got to work and before they knew it, it was dark out. Inside the duffel bag, they found a document confirming it belonged to Wilhelm.

"I guess he still has some friends around here," Kabhat said. The others nodded.

She called the station and asked a sergeant to deploy a surveillance unit outside the house overnight, in case Wilhelm decided to come back for the bag.

On her way to her car, Kabhat called Sara to tell her what they'd found.

They were both relieved the boy seemed to be alive. But they also wondered what he was doing in Falun. As they saw it, there were two possible reasons. Either he had murdered his parents, or he was running from something back in Lund. Maybe he was involved in Reza's murder after all?

"If we find him, I'll drive him to Lund myself," Kabhat said. "I would love to see how you guys work down there, and it would be nice to see you and Torsten again."

"Sounds like a great idea. But I don't actually think this guy has murdered his parents. It seems too obvious somehow," Sara said.

"But we can't rule it out," Kabhat answered.

"By the way, we found Amanda Svensson. She's helped us quite a lot, although she was acting very hostile to start with." Sara paused to allow Kabhat to react.

"Wow, that's great," Kabhat exclaimed. "How did she know Carola and Tom Karlsson? What could she tell you?"

Sara told her what Torsten had found out during the interrogation.

"I'm impressed. I'm sure you guys will solve this thing soon. I hope we can get some momentum going with our murder investigation too. At least when we find Wilhelm, it probably means we've found Karl-Axel too. But that's a different story."

"Yes, I think it's fair to assume that's the case. But hey, did you find anything on Tom's and Carola's computers that could explain why they were murdered?"

"No, not really. But we'll keep looking, of course. These Nazis are good at keeping things hidden. They use firewalls or whatever it's called. I've got a couple of guys from IT forensics looking through the computers as we speak. Carola's computer was mostly full of Facebook posts and things like that. But there is a mountain of data on Tom's computer, so we're still working on it. He also had a second computer in his office. We haven't had the time to look at that yet. But we'll get there. By the way . . . I think Tom abused Carola for years. We can't be sure, but the autopsy revealed she had a bunch of old scars and fractures. And the medical examiner confirmed that the trauma causing the strangulation mark you saw when we talked to Carola must have happened recently. This makes me think that Wilhelm might have had something to do with their murders after all . . ."

"How come you haven't told me this until now?" Sara asked, feeling slightly annoyed.

"There have been so many twists and turns during this investigation that I must have forgotten."

"So Wilhelm might have had a reason to kill his father after all . . . But why kill his mother? I don't understand. This case is getting more complicated as the investigation goes on. Would you please get back to me as soon as you know more about the computers?" Sara asked.

"I will. Hopefully soon. If nothing else, I'll call you to talk about Wilhelm. I hope we'll find him tonight. Bye for now." Kabhat ended the call and sat down behind the steering wheel.

"There are still a lot of unanswered questions when it comes to this case," she said, and glanced at her two colleagues in the back seat.

"Oh, is it more complicated than we thought?" one of them asked.

"Yes, without a doubt," Kabhat answered, and told them about the Karlsson family, Wilhelm's potential involvement in the murder of an Afghan refugee boy, and everything else that Sara had told her.

Her colleagues' jaws dropped as they listened. It amused Kabhat but she held back her laughter. *Better to stay professional,* she thought, and left the crime scene as soon as Forensics arrived.

"It'll be a long night," she said, and they all fell silent.

42

Rita waited for Linda to arrive. She had suggested going out for dinner to avoid being alone with her. She felt like a coward but also knew being a coward was sometimes better than being brave. She needed to think about herself, and Linda's temperament was very different from her own. Rita was alert and driven, but not aggressive. Not at all. She was strong both mentally and physically, but she had a hard time dealing with aggressive people and almost always became physical when confronted by them. Her approach didn't go down well with Linda, so she knew it was safest to meet at a restaurant.

Linda had sounded suspicious when they talked on the phone earlier, and Rita knew she was expecting her to deliver bad news.

Just to be safe, Rita had picked a simple outfit—jeans and a shirt. She didn't want to dress too fancy and give Linda the wrong idea.

She heard the key in the lock and then she stood there. Linda was beautiful and radiated intelligence and energy, which was exactly what Rita had fallen for that first time when she met Linda at a restaurant in Lund. She smiled at the memory of the two of them walking out of a dinner full of boring and pretentious snobs.

Rita wasn't sure. Did she really want to end her relationship with Linda? *Shit*, she thought. *What am I doing?*

She walked up to Linda and hugged her. Linda leaned in and kissed her. Rita kissed her back. *God, she tastes amazing*, Rita thought.

"Hi, baby," Linda said after the kiss.

She seemed nervous. Anxious. It made it so much worse. Did she really want to hurt Linda? *You're out of your mind, you idiot*, she thought to herself.

"Let's go to Klostergatans," Rita said. "Let me change really quickly."

She could hear how stressed her own voice sounded. Linda looked sad. But she didn't say anything.

Rita changed into a pair of black trousers and a white blouse. She wanted to match Linda. And she felt utterly annoyed with herself.

"Come on," she said to Linda, who was waiting for her in the hallway with her coat on. She hung her head and Rita placed a hand underneath her chin. Linda's eyes were full of tears.

"Don't be sad. There is nothing to be sad about," Rita said, and kissed her again. "I love you. Let's go eat. Come on."

They held hands as they walked from Grönegatan and up to Lilla Fiskaregatan, took Stora Gråbrödersgatan up to Klostergatan and rounded the corner to arrive at Klostergatans Vin & Delikatess. They agreed it was one of the best restaurants in Lund. The walk took seven minutes, which was perfect for a cold night.

Rita kept talking nervously, certain of the fact that Linda was the one she loved. What did she know about Ali, except that she was attracted to him? Also, she forgot all about that attraction when she kissed Linda.

Once they had taken their seats and ordered a glass of wine, Linda looked at Rita.

"Just tell me. You want to break up with me, right?"

Rita was caught off guard.

"No, I don't want to break up with you. I love you."

"Did you cheat on me?" Linda asked, locking eyes with her girlfriend.

"No, I didn't cheat on you," Rita answered. And it was the truth.

"Okay, but are you sure you want to be with me?" Linda didn't look angry at all, just sad. Maybe the night had made her question her love for Rita.

"Yes, I'm sure. How do you feel?"

"I love you," Linda said, and took Rita's hand.

Now Rita wasn't the one in charge of the situation anymore—Linda was. Rita realised this immediately, just as she realised how uncomfortable it made her feel. Did she prefer being in charge of Linda and people in general? *Wow*, she thought, *what a mess I made of all this.* She decided to enjoy the evening instead of trying to figure out who she really was. She would leave that for a later time.

"And I love you. So let's eat," she said, and aimed a loving smile at the most beautiful person she had ever met.

When the food arrived, they were both in a better mood.

43

Rita woke up early. She was tired and her head hurt. Linda was sleeping next to her and Rita stroked her back and kissed her cheek. Her hands wandered up her stomach, towards her breasts. They were plump and beautiful with nipples like rosebuds. Despite her headache, Rita felt aroused. She continued caressing Linda until she woke up and answered her advances. It was among the best sex Rita had ever had. Afterwards, Linda's eyes sparkled. Rita was pretty sure the same went for her own. Her head wasn't hurting anymore.

"I have to go," she told Linda, who lay down on her stomach to go back to sleep. "See you later."

Linda mumbled something and Rita stepped into the shower. After, she felt refreshed and she smiled as she brushed her teeth. Before she went to the police station, she had a meeting with Reza Mahmoudi's psychiatrist. She had scheduled the meeting mostly because she felt the need to know more about what it was like to be a refugee and completely alone. She hoped it would give her a better idea of what Reza's life had looked like. She wasn't sure why it felt so important to know more about him. They had a good idea of who had murdered him by now, so knowing more about the boy wasn't necessary for the investigation.

She hurried to the psychiatrist's office. When she got there, she rang the doorbell and a receptionist let her into the building.

"Rita Anker, Lund Police Department. I'm here to see Berit. I can't remember her surname, I'm afraid."

"Berit Stjärna," the receptionist answered. "She's expecting you. Have a seat and she'll be right with you." The woman pointed at a couple of chairs in a corner of the room. Rita walked over to them and took a seat.

Three minutes later, Berit Stjärna showed up. She reached her hand out and welcomed Rita.

The window in Berit's office faced the west. Rita thought about how warm the office must be in the summer. At least on sunny days.

"What do you want to know about Reza?" the psychiatrist said when they were both seated. "Do you want a cup of coffee, by the way?"

"I would love one. I left home without having breakfast today," Rita said.

"Maybe I can find you a roll or something, if you're hungry?" Berit Stjärna offered without smiling.

"Thanks, that would be lovely," Rita said.

The psychiatrist stood up, left the room, and returned a minute later with a cup of coffee and a sandwich. The cheese on the sandwich looked sweaty, and the lettuce leaf had definitely seen better days. But Rita didn't care. She was starving.

"Let's start over. What do you want to know about Reza?"

"I wonder if you could tell me how he was doing. He was young and lonely . . ."

"Well, these young people have often experienced trauma that we can't even imagine. He was eighteen years old. He had been here for two years. He was a very ambitious young man but suffered from anxiety. Running made him feel better. Moving is good for anxiety," she told Rita, who knew exactly what she meant.

She studied the psychiatrist, who was plain-looking with grey hair, grey-blue eyes, and pale skin. She was Rita's polar opposite, and her greyness stood in stark contrast to Rita's almost white hair, ice-blue eyes, and golden-brown skin.

"He had a really rough time getting to Sweden. For example, he was sexually abused by a smuggler. He rarely had enough to eat or drink. It must have been a struggle to say the least. Reza and his family were Hazara. The Hazaras are considered to be one of the most persecuted groups in Afghanistan. His parents seemed very loving—at least judging by the way Reza described his mother. He was very well-behaved, but stubborn and strong. I would describe him as fierce. His parents fled Afghanistan when he was very young, because the Taliban were after them. This is not unusual at all, on the contrary. Like many in the same situation, they were forced to live like undocumented migrants in Iran. He talked a lot about his mother. He missed her a lot. And he worried about his future. He wasn't sure if he would be allowed to stay. But still, he did great in school and spent a lot of time learning Swedish. He studied together with a group of other students at the university. What a great initiative, right?"

"It was actually a group of students who decided to get together and help unaccompanied refugee youths with their studies," Rita clarified.

"Yes, and he was very grateful. I'm so sad to hear he's gone." Berit took off her glasses and wiped a tear from the corner of her eye. "I'm sorry. I know I should be used to these things in my line of work, but I really care about my patients," she said, and smiled solemnly.

"Naturally," Rita said, and smiled back at her. "This must seem like an odd question, but do you have any idea why anyone would want to kill Reza?"

"It's hard for me to speculate, of course, but I can imagine that people with anti-immigration attitudes would be provoked by him. He always stood up for himself, and if someone offended him, he would fight back. He was brave. And strong. But I guess that doesn't matter if you're attacked by a group of aggressive young men," she said with what looked like a bitter expression on her face. Or was it anger?

"No, unfortunately not," Rita said.

The conversation was over.

"I'll help in any way that I can," the psychiatrist said, and stood up. "Thanks for coming, and for a good conversation." She took Rita's hand.

"No, thank *you* for taking the time to see me. It means a lot."

Those fuckers, Rita thought as she biked back to work. She couldn't come up with a better word to describe the men who murdered Reza.

44

Rita And Torsten were on their way to Staffanstorp to pay a visit to an address where a twenty-two-year-old unemployed man called Greger was supposed to live. Greger had worked at a car repair shop for a while, but the shop had unfortunately gone bankrupt. According to the shop owner, the young man had lost his flat as a result of losing his job.

The shop owner described him as a nice guy who wasn't the smartest person, but harmless. Greger's former boss had no idea where he lived now but gave them his mother's address.

Although Staffanstorp was quite close to both Lund and Malmö, neither Rita nor Torsten had ever been there before. Therefore, they trusted their GPS to take them where they wanted to go.

"I can't see why anyone would come here," Rita said, and let out a little laugh. Torsten wasn't sure if the laughter was mocking or not.

"I don't know. Or, well . . . I know there is a café on the outskirts of town as well as a plant nursery. But a visit there doesn't take you into town though," Torsten said as it was all he could think of.

"Yes, but I've never been there either."

He sighed.

"Me neither. But then again, all I do is work."

After Torsten's comment, they both fell silent.

Rita and Torsten were both closer to Sara than they were to each other.

They stopped outside an apartment building in an area called Åkershus. The entrance door was propped open, so they stepped inside.

Gun Johansson lived on the third floor. They walked up the stairs. The whole staircase smelled of fried food and cigarette smoke, but was kept clean and tidy. The building looked like it was built sometime during the sixties or seventies.

They rang the doorbell and heard dragging footsteps in the hallway.

"What do you want?" a woman asked. Judging by how hoarse her voice was, she was a smoker.

They showed her their badges.

"What did he do now?" she said before they had even introduced themselves.

"Could we come inside?" Torsten asked in a friendly tone.

The woman opened the door wider. The flat reeked of cigarette smoke. Although the smell was one of Rita's least favourite, she pretended not to notice it.

"We're looking for Greger," Torsten said after sitting down on one of the rickety chairs in the kitchen, which was clean but outdated.

"I have no idea where he is," she said while she pulled a cigarette out of the package in front of her on the table and lit it.

"No, he's an adult," Torsten said. "But when was the last time you saw him?"

"Months ago. He has his own flat now."

Gun Johansson obviously had no idea her son had lost both his job and his flat.

"No, he actually lost his flat. The company he worked for went bankrupt," Rita said, and resisted an urge to cough.

"Really? He didn't tell me. I spoke to him a week ago. He didn't mention it then."

The smoke settled like fog around her face, and Rita noticed that her gaze was heavy with another type of fog. *Grief*, she thought.

"No, I guess it might be hard for him to talk about. We need to talk to him though. Do you know where he could be? Maybe with his father?"

The woman let out a hoarse laugh, deprived of all joy.

"He's never cared about the kid," she said. "We were never married. He knocked me up and ran out. He was married with children when I met him. He's a hillbilly on some farm outside Staffanstorp. I think it's close to Lyngby, but I'm not sure. I don't think they talk to each other at all. Not as far as I know, at least."

The woman looked defeated.

"That boy has always been trouble," she said. "He's always struggled in school and all that. I guess I haven't been the best support either, to be honest. But what did he do now?"

"It's nothing you need to worry about, we just need to talk to him. By the way, do you know if he has any tattoos?"

The woman looked upset.

"Tattoos," she exclaimed. "Does this have something to do with those Nazi arseholes?"

Rita and Torsten raised their eyebrows and glanced at each other, silently agreeing not say anything for now. A strange silence spread in the room.

The woman brought her hands up to her chest as if she was in pain. Rita stood up and walked up to her.

"Are you okay?"

"Bloody hell," she said. "Those monsters will ruin his life. And no, I'm not in pain. I'm grieving. Greger is weak. He started hanging out with a strange group of guys, got a swastika tattoo, and moved out. I have no idea what those guys are up to, but it can't be anything good."

She started crying.

"If his father had only been man enough to be a father, and if he hadn't left me with it all . . ." she whimpered as big tears trickled down her face.

"Can you try to explain to us what happened?"

Torsten and Rita could both see how she struggled to compose herself. She bit her lip and wiped the tears from her eyes with the back of her hand. Then she stood up and went over to the kitchen counter to get a roll of paper towels.

"I'll try," she said, and blew her nose. "Greger isn't very smart. As I said before, he's always struggled in school and he was bullied. I tried to help him, but I'm not a great student myself. And nobody wanted to help us. The school didn't give a shit about him and he suffered through it. Because he couldn't keep up. He went to high school but didn't do well there either. He kept failing. I decided to let him drop out, for his own sake. And I got him a couple of odd jobs around town, helping out in the supermarket and cutting grass and things like that. Then he got this job and moved out when he was twenty-one. It didn't last for long—his employment, I mean. But then a couple of years ago, he started hanging around with a group of Nazis. They're not from here, but I know they're Nazis. One time when I got home from work, they were all here. They didn't even say hello to me. They had stolen my cigarettes and basically eaten everything that was in my fridge. I didn't recognise any of them. But anyway . . ." She paused to blow her nose while Torsten and Rita waited patiently.

Rita felt incredibly sorry for the woman.

"He came home dressed in brand-new clothes. White shirt and black fancy trousers. He told me he'd been to some training camp in the forest. He said he'd learnt a lot. I asked him if the people he was hanging out with were Nazis. He said they were, and then he got upset and left. And then he got that tattoo. I've been terrified of what he's doing. But I haven't had anyone to turn to."

"What do you think they were doing in the forest?" Torsten asked while Rita stroked the woman's hand.

"I think they were doing combat training. He kept talking about combat. I guess it had something to do with their plan to take over. I've lived my whole life as a straight and honest citizen, but I don't have much to show for it. All of a sudden, I wasn't good enough for him. I wasn't fancy enough, I guess." She started crying again.

"I'll see if I can get you someone to talk to . . . I'll call you about it later," Rita said, and looked at the woman, who never seemed to run out of tears.

"Thanks," she said. "I could have used someone to talk to ages ago. But thanks anyway."

"What's Greger's father's name?" Torsten asked, interrupting the two women's intimate moment.

"Jens Pettersson. He's married with adult children. As far as I know, Greger has no contact with him whatsoever."

"Has Greger ever been evaluated for ADHD or some other dysfunction?" Torsten asked further. Rita thought it was a wise question.

"Nope, never," the woman answered.

"And you don't know the names of these young men who you call Nazis?"

"No, no idea. Greger didn't tell me anything about them. I told you that already."

Torsten nodded.

"I just wanted to make sure," he said. "Thanks for taking the time to talk to us."

She waved her hand dismissively.

"Do you have anyone who you can call? I'm thinking you might need some support, being as upset as you are?" Rita asked. She was seriously worried about the woman's mental well-being.

"No. I don't have anyone," she answered.

"Not even a friend?"

"No, not even a friend. I had a good friend, but she died a year ago. Cancer. I have nobody else."

"I'll see what I can do," Rita said, and took the woman's hands and held them for a while. It seemed to calm her down slightly.

They both left the flat knowing that what the woman's son had done would break her completely. Rita felt saddened by the interview with Greger's mother and decided to contact the women's association when she got back to the station. Maybe they would be able to offer Gun Johansson some support.

They went back to the car and found the address for Jens Pettersson. They drove out to the countryside. Although it was a wet and cold day, it was beautiful outside. Everything looked brown and grey, and the landscape was covered in a blanket of fog. Rita thought it mirrored their mood perfectly.

There were no real addresses in the area—only the names of the farms—so their GPS wasn't very helpful. After a while, they finally arrived at a large farmhouse surrounded by a couple of barns.

"Big farm," Torsten said dryly.

Rita scoffed. She was pissed.

"I can't believe this guy."

"Well, let's remember that we've only heard the mother's version of the story," Torsten said.

"I know, but why the hell hasn't he taken responsibility for the boy?"

"I don't know."

They drove up to the house and stepped out of the car. The raw and damp air made Rita shiver. It was quite windy.

45

It had been a long night for the two officers from the surveillance unit who were parked outside the empty house in Falun. Nothing had happened all night and when their shift was over in the morning, they were both in a horrible mood.

Once they got back to the station, they were met by the chief inspector with the dark eyes and amazing hair. But the two officers were too annoyed to be charmed by her.

"You should really get your own surveillance unit," one of them said.

"We're working a drug case," said the other.

"I know, but this is important," Kabhat said with a smile.

Both the officers had worked with the energetic chief inspector before.

"We know, but we have things to do other than support your team all the time," the first officer said.

"But that's your job. To support us."

"Either way, we have nothing to report," they said, and left before Kabhat had the chance to thank them. Kabhat refused to let the two officers' bad mood affect her and went to talk to her team.

"Nobody showed up at the house tonight," she told them. "But I have a brilliant idea. We'll have to assume Wilhelm knows something happened to his parents. He has probably tried to get ahold of them. Maybe he tried to call them? Even if their phones are dead, maybe he recorded a voice message? If he did, we might be able to trace the call. As the DNA we found at the house and on the hat all comes from the same person, it's also possible that he murdered his parents. In that case, he probably didn't call them. He might also be in hiding and too scared to contact anyone. If he is hiding, I have a thought . . . Carola's beauty salon. What do you say? It's possible, right?" She looked at her team.

"Smart," a female officer in her fifties said. She was Kabhat's closest colleague and they got along great.

"Can someone check Tom's and Carola's mobile phones? They should be with Forensics." She pointed at a man who looked tired. "You, get up." He got the hint and slowly stood up.

"I want two of you to head over to Carola's salon. Be careful. He might be there. He's arrested in absentia, suspected on reasonable grounds of complicity in the murder of the young Afghan in Lund, and possibly also for murdering both of his parents. We'll swab him here and then I'll drive him down to Lund with two of you. There, we'll interrogate him about all three murders at the same time as the investigation continues here."

She pointed at the colleague who had just complimented her, and then she pointed at a male officer, who was balancing his chair on its two rear legs. He was alert and always ready to work. And he was a great interrogating officer, which is why she had decided to take him with her.

The three of them left and she asked the last member of her team to go through everything in the case file again.

Kabhat got herself a cup of coffee and called Sara. It felt like they were close colleagues by now.

Torsten and Rita—whoever that was—had found one of the Nazis who had murdered the young refugee, and Sara was still a bit worked up about it. Therefore, they kept the conversation short.

A moment later, the officer who had been given the task to go through the mobile phones returned. He'd found nothing of interest.

"Shit," Kabhat said, and gave her colleague another assignment. She wondered why Wilhelm hadn't tried to contact his parents. As she had said during the meeting, she could think of two possible reasons.

Suddenly, her phone rang. It was one of the officers who had gone to Carola's salon.

She sounded excited.

"We've found him. He was at the salon. He's not saying anything though. And I've told him he'll have to come with us. He seems stressed. We'll bring him in."

"Wow, great!" Kabhat said, and hung up. Then she called Sara again.

"We've found Wilhelm. We'll question him here and then two of my colleagues and I will drive him down to Lund. We'll swab him for DNA and ask for a quick comparison to the DNA we found at the scene of the murders. I'll call the NFC before he gets here and tell them to hurry up."

"Excellent," Sara said, and Kabhat could hear how relieved she was. "I look forward to seeing you again. Our guy will be here any minute now, so I've got to go."

"I understand, I'll let you know when we're on our way."

They ended the phone call and Kabhat started preparing for Wilhelm Karlsson's interrogation. She knew it would be a tricky one. She prepared the custody suite for the DNA test and then she called the prosecutor in charge of the double murder case to tell him that Wilhelm was expected in Lund, where he was arrested in absentia. The prosecutor asked her to call him once they'd interrogated the suspect.

When she grabbed her notebook and her phone to head over to the interrogation room, her heart beat a bit faster than usual.

46

Torsten and Rita brought a very angry young man into the station. He was kicking and fighting. *For his life*, Sara thought when she met them down by the custody suites.

Torsten and Rita stayed calm and held onto him as he kicked and squirmed. On his wrist, they could see a black-and-red rose. Just as the one Amanda Svensson had described.

The guards took over from Rita and Torsten and removed the man's jacket, belt, and shoes. Then they basically dragged him to the cell door. One of the guards opened the door and pushed him inside. He screamed at the top of his lungs.

Rita shook her head.

"We spoke to his mother first. It was so sad. She was lonely and had nobody to talk to," she told Sara.

Sara asked them both to come with her to one of the interrogation rooms. She didn't want to talk about the case down by the custody suites. There were too many curious ears there.

"Then we went to see his father. They had been in contact for years behind the mother's back. The father told us about how Greger arrived at the farm all cold and desperate, but he claims he has no idea what he was up to before that."

"So now we're sitting here with a murderer on our hands—because it's fair to assume he's a murderer. It looks like this guy has two devastated parents and a future in prison to look forward to. He's not the brightest, but he's never struggled enough to get professional help. My guess is he ended up with the Nazis because they saw him as easy prey. He hasn't said a word since we picked him up. He keeps screaming and kicking."

They told Sara about what Greger's mother had told them. Sara leaned back and closed her eyes as she listened. She didn't want to miss a word.

"I think it's best if I interrogate him," she said when Rita was done talking.

"I agree," Torsten said.

Rita nodded.

"He won't talk to us, that's for sure."

"I'll give it a try, but I think it's safest if we get a defence lawyer here right away. Could you take care of that, Torsten?" Sara asked.

"Of course. Does Baum know we brought him in?"

"Yes, or at least he knows he's on his way to the station."

"Good. I'll make sure the lawyer gets here as soon as possible."

"And by the way . . . Kabhat found Wilhelm Karlsson in Falun. He was hiding out in his mum's beauty salon. Once they've questioned him up there, she'll drive him down to us. It'll be interesting to hear what he has to tell her."

Torsten high-fived Rita and before he left, he turned to Sara and gave her the thumbs-up.

"Finally, things are starting to come together," Rita said, and smiled at Sara.

"I sure hope so. Also, they're going through Tom Karlsson's computer as we speak to see if they can find something that might tell us why he and his wife were murdered. I don't think Wilhelm did it."

"Why not?"

"It's just a gut feeling," Sara said. "Now I need to prepare for the interview with Greger Johansson."

She wrote a long list of questions she hoped Greger could answer. She was also going to let Greger know they had reasonable grounds to suspect him of murder. But she needed to wait for his lawyer to arrive. It was especially important to do everything by the book when dealing with a person like Greger and a crime as serious as the one he was suspected of committing. She was sure it wouldn't take too long to find him a lawyer.

"Who will it be, you think?" Sara shouted to Torsten as he walked by.

"What? Oh, the lawyer. I don't know. Baum told me he would be here quite soon. Maybe this little break is for the best as the suspect needs to calm down anyway."

"Yes, I'm just being impatient," Sara said as her eyelid started to droop. "And I think I've been working too much lately."

She massaged her eyebrow with a finger and the eyelid slid into place again.

"I'm so sick of this eyelid," she said. "Why does it keep doing that?"

Torsten laughed and disappeared into his office.

Sara suddenly felt just how tired she really was. She hoped she would get some rest once they had solved the case. She sat down on the sofa and leaned back. Before she knew it, she drifted off to sleep.

47

Someone shook her gently, but it felt like a dream and it took her a while to open her eyes. It was Rita, trying to wake her up.

"The defence lawyer is here. Time to interrogate."

Sara yawned and stretched.

"What a nice nap. I'll be there in a minute. Can you give the lawyer a cup of coffee and tell him I'm on my way? I have to pop into the bathroom and wash my face."

"Of course," Rita said, and left.

Sara introduced herself to Greger's lawyer and then she went to get the suspect from his cell.

He had calmed down and came with Sara without putting up a fight. Sara got the feeling he was a bit jaded. But it wasn't all that strange as spending time in a cell could have that effect on people. It wasn't unusual.

They entered the interrogation room. It was gloomy and little, matching the cheerless nature of the criminal procedure.

Being in the interrogation room was never a nice experience for anyone—except for maybe an inspector who managed to crack a case. But that was another story.

She started recording the interrogation and spoke the date, time, and names of those present into the microphone.

She told him they had reasonable grounds to suspect him of murder and shared the timeline of what they thought his recent movements and activities had been.

"What do you have to say about that?" Sara asked the young man.

The lawyer stayed silent next to Greger.

"Huh?"

Sara realised she would have to use more direct language.

"I've just told you that you're suspected of murder and now I'm wondering what you have to say about that."

Greger looked confused and glanced at his lawyer, who gave him an encouraging nod.

"I didn't do anything," he said, and looked perplexed for a second. "I didn't kill anyone."

"So you're denying committing a murder?" Sara confirmed.

The young man looked at her as if she was an idiot. She forced herself to hold back a laugh and stay neutral.

"Can you please tell me what you were doing during the night between the seventh and eighth of March?"

"I don't remember."

"You spend a lot of time together with a couple of young men. Who are they?"

"Friends," he answered.

"Yes, but you know who they are, and I would like to know who they are too."

"I have many friends."

Sara tried a different angle.

"You have a rose tattooed on your wrist. What's underneath the rose?"

"Nothing." He aimed a blank look her way.

The interrogation continued and Greger kept giving short answers without any relevant information. Sara grew more and more irritated.

She turned to Greger's lawyer, who hadn't said a word yet. She knew he was only doing his job. He was only supposed to speak if asked to speak, or if he himself had asked to speak. But he didn't seem *interested* in saying anything.

"Maybe it's time for you to have a chat with the suspect," she said, and looked at him.

"I'd love to," the lawyer said, and Sara left the room.

* * *

Fifteen minutes later, the lawyer asked Sara to return.

"Let's start over," she said after sitting down again.

Greger didn't answer her. Sara waited. She had asked Torsten to join them as he was a better interrogating officer than she was. She wanted him to take over.

Torsten entered the room and introduced himself to the lawyer. Then he reached his hand out towards Greger. Greger looked reluctant, but after a stern look from his lawyer, he finally agreed to shake Torsten's hand.

Sara stood up.

"Torsten Venngren will take over the interrogation," she said to get it on record and to inform the others. The lawyer looked surprised, but Sara didn't feel like explaining herself.

She left the room and felt relieved, which was both unexpected and unusual.

She called Kabhat to check how close they were to Lund. Kabhat told her they wouldn't be there until 7 p.m.

"No worries. The team and I will stay here until you arrive. We can't wait to hear what Wilhelm had to say."

"I've booked a hotel in town, although I can't remember the name of it now," Kabhat said, sounding excited.

"Oh, you shouldn't have. I didn't think about it until now, but you could've stayed with me," Sara said.

"I only booked one night, but I might stay for two as this is relevant to our murder case too. In that case, maybe I can stay at your place," her colleague from Falun answered.

"Of course!"

48

Torsten interviewed Greger for two hours. It was difficult to get him to speak, but Torsten refused to give up.

After the interrogation, he called Åke Baum, who placed the suspect under arrest. Torsten headed back to his office after saying goodbye to the lawyer and walking Greger Johansson back to his cell.

The team met in the conference room and Torsten told them about the interrogation.

"The kid told me about his tattoo. It was a swastika until the leader of the Nazi group ordered him to cover it up with a black-and-red rose, just like Amanda Svensson told us."

"Great work, Torsten," Ali said, and smiled.

"Well, I kept asking questions and gradually let him realise how much we already know. Then he finally agreed to tell me more." Torsten paused for a couple of seconds. "He refused to tell me about the others though. The only person he named was Will. I assume this is Wilhelm Karlsson. He told me he wouldn't tell me about the others even if I tried to beat their names out of him. I told him I would never beat him, but that I would really prefer it if he just told me. Then he admitted to beating Reza up and leaving him in the water. He told me they came back the next night only to realise he was still there. He swears the boy wasn't dead when they left him in the water though. What's interesting is that he mentioned Will in connection to the recording of the murder video.

But he refused to give me a straight answer when I asked him more about it. What will be the downfall of these Nazis is the way they left Reza face down in the water. There is no way they didn't realise he would drown. It will be considered extremely ruthless and an obvious murder."

"Okay, but we still don't have reasonable grounds to suspect Wilhelm Karlsson," Sara said. "Did you manage to get him to tell us who the others are in the end?"

"No. I think he's been told he's fighting a war in which casualties will be inevitable, or something along those lines. He'll give us names eventually, but only when he realises he'll be left carrying the guilt alone if he doesn't. He came across as tired and restless to me. And not dumb in any way, just short-sighted. At least that's what I think."

"What did he say about harassing the student group?"

"He admitted to that too, but claimed it was a joke. He also told me that's when they decided to go after Reza. He told me he doesn't consider Muslims to be people. He calls them rats. I've seen the rhetoric before. Judging by our meeting with his mother, I'm not sure these thoughts are actually his own. But he's a young man with a sad little boy's soul. His parents haven't given him what he needs. Even if they both come across as loving to me."

Rita nodded and scratched her head. She clearly had a question.

"What did he have to say about Wilhelm?"

"Will was the only name he mentioned, and as I said, he was very careful avoiding the names of anyone else who was present during the murder or the harassment. He seems groomed somehow, if you know what I mean. And I'm not sure if he's being loyal or if he's scared."

"This is a step in the right direction. We'll interrogate him again and I bet you we can get him to tell us more," Sara said, looking pleased. "And tonight around 7 p.m., we'll get a chance to talk to Wilhelm too. The police up in Falun held a short interview with him and it'll be interesting to hear what he had to say. Very interesting."

Torsten suddenly thought of something and signalled to everyone to stay seated.

"I realise now that Greger accidently let something slip at one point."

The rest of the team looked curious.

"He used the word 'leader' one time, and the way he said it made me feel like he was referring to someone he had never mentioned before.

To me, it felt as if he was talking about someone higher up in the hierarchy. Someone who wasn't there physically when these crimes took place. We've been suspecting that it's an older individual who controls Action Now! and I'm convinced this is the guy he referred to. I don't remember the context exactly, but when I asked him what he meant, he answered evasively at first. I think he was trying to buy himself some time to think. Then he assured me that he was talking about one of the young men who were there when the crimes were committed. But his answer took too long. As you know, it's possible to answer too quickly—or not quickly enough. An experienced interrogation officer will pick up on these things straight away. Either way, I think we should listen to the recording to see if we can read something more into it."

"I'm convinced he'll tell us more during the next interrogation. Let him ripen in the cell," Sara said a bit too callously.

Her outburst surprised Torsten. *I guess she's tired*, he thought, and let her comment slide.

They all stood up and returned to their separate offices. It was Torsten's job to make sure the interrogation was transcribed. It had to be done. Despite it all, he felt satisfied with the interview as it had led to a confession. Also, there were plenty of other things that made Greger look guilty. The tattoo and Amanda Svensson's statement, for example.

"Sara," he shouted, and a moment later Sara came into his office.

"I've been thinking. I think we need to bring in Amanda Svensson and show her the video, or at least a still image of the tattoo. We need her to confirm she's the artist behind it. We have to build a strong case here."

"Absolutely. Bring her in as soon as possible," Sara said, and kept walking.

Torsten called Amanda. To his surprise, she picked up.

"Hi, Amanda. This is Torsten from the Lund Police Department again."

"What do you want now?"

Amanda's rudeness threw him for a second, but he recovered quickly. *Young people today*, he thought.

"I would like you to come to the station to have a look at a couple of pictures. Could you come in right away?"

"Yes, if you'll pay for a taxi," she said. "I have to be back here at 4 p.m. and there is no way I can make it in time if I take the bus."

"I'll send a unit to come pick you up," Torsten said. "Plainclothes offi-cers in an unmarked car," he added.

"Fine," she answered.

"That's my tattoo," Amanda confirmed after looking at the photos.

"Are you sure?"

"Very sure." She pointed with a long nail at a corner of the tattoo. "Can you see those letters? That's my signum."

Torsten couldn't see any letters and brought out a magnifying glass to have a closer look. Then he saw it. *Miss A.*

"I call myself Miss A when I work, and I sneak the name into every single tattoo I make."

"Do you tell your clients?"

"I tell some. Not all."

"Why?"

"Sometimes I do it for fun, sometimes because I want to."

Torsten realised she wouldn't be able to give him a better answer than that.

"Before you go, I want to tell you that you'll probably be asked to take the stand if this goes to trial."

"That's fine," she said, which surprised Torsten as she had barely wanted to talk to the police to start with.

Torsten knew the soft approach of his interrogation style was efficient and hoped more people would understand that adopting a tougher inter-rogation technique was often useless, as one can never force a person to share information. It was all about being a good listener. He thought Amanda was a tough woman and admired her straightforwardness, even if he didn't share or like her political views.

He finally read his notes to Amanda and she approved what he had written.

She waved and smiled before she left. He hesitantly waved back.

49

Wilhelm looked pale sitting across the table from Sara and Rita. They gave him a moment to process the fact that he had been taken to a new police station in a new city.

"I don't get it," he said suddenly.

"What do you mean?" Sara asked.

"What am I doing here?" he said, and shook his head.

"I'll tell you," Sara answered in a friendly tone while keeping her guard up. The DNA results were back from the lab. Wilhelm's DNA had been found on the hat, napkin, and door handle. But she wasn't going to tell him yet.

"The cops up in Falun told me I'm suspected of murdering my parents. So why am I in Lund?"

The young man seemed strangely unaffected by his parents' death and the fact that he was suspected of killing them. A less experienced police officer might have interpreted the lack of tears and emotion as a sign that he was guilty. But Sara knew better. She knew people reacted differently when facing a catastrophe, which meant his reaction couldn't possibly tell he if he was innocent or guilty.

"That's a relevant question," Sara answered. "You're suspected of murdering Reza Mahmoudi together with at least four other men sometime between the seventh and eighth of March. Also, as you've already mentioned, we have reasonable grounds to suspect you of murdering

Tom and Carola Karlsson in their home in Falun on March 10, 2018. In addition, we have reasonable grounds to suspect you of harassing several students at Juridicum on the first of March, as well as molesting two of the female students on their way home on the fifth of March." Sara paused for a second. "And you have the right to a defence lawyer."

Wilhelm sighed.

"I confess," he said suddenly. "And I don't need a lawyer." He stared at Sara and didn't even look at Rita.

"You confess to what?"

"I confess to harassing those students on the first and fifth of March," he said without flinching.

"Okay, let's talk about that in a minute. Would you like to comment on the fact that you're also suspected of being involved in the murders?"

"I didn't kill my parents," he said, looking almost smug. "And I didn't murder the Afghan either."

Sara and Rita glanced at each other.

"I think we might want to get you a defence lawyer anyway," Sara said, looking at Wilhelm.

He shrugged his shoulders.

"I have nothing to do with any murders, but sure, if you say so. Get me a lawyer if you want."

Rita left the room to call Baum, who promised to send over a defence lawyer as soon as possible.

"Let's pause the interrogation until the defence lawyer gets here," Sara said, turning off the recording.

"What? We're stopping?" Wilhelm said, holding back his rage. His gangly body was stiff and he kept his distance. He stared into space.

"Yes, Wilhelm. This is serious," Sara said. "You need a lawyer here."

Rita walked him to his cell, where the guards took over. Then she went with Sara to meet the rest of the team on the third floor. Their colleagues looked at them in a way only people who were expecting to hear news would look at someone.

"So?" Torsten said impatiently.

"He confesses to the two cases of harassment, but not to the murders. We're waiting for his lawyer."

"Did you really think he would confess to the murders?" Jonny asked, raising his eyebrows.

They had a seat in the conference room where the walls were white and basically covered with framed posters from years and years of the Lund Carnival. The carnival was a spectacular event that was known far beyond the limits of Lund.

They allowed themselves to lean back for a moment, but they knew they needed to keep moving forwards. Who were the men in the video? Who was the leader? How involved was Wilhelm Karlsson in Reza's murder? Was he the one behind the camera? All they had on him was his connection to Action Now!, which didn't really mean anything at all. Was he too smart for his own good? Or was he nothing but an insecure teenager acting tough?

"Even if we're close to solving this case, there are still too many questions," Sara said. The others seemed lost in thought and stayed silent for a couple of seconds.

"And not enough answers," Rita said finally.

Sara stood up and walked up to the whiteboard with a marker in her hand.

"Shoot," she encouraged her colleagues. "What questions still need to be answered?"

When they were done, the whiteboard was covered with questions.

Sara took a photo of it with her phone and the others did the same.

A couple of hours later, the defence lawyer arrived. When Sara and Rita went down to reception to get him, he wanted to know what his client was being accused of.

Sara briefed him and asked the guard to bring Wilhelm to the interrogation room.

"My name is Tomas Mood, and I'm your defence lawyer," the lawyer said, and shook his client's hand.

"Wilhelm Karlsson. I'm a law student."

"Oh, I see. Don't you think this is quite a dumb situation to put yourself in, then?" the lawyer asked, and cleared his throat.

Wilhelm looked bothered and didn't answer the question.

Sara started the recording and stated for the record that defence lawyer Tomas Mood had joined them in the interrogation room.

Then she started asking about the murders. She realised quickly that it was meaningless and started over from the beginning. The lawyer didn't say a word.

"You realise the harassment will be considered a hate crime?"

"Yes, I know the law," Wilhelm said, looking at his hands.

"Let's talk about this," Sara said. "Who were you there with and why?"

"I'll tell you about it, but I won't give you any names."

"How come you decided to harass the study group at Juridicum?" she asked.

"I'm a nationalist. I'm a member of the Moderate Party, but I've been thinking about joining a different political party. One that suits me better. The Swedish Democrats, or something else," he said as if the most natural thing would be to choose something more far-right. "I'm not a member of the Nordic Resistance Movement like my old man, but I see myself as a nationalist, and it's important to me that Sweden is kept Swedish." He paused.

Sara noticed how he seemed to confuse the concepts but decided to not interrupt him.

"Anyway . . . When I got back to Lund after the Christmas break, I started talking to a group of guys who told me they were nationalists just as I am. But they weren't. They were Nazis. Just like my dad. But worse, if possible."

"How did you get in contact with them? Not through the Moderate Party, right?"

"No, of course not. I heard about a website. As I said, I thought they were nationalists, but they turned out to be Nazis. So yeah, to answer your question, I met them online. We normally don't meet IRL, if you know what that means?"

Sara and Rita nodded.

"Who told you about the website?" Rita asked, interrupting his story.

"I think it was . . ." he hesitated for a second. "I don't remember."

Sara shot Rita a look that told her to take it easy and not force anything.

"Continue," Sara said, encouraging him.

"I didn't realise they were Nazis at first as they kept calling themselves nationalists when I told them that's what I was," he repeated. "When we met up I told them about these two chicks who run a study group for luxury refugees."

"Luxury refugees?" Anyone who knew Rita would be able to see how angry she was.

"Yes. They come here to take advantage of our wealth. Like parasites," he clarified.

Sara noticed that his blue eyes looked like ice.

"In here we express ourselves respectfully, regardless of what we think," Sara said without letting her feelings show.

Wilhelm shrugged his shoulders.

"When I met them the next time, I realised they were Nazis. But it didn't matter because we all agreed those luxury refugees had no right to be here. So we followed through with our plan and went there to bother them. One of the guys—an Afghan guy, I assume—got up to protect the girls. But we ignored him. One of the girls in charge of the study group studies law too, by the way. I recognised her. She's hot. But I didn't care at the moment."

"And what did this girl look like?" Sara couldn't stop herself from asking.

"I mean, there are two of them so I guess they're twins. Both of them have curly hair. Like yours," he said, pointing at Sara.

Sara kept a straight face.

"Tall, reddish hair, blue eyes, and cool. Super-hot." He paused for a second. "They remind me of cats. They look flexible."

Sara had to fight the urge to correct him about the girls' eye colour.

"Did you see this group of men again after that?"

Wilhelm shook his head, but then he changed his mind and nodded instead.

"Once, but then I told them I was going back to Falun and they seemed to be okay with that. It was after we followed the twins."

"Why did you follow the twins?"

"To scare them," he explained.

"Did you say anything to them?" Sara clenched her jaws and tried her best to relax.

"I don't remember. I think we called them whores or something like that." He sat with his back straight in the uncomfortable chair and didn't seem to care at all about what effect his actions had on others. Sara held back her anger and it felt like imaginary horns had grown out of her forehead. She tasted blood and her heart was pounding. Her eyelid started to droop and she blinked hard.

"Did you get close to them?"

"Yes, we were right next to them."

The audacity of this guy, she thought. *Someone should give me a medal for my patience.*

"Who are these guys?" Rita asked again.

"I don't know. But I can tell you one of them is called Greger. He's not very bright and has a tattoo of a swastika on his wrist. The others used code names inspired by Nazi Germany. Goebbels, Himmler, and names like that . . ." he paused for a second and a grin played on his lips. "Sick fuckers," he said.

"You told us you didn't realise they were Nazis until you met them a second time. That sounds strange to me as you're telling us they used old Nazi names as code names."

"I thought it was a joke," he said, and turned his eyes away for the first time since the interrogation had started.

"Funny guys," Rita scoffed. "What can you tell us about Reza's murder?"

Sara glanced at Rita, who understood that she didn't want her to tell him about the video just yet.

"I have nothing to say as I don't know anything about it, except for the fact that they planned to kill him."

Considering what Greger had told them, Wilhelm sounded cockier than he should have. But Sara wasn't going to tell him about the evidence they had against him until he let his guard down.

"How come you decided to go home to Falun?" she asked.

"I heard how these guys were planning something that I wasn't interested in being a part of," he said, and stared at Sara again with his ice-blue eyes. Then he looked at Rita the same way, as if he was trying to show how tough he was.

"And what was that?" Sara asked, knowing what the answer would be.

"They planned to kill that guy from the study group—the Afghan—because he had the balls to stand up to them. The same guy that you accuse me of murdering, by the way. Apparently, they videoed it," he said as if he didn't care at all. "I wasn't prepared to risk my whole future for a stupid thing like that. Even if I want Sweden to be free from all Muslims just like them."

Sara wasn't sure if she had mentioned the video to Wilhelm.

"What do you mean when you say they apparently videoed the murder?"

Wilhelm's face turned white.

"That's what you said," he tried.

"No."

"Then I don't know."

"What don't you know?"

"I just don't know."

"You don't know why you said the murder of the Afghan boy was videoed?"

"That's right," he said after composing himself for a second.

The air in the room suddenly felt harder to breathe. Sara knew she had to stay on course.

Wilhelm suddenly looked confident again and Sara decided to leave the video for a second.

"When did you go to Falun? Do you still have the ticket?"

"I left on the eighth," he answered, looking slightly unsure. Maybe he was trying to remember what date Reza was murdered. "The ticket should be on my phone, if I didn't delete it. The police up in Falun found me in my mum's beauty salon, so you already know I've been there." He looked at Sara as if he thought she was an absolute idiot.

The young man clearly lacked self-insight.

"We'll have a look at it once Forensics have gone through your phone. As you probably understand, it's been confiscated," Sara answered, locking eyes with Wilhelm. "How come you decided to go to Falun instead of just avoiding these guys?"

"Do you seriously think I wanted to stay in town when I knew they were planning a murder? I didn't want anything to do with it."

"So what did you do on the seventh of March?"

"I guess I studied," he said, and started picking his cuticles.

"You heard me when I told you what date Reza was murdered, right?"

Sara noticed a change in the young man, and it looked like he wasn't sure how to act for a second. But then he gathered himself and locked eyes with her again.

"Yes, so? I studied." It was obvious that he tried his best to sound dead certain.

Sara had seen a lot of interrogations. The difference between inexperienced criminals and hardened, professional criminals was that the latter never said anything. They kept denying any involvement and provided no information whatsoever. There was an obvious explanation for this behaviour. The less you say the less you risk getting tangled up in lies. Wilhelm Karlsson wasn't a hardened criminal. And he talked too much.

"Where did you study?"

"At uni."

"Okay, but *where* at the university?"

He hesitated again.

"Mostly . . . in the cafeteria, I guess. I wasn't sure what to do about the plans I overheard."

Sara was convinced he was lying but decided to let it go for now.

"So you went to Falun on the eighth of March? Where did you go?"

"What do you mean?"

"Your parents were alive then. Why didn't you go see them?" Sara sounded sterner than she had planned to.

The silence in the room spoke for itself.

"Where did you go?" Rita asked.

"I went to a friend's house," he said, and looked away again.

"What friend? Look at me, please."

Wilhelm scratched the cuticle on his right thumb. It started to bleed.

"A girl."

"What girl?" Sara asked.

"Just a girl," he said. His lawyer raised his hand.

"I would like a word in private with my client." It wasn't a question.

"Of course," Sara said, "how long to you need?" She turned to the lawyer.

"Half an hour will be enough."

Sara looked at the young man. He looked tired. Sara was tired too, just like Rita. She came to a quick decision. She knew it was time to start reeling Wilhelm in like a fish on a hook. She decided to take the chance. It was now or never. It was important to not give him a chance to think too hard about what she was about to say.

"Maybe we should continue after all. There aren't that many questions left. You two can talk after we're done here."

The lawyer shrugged his shoulders and looked helpless.

"I think my client could use some rest, and I need to have a conversation with him . . . But fine."

Sara took a moment to breathe and refocus.

"Who is this girl?"

Wilhelm hesitated.

"I lied. I went to the salon and then I wandered around town. Then back to the salon again. I didn't feel like going to my parents' house."

"Great, then I only have two more questions." Sara tried to sound as friendly as possibly.

He nodded.

"First . . . You mentioned that Reza's murder was videoed. Nobody told you about this. How did you know?" Sara asked, dropping the first bomb.

Wilhelm and the lawyer both looked shocked, but the suspect looked slightly more surprised than his lawyer.

"I . . . I didn't record it," he said.

"So, how did you know the video existed?" Sara asked.

Wilhelm's Adam's apple moved up and down. He swallowed a couple of times.

"I saw it online," he said finally.

Sara kept going.

"And how would you explain the fact that we found one of your belongings outside your parents' house and your DNA inside the house, although everything else was wiped clean?"

Wilhelm's eyes turned big and round. Their ice-blue colour suddenly looked grey.

He shrank in his chair and looked small. Then he shook his head.

"That's it," the lawyer said, raising his hands. "We need a break."

"That's fine," Sara said, feeling strangely satisfied. She had dropped both of her bombs.

50

Torsten had finally heard back from Staffan Ehn, who apologised for being unavailable before asking what he could do to help.

"Did you know a woman named Carola when you lived in Falun?"

"Yes, I knew a Carola," Staffan answered after thinking about it for a few seconds. "I had completely forgotten about her. Why do you ask?"

"I would like you to tell me about your relationship. That's all I can say for now. So please, tell me," Torsten encouraged him.

"We were an item for a while. But she was quite difficult. When I broke up with her she refused to accept it. She stalked me and wrote letters where she threatened to report me to the police for a bunch of different things I never did. But when I moved from Falun to Kristianstad, she stopped."

"In what way did she stalk you?"

"She could wait for me outside my door, and she sent me those letters that I told you about. I think she threatened to kill herself a couple of times in those letters as well."

"Did you save the letters?"

"No, I threw them out as soon as I left town. And I haven't heard from her since."

"Do you think she could have anything to do with Karl-Axel's disappearance?" Torsten wasn't going to give anything away.

"No, I really don't think so," Staffan said. "But what do I know? I'm no psychologist. Did you find Karl-Axel?"

"We're not there yet," Torsten said. "How come you never mentioned Carola twenty years ago—or now?"

Staffan cleared his throat.

"I don't know. I forced myself to forget about her. She was out of her mind, but I never considered her a real threat."

"That'll be all for now, but we'll talk again soon," Torsten said as he couldn't come up with any more questions to ask. "Thanks for calling me back."

Torsten hung up the phone and stood in front of the window for a while. At least now they knew that Carola and Staffan knew each other and that there had been a connection between the two families all along. The fact that she was a stalker and probably extremely jealous could very well be reason enough for her to come up with the idea to travel south and steal Staffan's stepson. It was all very relevant information, but it didn't make Torsten feel any wiser.

He couldn't get ahold of Sara as she was busy interrogating Wilhelm Karlsson, so he called Åke Baum.

"Prosecutor Baum."

Torsten introduced himself and told the prosecutor about his conversation with Staffan Ehn.

"Isn't it strange that he never mentioned her back then? Or now?"

"Yes, I sure think so. I think I'll have to bring him in for questioning."

"Yes, as soon as possible," Baum said. "I have a bad feeling about this."

"Me too."

Torsten ended the call and phoned Staffan Ehn back right away.

"I don't really know what more I could possibly add to what I've already told you," Staffan said. "And by the way, I'm in Luleå attending a conference. I'll be back the day after tomorrow. Can this wait until then?"

"I'd rather talk to you today, actually," Torsten said with a strange feeling in his gut.

"I can't, I'm afraid. I'll come to the station the day after tomorrow, after lunch."

Torsten had no other choice than to accept. Maybe it wasn't as urgent as he thought. Carola and Tom didn't exactly pose a threat anymore.

Luckily, they'd managed to keep the double murder in Falun away from the press. Media generally respected the confidentiality of judicial proceedings and Kabhat had friends at the local newspaper, which meant everything was kept out of the news for now.

51

Kabhat sat in Sara's office with headphones on and a laptop in front of her. She pointed to her phone and Sara sat down on a chair across the desk from her.

Kabhat listened attentively and hummed here and there. After ending the conversation, she turned to Sara.

"I've got some news about Tom and Carola Karlsson."

"Tell me," Sara said, and walked around the desk to stand next to Kabhat.

"You're like a child," Kabhat laughed. "I'll tell you, but please have a seat."

She shared the news with Sara, who clapped her hands.

"Wow, that's perfect."

Sara told her about the interrogation with Wilhelm Karlsson and how shocked he'd been when she dropped the information about the video and the evidence.

Kabhat laughed again.

"We're definitely moving now," she said.

"Yup. Let's go tell the rest of the team."

Kabhat and Sara got up and walked over to the conference room. Then Sara went to get the rest of her team. She also asked Beatrice if she wanted to join.

"Maybe you'll learn a thing or two about how to conduct an investigation," she said with a grin.

"You've got some nerve," Beatrice said, laughing, and came with Sara.

When they stepped into the conference room, the air smelled like impatience and adrenaline.

Kabhat cleared her throat. Then she started her computer connected it to the projector, and showed an evidence board to the whiteboard.

"As you can see here, we've now identified a connection between Reza's murder, Action Now!, and Tom Karlsson. We've found evidence on Tom's computer that proves he's been chatting with the members of Action Now! online. The people who are using the chat all go by code names, and no real names are used, of course. But we've managed to figure out what code name Tom used, as the IP addresses of both his work computer and his home computer are connected to posts written by a man called The Romanian. The men in the chat group talk a lot about someone they call the Führer. Unfortunately, we haven't been able to figure out who this person is, but we think he's the leader, judging by his code name. And we're pretty sure it's a man. But it could of course be a woman. Either way, it's mentioned that a Muslim is going to die to prove how powerful they are. We're assuming they're talking about Reza Mahmoudi. I don't think Tom was aware that his son, or his pretend-son, was involved with these guys. It doesn't seem like it anyway. They do, however, talk about a group of guys who use code names referring to Hitler's closest men. Greger doesn't seem to have a code name like the rest of them, but we're quite sure he's the person they call GJ. It seems as if they've mostly used him as an errand boy. We found the whole chat history on Tom's computer. It took some digging, but we found it in the end."

"But did you find anything at all that could explain why Carola and Tom were murdered?" Ali asked.

"No, nothing. Probably because Wilhelm did it on his own. I think it's fair to assume he's the perp."

"And who's the leader? How will we find out? Do we think Wilhelm or Greger will tell us?"

"Considering their behaviour, I think they might," Sara said, and crossed her arms.

"I think so too," Ali agreed. "And we can keep investigating it from other angles until one of them decides to talk."

Torsten took the opportunity to tell them about Carola and Staffan's past relationship.

"It's impossible to say what it means, but it sure is strange that he hasn't told us about her."

"I don't like the feeling of this at all," Sara said. The others agreed.

"Something else that's quite interesting is that Amanda Svensson knows Tom and Carola. She's also met Wilhelm, although it was years ago. Could she know more than she's telling us? Are we being naive about her? Maybe she's more involved with these guys than we think? Maybe even she's the Führer?"

They all fell silent and you could hear a pin drop.

"We never even considered that," Kabhat and Sara said in unison.

"But she's told us quite a lot," Rita said. "Why would she do that if she was in fact involved in it at all?"

"Sometimes things don't make sense in this world," Ali said, then sighed without looking at Rita.

"No, you're right about that," Rita said, and tried to smile at him.

"I'll call Baum to ask for permission to bring her in again," Sara said, frowning. She spoke so loudly that it made Ali jump.

"Is that really necessary? I think she'll come if we ask her," Torsten interjected.

"I don't want to take any risks here," Sara said. "Let's wait until we have a plan. And I still want to call Baum to get his go-ahead."

Sara spoke to Baum, who okayed her plan.

"I want to sit in on the next meeting," he said. "I want to be there when you compile all this new information."

"Sure; it'll probably happen tomorrow morning. Kabhat Celali, from Falun, is here, so we'll try to be as efficient as possible. Now we just need to find a way to get Amanda Svensson to tell us what she knows. We'll interrogate both Greger and Wilhelm again. We've sent Wilhelm's DNA off to the lab to see if it matches Molly Altenius. We need to know if they're related or not."

"Sounds good. See you tomorrow morning, then."

52

A blanket of grey fog had settled over Lund. The air was humid and the people who walked the streets on their way to work looked tired, cold, and defeated. Spring was around the corner and it always arrived in the south of Sweden before the rest of the country. In a month or so, nature would begin its shift from sleep to new life and vigour. Sara felt a similar shift in herself. She was full of energy and hope for the future. Things would work out fine, even if she knew it might take a while.

She felt grateful for how well she was doing. Her life had regained its shimmer. To be in love made everything feel easier. She felt like a new person. That morning, she forgot all about her history of fighting, difficult experiences, and failure.

Kabhat was waiting for Sara when she arrived at the station. She told her that the DNA results had returned from the lab. They showed Wilhelm was indeed Molly's son. Torsten came into the office and his eyes welled up when he heard the news.

"Finally," he said. "Finally, I can let this case go once and for all. I've been carrying it on my shoulders for almost twenty years. But I'm so sad it had to end like this. Instead of Molly celebrating that her son has finally been found, she'll find out he could be a murderer." He sighed.

They stepped into the conference room and waited for the rest of the team and Åke Baum.

When they were all there, Sara told them about the DNA results. Everyone gasped.

"Wow," Jonny said. "What are we going to do now?"

"I've never heard of anything like this before. And it doesn't make things easier that Wilhelm is in custody, suspected of three murders. I'm not sure if we should tell Wilhelm—or Karl-Axel—first, or if we should begin with Molly? We can't tell her he's in custody though. So I'm not sure how to approach this. Maybe we'll have to hold off telling Molly," Sara said. "Or what do you say, Åke?"

"First of all, I want to say this is fantastic," the prosecutor said. His eyes sparkled. "Never during my thirty years on the job have I seen anything like this. The problem now is that Wilhelm is in custody with a detention hearing scheduled for today. I'm not sure what we should do. I suggest we wait. Wilhelm needs to know about this, but there is no panic. We can wait a little."

"Okay, that's what we'll do, then. But whatever we do, this won't be easy." Sara shook her head.

Kabhat waved to get everyone's attention.

"I received a message this morning telling me there has been activity among the Nazis in Action Now! They have no idea that we're looking into them and that we're searching Tom's computer. And now it looks like things are starting to move," Kabhat said.

"What? What do you mean?" Sara said, and forgot all about the rest. "What's going on?"

"Someone who calls himself Goebbels contacted the Führer. He told him G has been caught and asked him what to do next. The Führer told him to stay away and avoid getting caught too. He also told him that if anyone so much as mentions the Führer, they will pay."

"Is there any way we can find out who sent these messages?" Baum asked Kabhat, looking curious.

"I'm not sure."

"Ali?" Sara said, and turned to her colleague.

"I looked into it last night. But I don't know, I'm no expert."

"Do we have the IP addresses?"

"Don't we need access to the computers to get those?" Jonny asked, and glanced at Ali.

"Well, not really. But we would need expert help to get our hands on the IP addresses. I think we should leave it to the forensics team up in Falun as they already have access to Tom's computer."

"Is it really that complicated?" Baum asked.

"Yes, it's complicated. A site like this contains a bunch of secrets and the users go through a lot of trouble to keep unwanted guests out. Everything is encrypted, which means that if you don't know how to work around the encryption, nothing makes sense."

"You seem to know quite a bit about this," Jonny said.

"Yes, but only in theory," Ali answered Jonny with a smile. "The site was open on Tom's computer, which seems a bit odd. These sites are normally protected by a timeout function, but they might not have thought about that. I'll reach out to your IT guys, Kabhat. I'm sure they'll find a way to sort this out."

"They might even be working on it as we speak," Kabhat said. "But give them a call. I think it's a good idea if *you* call though. I can never keep up with what they tell me anyway."

"They'll have to submit a request to the operator as well to get the IP addresses—if they're available. A problem is that we still won't know who the users are though. We could try to get information via social engineering, which is a bit complicated as it could be considered entrapment. We'll see what the IT guys think we should do next."

"And what's 'social engineering'?" Sara asked.

"It's a combination of technically hacking into the page you want to access and socially manipulating people in an attempt to get your hands on information. A lot of companies encounter this. What it really means is that you exploit weaknesses in the human psyche and manipulate people into sharing confidential and private information. This can happen via messages or emails, for example. In other words, you trick people. And to do anything like that, we need approval from the prosecutor. What do you say, Åke?"

"You officially have my approval," Åke said. "And move quickly. There is a real risk these guys will leave the country if we don't hurry up."

"I'll take care of it, but let's keep our expectations realistic," Ali said, and left the room.

"I wonder who the Führer is," Kabhat said, "and if this person has something to do with the murder of Tom and Carola. It sure seems as if he or she was involved in Reza's murder. Sara, what do you think Wilhelm will be able to tell us?"

"No idea, but I have a feeling it'll be hard to get him to collaborate. I think it would be faster to find another angle, like the one Ali suggested, for example."

"I have another idea," Rita said. "Maybe Ali's contact can help us."

"You're right!" Sara exclaimed, and rushed after him.

She caught up with him just as he entered the forensics department.

"Your contact!" she panted.

Ali looked confused for a second.

"Yes, do you think he would be willing to help us some more?"

"I'll ask him, but we still need Forensics to help us out here."

"Absolutely, but I'd really appreciate if you could call him and ask him to help us. Maybe he knows more now?"

"I'll call him as soon as I get back to the office. Okay?"

"Of course, and thanks," Sara answered, and headed back to the others.

"Ali will talk to his contact. I'm hoping he'll be able to find something now that we have some new information to share with him. I wonder who this guy is . . ."

"Great," Baum said. "Do you mind telling me a bit more about how these different groups are connected? I don't think I'm completely up to speed."

Kabhat started her computer again and projected her evidence as well as Ali's onto the whiteboard to compare the two.

Baum was impressed. He smiled and clapped his hands as they spoke. Kabhat looked baffled. It was clear she had never met someone like Baum before.

"You guys have done an amazing job," he said, still applauding.

Kabhat laughed with her mouth open wide. Her laughter was contagious and filled the room with joy and hope.

"We're very happy about this collaboration," she said. "It's truly amazing how much we've accomplished by working together like this," she continued with a wide smile spread across her face.

"Yes, that's exactly what I meant," Baum said, turning serious.

Torsten was on his way to interrogate Greger while Sara was preparing to talk to Wilhelm again. Hopefully, they would be able to get both to tell them something relevant. Also, it was time to tell Wilhelm who his biological mother was.

"I'm not looking forward to this," Sara said seriously as she went to get Wilhelm from his cell.

Torsten had to wait for a while to avoid the two suspects bumping into each other in the corridor between the custody suites and the interrogation rooms. It would be disastrous if Greger found out Wilhelm was there too.

53

As she sat across the table from Wilhelm Karlsson, she saw him in a new light. He looked small and not at all as cocky as before. He had probably realised the gravity of his situation by now. Sara had regained her balance. She wasn't angry anymore. She thought about all the young people she'd talked to during her years as an emergency buddy and how lonely and let down they had all been. The adults in these youths' lives absolutely carried some of the blame for not seeing what they were going through.

She braced herself. She knew she would have to break through Wilhelm's barrier, regardless of how bad she felt for him.

"I would appreciate it if you could tell me the whole story about your Nazi friends and the murder of Tom and Carola."

He stayed silent. Sara wasn't sure if she would be able to get him to speak at all.

"All I have to say is that they were already dead when I got there," he blurted suddenly.

"Then why did you wipe everything down with the napkin?"

"I was afraid you would think I did it if you found my fingerprints there."

"Yet, you trying to cover up your tracks had the opposite effect," Sara explained.

Wilhelm told her that he walked over to his mother's salon after stepping off the train. He didn't feel like going to his parents' house. But eventually, he called his mother, who picked up the phone and asked him to come home. He didn't want to go there but realised he had no other option. He took the bus from town and got off at the stop outside their neighbourhood. He walked over to the house without meeting anyone on the way there. The door was open so he walked into the house and called out to his parents. But nobody answered him. He found his mother in the kitchen.

"I panicked and ran into the living room. Then I saw my dad. I got the napkin and wiped all surfaces clean. Then I ran away. I dropped my hat as I ran. I assume you guys must've found it."

Sara nodded and encouraged him to keep talking.

"And I didn't kill them. It was probably the Autonomous Left," he suggested.

"Did you ever hear about a murder committed by the Autonomous Left?" Sara asked.

"What about Baader-Meinhof and the Red Army Faction?" he said, and grinned. He was incredibly hard to read.

"Yes, but they were never active in Sweden, and they didn't belong to the Autonomous Left. I think they were revolutionary, if anything, and they operated in the seventies."

"Hmm."

Sara wondered what was going on in his mind. There was something lifeless about his tall, gangly body, as if it lacked the ability to react and act. And in a way, his personality seemed equally lifeless. The boy had a polished appearance and looked very put together, but he came across as flat and empty, like a paper doll.

He answered her questions but didn't say anything. Sara paused for a second to come up with a new strategy. She decided to be non-confrontational. Instead, she would allow him to tell his story from his own perspective. It was worth a try.

It turned out she was right.

He slowly let his guard down and started from the beginning.

She listened to him and was baffled by what was hidden underneath his polished surface.

Sara felt done with the interrogation and Wilhelm looked exhausted. He was to be detained during the afternoon, so she knew he needed to rest.

Now it was time to drop another bomb, and it was about something completely different.

"Do you know what we found buried in your parents' garden?" she asked.

He shook his head.

"The police found the skeleton of a little boy. Barely two years old," Sara said. "He was Tom and Carola's son."

There was a moment of tense silence.

"What? Who?"

Sara was convinced that if Wilhelm's skin could turn any paler than it already was, it would have.

"A little boy named Wilhelm Karlsson," Sara said.

"But-but . . . That's me!" he stuttered.

"Here's the thing," Sara said. "A young boy was kidnapped from Lund in 1998 and he was never found. Now we know you're that boy. I'm sorry that I have to tell you like this, but it's the truth."

"What? What are you talking about?" Wilhelm seemed utterly confused. "And who are my parents, then?"

"Your mother's name is Molly Altenius, and she still lives here in Lund, in the same house in which you once lived. She's a doctor. Your father died when you were a baby."

Wilhelm was quiet for a while.

"Why did they kidnap *me* of all children?" For the first time since the interrogation started, his eyes teared up.

"We don't know, but we suspect it had something to do with the fact that Carola had a relationship with Molly's husband—your stepfather—many years ago. She was very angry with him, or rather obsessed with him, it seems. Maybe it was to get revenge on him for being happy. We don't really know."

"So, what's my name?"

"Your name is Karl-Axel Altenius."

The young man looked strangely happy and Sara saw a sparkle of hope in his eye—one that she had never seen before.

"Sounds posh."

"Oh, does it?" Sara asked him.

"I'd like to know more about Molly. My mother," he said, sounding hopeful.

"Another time. We must end the interrogation here. It's time for lunch and you need to rest before the detention hearing."

"When can I see her?"

It was as if he had forgotten the fact that he was suspected of murdering three people. It surprised Sara as much as it felt completely natural.

"It'll probably be a while," she said, and saw how disappointed he was by her answer.

54

Ali and one of the IT technicians from the forensics department had joined a video call with the forensics department in Falun.

They could see that two users had logged into the chat recently, although there was no way of knowing who they were. The operator had helped them trace one of the IP addresses to Staffanstorp though.

"Lucky," the technician from Lund said, "in that area the towers are put up so close to each other that it's basically impossible to pinpoint a location."

Ali felt overjoyed. He clenched his fist and pumped it in the air a couple of times.

"Yes," he whispered. "Yes, yes, yes."

It was an incredible feeling of victory. Not only did they have Greger and Wilhelm in custody, but now they had a chance of finding more Nazis.

"How close can you get?" he asked the technician next to him.

"Pretty close. The neighbourhood is called Åkershus. There are a couple of apartment buildings there, but at least it's quite a small area to search. Some of the buildings have basements. I'm sure you'll find the people you're looking for," she said, and smiled.

Ali asked for a report and she got it ready for him quickly.

He thanked her for her help, and without thinking, he kissed her on the cheek. She just laughed at him.

* * *

Ali ran upstairs and found Rita, Sara, and Kabhat. The prosecutor had left and would be back later that afternoon. Torsten and Jonny were talking to Wilhelm.

Once Ali had told them what the technician had just said, he hurried downstairs to ask a sergeant for help. After listening to Ali, the sergeant called the operations centre, who agreed to send two units to help them.

Ali ran back upstairs to put on his bulletproof vest and check out his weapon. Kabhat was already dressed and ready to go. She had borrowed a bulletproof vest from Sara. It fitted her perfectly even if she was wider and taller than Sara, who was strong but slim. Each woman tied her hair up in a knot while adrenaline made their fingers shake slightly.

They decided to take two cars to leave room for additional passengers, and then they waited for the units that had promised to come along as backup.

The tension was almost unbearable, and when the backup units arrived in unmarked cars, they stopped next to Ali and rolled down their windows to receive further instructions.

They took two different routes to avoid attracting attention.

It was getting dark.

Sara called Torsten and told him about what had just happened. She asked him and Jonny to question Greger as she hadn't had the time to do so yet. She also told them they were welcome to join them afterwards, if they had time. She hung up the phone.

"Okay," she told her colleagues, "once we get there, we'll split up in teams of two and search basement after basement. Isn't it strange that we're going to the neighbourhood where Greger's mother lives, by the way? The same block, even. I wonder if she knew where they were all along. What do you think, Ali?"

"No idea. I don't think Rita and Torsten asked about it. But as I understand, she felt horrible about what her son was up to and I think she would have told us if she knew."

"If they hang around in the area often, maybe someone has seen them?" Sara said.

"You never know," Ali said. "I guess we'll find out."

* * *

Ali and Sara were the first ones to arrive at their destination, followed by Rita and Kabhat. A couple of minutes later, the two other units arrived. They met up behind the buildings and hoped nobody would notice them. They had parked in different car parks and there was no way a civilian would be able to tell theirs were police cars.

"Right, let's team up. I want everyone to keep their radios turned on. The operations centre has sorted us out with our own channel."

Sara made sure they had an operator on the line, and then they spread out as they approached the apartment buildings.

"People will realise something is going on," Ali said to Sara.

"Yes, but they won't know *what*, and that's enough. If someone leaves the building, they'll run right into our arms."

"Okay," he said, and let the rest of the officers know what Sara had just said. They all needed to know the plan.

Sara and Ali walked down the stairs and into one of the basements. It was dark and empty. They looked everywhere but couldn't find a single trace of anyone or anything.

Ali heard a sound and froze. Sara held her breath.

"Rat," he whispered when he saw the rodent scurry across the floor in front of them.

After looking for a while, they decided to leave the basement. It was even darker out now, but the streetlights were on, so it didn't matter.

Suddenly, they heard a voice over the radio.

"We've found a room that looks like a meeting place of some kind. Could you head over here? Get the forensics kit from the car." It was Rita. She told them which building they were in, and Sara and Ali headed for the car to get the forensics kit.

They walked into the basement where Rita and Kabhat were waiting for them outside the door.

Sara called the backup units, who let her know neither of them had found anything of interest in the other basements.

"Do we have the operations centre with us on the line?"

"Yes, do you need backup?"

"No, there is nobody here, but we need to check for prints. Could you send a forensics team over?"

"I'll take care of it immediately. Maybe it's better if you don't touch anything for now? Wait until the technicians show up."

"You're right, but we'll stick around here in case someone shows up. I'll send the backup units back to Lund. We don't need them anymore. If anything unexpected happens, I guess you can always send them back this way."

"Sure," the operator said, and called the two backup units, who were already on their way back to their cars.

Sara wanted to see the room with her own eyes, so she put on plastic gloves and carefully walked in through the door. The floor was covered in soda cans, blankets, pizza boxes, and other things that would definitely be interesting for the forensics team. It looked like the room would be full of DNA.

"This is great," she whispered. "If any of these guys appears in our records, it'll be an easy match. If not, it'll be more of a challenge. But we'll find them."

They whispered to each other in case someone would return to the basement while they were still there. They didn't want to spook anyone.

"Look," Ali said after joining them in the room. He showed them a necklace. "This is a Nazi symbol. It's called the Black Sun."

"The symbol has existed in many occult sects, but just like the sun cross, it's been co-opted by the Nazis," Kabhat clarified.

"I've never seen it before," Rita said, and had a closer look at it. "But I think it's fair to assume we're on to something here."

Half an hour later, two forensic technicians arrived from Lund. They were annoyed as they had just finished their shift and were heading home to enjoy a quiet night off when they got the call.

"Isn't it typical that this kind of thing always happens when we're on our way home?" one of them said, and glared at Sara.

"We're in the middle of a murder investigation so I'm afraid we don't have time to worry about things like that," she answered, and grinned.

The technician popped his head into the room.

"Wow, we've got a lot to work with here. This is a dream for anyone in my field," he said, and rubbed his hands together. And just like that, his frown was turned upside down.

"We'll be around," Sara told them before leaving them alone to do their job.

Then she turned to her colleagues, who didn't quite know what to do.

"I think we should knock on some doors in the area. We need to ask people if they've noticed any suspicious activity in their basement.

Maybe someone has seen these guys—assuming they're all guys. Maybe someone even knows who they are? Good or bad idea?"

"Good idea," Rita answered. "A constructive and good idea."

"Anyone feeling up for the job?"

Rita and Ali raised their hands while Kabhat looked hesitant.

Sara looked at her.

"I've never been here before," she said. "And what if they don't understand my accent?" Kabhat laughed, showing all her teeth. As usual, her laughter was contagious and made them all smile.

"Yes, that's a real risk." Rita grinned. "I've had the same problem down here from time to time."

"Me too," Sara said, and they all laughed together for a while.

Their colleagues from Forensics were hard at work inside the room, placing old food, cigarette butts, and everything else they could find into different bags.

Sara, Rita, and Ali decided they would all go talk to the people living in the buildings in the area while Kabhat stayed behind to guard the basement. Sara told Kabhat to call them over the radio as soon as the technicians were done. She didn't want her to stay there by herself.

Sara, Rita, and Ali split up. There weren't that many floors and flats to cover, so they decided to take one building each. Most likely, nobody would have seen anything and it would all go quickly. The only person they tried to avoid was Gun Johansson, Greger's mother. Simply because they had already talked to her, and because it would be difficult for them to answer any potential questions about her son.

"Can you guys imagine how amazing it would be if we found someone who knew something?" Sara said before they all went their separate ways with strict orders to stay in contact with each other.

55

Torsten talked to Greger and his lawyer for hours before he finally had to give up. Torsten rarely failed to produce results during his interrogations. He had the ability to get people to share things they thought they would never share. But this time he couldn't get anywhere. It bothered him.

Torsten called Baum to tell him he hadn't been able to get Greger to give him anything at all.

"Even the sun has its spots, I guess," he said, sounding surprised but cheerful. "By the way, I've prepared the detention order and I'll send it over in the morning. It shouldn't be too complicated. I guess you'll have to give it another try after the detention hearing. He might need some time to think. Maybe he'll realise eventually that he's the only one who'll be paying for this. It's never fun when that happens."

"I think he's scared. Too scared to snitch on his leader. Hopefully, we'll get some more of these guys in here soon. Did you hear Sara is out searching basements in Staffanstorp?"

"Yes, I heard. I hope she finds someone. She hasn't called me yet."

"I'm sure she'll call soon. She knows you're about to leave for the day."

"I hope you're right."

Torsten thought about everything that had happened. He felt immensely relieved that Wilhelm had finally been found. But he also felt like something was off when it came to Wilhelm and the murders of Carola and Tom. His understanding was that the boy was naive, but not stupid. What if Wilhelm was being framed? Maybe this was something personal and maybe someone had carved swastikas into the victims' foreheads as a diversion, only shortly after the Afghan boy was murdered and had an identical symbol carved into his face? It didn't make sense, and the more he thought about it, the more convinced he became that the murders were connected. They had to be. The question was only *how*.

He went into Jonny's office. It looked like he was packing up for the day.

"Oh, you're on your way out? You don't want to come with me to Staffanstorp to see if we can help somehow?"

"Not today. I've got a date at 6 p.m. So I've got to go."

"A date?" Torsten repeated, and raised his eyebrows.

"Yes, why not?" Jonny said, and flipped him the bird.

"Well, I don't know. I guess I've never heard you say you're going on a date, that's all."

"Just because I don't tell you about it doesn't mean that I don't date women . . ." Jonny pulled a face.

"You're right. But do you think you could stick around for a couple of minutes? I need your input on something." Torsten aimed a crooked smile his way.

"Fine, I'll catch the next train."

"Thanks, buddy."

"So, we've got two murder scenes and three murdered people," Torsten concluded. He wasn't sure what he wanted to say and took a moment to try to figure it out.

Jonny shifted his weight from one foot to the other and looked impatient.

"Yes, that's what we got," he answered, and shrugged his shoulders a little.

"I mean, the murders have two things in common. They're both connected to Nazis, although in once case the Nazis are the murderers and in the other case they're the victims. The strangest thing is that all victims had swastikas carved into their foreheads. But how is it all connected? I know there is a link there that we must have missed." Torsten paused.

"I have no idea," Jonny said, and squinted. "You think too highly of me. You're the detective here, not me."

"Well, that's not true. In fact, you're not giving yourself enough credit. My expectations are appropriate for your expert detective nose."

"Okay, I'll give it a think."

Jonny sat down and pulled out a piece of paper and a pen. Torsten sat down next to him.

"I mean, we've already talked about this. And now when we know about Tom's involvement in Action Now! it sure looks like it's all connected. But why would Wilhelm murder his parents—if he wasn't dragged into their Nazi mess? If Wilhelm didn't do this, the question is what did Tom and Carola do to be murdered? Do you think one of them threatened to expose the Nazis? Or is this about something private?"

"Private." Torsten jumped up. "It's bloody private! Staffan Ehn. Can this have something to do with him? Maybe he murdered them for kidnapping Molly Altenius's son?"

"But was he even aware that we knew the boy's real identity at the time of their murder? And why would he carve swastikas into their faces after murdering them?"

"You're right, he didn't know. He didn't tell us about Carola until after her death. Man, I don't know . . ."

Torsten thought about it for a while without getting anywhere.

Jonny stood up and put his coat on.

"I really need to leave now," he said, and left.

56

The forensics team had left and Sara joined Kabhat.

"It doesn't seem like anyone will show up here. But let's get a surveillance unit from Lund out here anyway," Sara said.

"Did you stumble upon anything interesting while talking to the neighbours?" Kabhat asked.

"No, nothing. But let's see what Rita and Ali say when they get back here. They haven't called me yet."

"They obviously haven't found anything, then," Kabhat said, and yawned.

"Obviously." Sara yawned too. "Long day."

"Yes, and tomorrow it's time for me to go back to Falun. I stuck around here for much longer than I thought I would, but I don't mind. It's been great. What an experience. Now we just have to figure out if Wilhelm murdered the Karlssons or not. Did you ever consider that maybe there was someone else with him?"

"No, actually, I didn't. And I don't think anyone else has considered that either," Sara said, and regained her focus.

Ali and Rita came walking down the stairs. They both looked pleased with themselves. Two of the people they had talked to had noticed a group of guys down in the basement, although they hadn't thought much about it. Both of them saw it as a good thing that the young men had found somewhere to hang out.

"The guy I talked to was young too, maybe twenty-five. I think that's one of the reasons he didn't care so much. He recognised Greger's name. He also thought he recognised one of the other guys as someone who had visited Greger at home a couple of times. Oh, I forget to say that the guy I talked to lives in the same building as Greger's mother," Rita explained.

"Could he tell you the man's name?" Sara asked curiously.

"No, but he knew exactly what he looked like. I thought the description sounded like Wilhelm at first, but then he told me he was just as tall as Greger, which makes me think it's not Wilhelm at all. Except for the height, the description sounded just like him though."

"I also talked to a young woman in the building next to Greger's," Ali said.

"And what had she seen?"

"Greger, although she didn't know his name. She'd noticed the swastika on his wrist when she dropped her car off at the garage where he worked. Then she'd seen him and a group of seven or eight other men walk down into the basement together. She didn't recognise any of the others, but she could tell me what they looked like. The next time she saw them, she snapped some photos of them from her balcony. How about that!"

"You're telling us this now?!" Sara exclaimed, and pushed him in pure excitement.

Ali pulled out a mobile phone from his pocket.

"This is her phone. I confiscated it and promised her we'd return it tonight."

"Of course," Sara said, and took the phone out of his hand.

"Code?"

"2525," Ali said, and grinned.

They aimed a flashlight at the phone and had a look at the photos.

They were taken from afar, but the technicians would surely be able to work around that.

Sara jumped up and down in excitement.

"This is great! No doubt the best thing that's happened today."

Sara called the operations centre and asked if the surveillance unit was on its way.

"Sure, they should be there in five minutes according to my map here."

"When they arrive, we'll leave right away."

"Let me know when they get there and I'll let you go."

"Ali and Kabhat, I want you to go back to the station to get the phone to Forensics," Sara said, pointing at them.

"Yes, ma'am,"Ali answered.

"Wait for me in my office," Sara shouted. "Kabhat, let's go for dinner around 8 p.m. Will that work?"

Kabhat raised her hand and Sara took it as a confirmation.

"You'll come too," she said, and turned to Rita.

"I can't. I'm seeing Linda."

Back at the station, they found Ali and a couple of technicians in front of a computer. They studied the photos they'd found on the woman's phone. The forensics team had been able to zoom in quite a bit.

"So, the photos get quite grainy when they're zoomed in like this, but I still think they give us a good idea of what these guys look like. At least the two whose faces are visible."

Sara leaned over Ali's shoulder to get a better look. Rita pulled up a chair.

"By the way, Torsten and Kabhat are working on trying to solve the mystery of the connection between these murders," he said. "I'll make sure we get these photos as clear as possible so we can put out a warrant for their arrest."

Sara giggled when she pictured two black-and-white posters with the text *wanted, dead or alive*, written under the men's faces.

Ali looked at her and raised his eyebrows. She aimed a dismissive wave his way.

"You, go home now," she said to Rita, and pointed towards the door.

"Let me change first, then I'm out of here."

Rita walked down to the changing rooms while Sara headed upstairs.

57

Dinner was enjoyed in the relaxed atmosphere at Italiano. Kabhat and Sara had each ordered a glass of wine with their food. Sara felt at ease. It would all work out in the end. They were closing in on Reza's murderers. Even if they didn't know exactly who they were, it was only a matter of time before they found them.

Greger Johansson was most likely guilty, while they weren't as sure about Wilhelm. They had been given a week to find more evidence, and after that, they would be forced to release him. And the reality was that Sara wasn't convinced he had anything to do with the murders. But she couldn't possibly know for sure.

Torsten seemed obsessed with finding a connection between Reza's and the Karlssons' murders and if he did, she hoped it would solve both cases at once.

They hadn't talked much lately. There was no need. But they both agreed they should spend more time together. If nothing else they would have to see each other outside of work.

"It's been fun working with you, and I've learnt a lot," Sara said.

"I agree and feel the same way. It'll be nice to get home though, even if we have a lot to do back in Falun too. Murders and a long list of other things. Business as usual, so to speak. But I hope I get to see you soon again."

"Me too. But I think it's time for us to go home and get some sleep now. I could really use the rest. And I need to talk to my boyfriend,

Anders. It's hard to keep love alive when you never see each other," Sara said, and let out a short laugh.

"Tell me about it. I've been married twice. Neither of the relationships were great. Not even in the beginning. I think the biggest problem is that you never stop being a police officer. Tragic, really. I guess it's the same if you work for a hospital or emergency services."

"Yeah, I guess. Let me pay for this," Sara offered.

"No, no, I'll pay," Kabhat said, and waved at the waiter.

Sara protested but there was no use.

They left the restaurant and said goodbye to each other. Kabhat was going back to her hotel. Sara walked home and felt grateful for getting to know the colourful and strong woman from Falun.

Her house was dark and empty, but she didn't mind. Klara and Bella were staying with their father for the night and Johannes was at his new girlfriend's house. *Thank God for text messages*, Sara thought once she had taken a seat on the sofa and started a show on TV.

She changed her mind and walked into the kitchen, where she poured herself a glass of wine and had a seat at the kitchen table. She lit some candles instead of turning on the light.

Then she texted the girls and asked how they were doing. Both texted her back at the same time. They were doing okay, but they were still upset that they hadn't arranged a search party for Reza before he died all alone in the cold night. She knew how they felt and understood how much it hurt. They didn't care about what had happened to them anymore. Compared to the murder, it was nothing. *What a world we live in*, Sara thought, and feared it would get worse the closer to the election they got. What she had always taken for granted felt more and more like it was in danger of disappearing.

She had a look at her own reflection in the kitchen window.

Pretty hot for being this old, she thought. She lifted her curls and spotted a couple of grey hairs. *Oh well. I can work with that.*

She finished her wine, placed the glass on the kitchen counter, and went into the bathroom to brush her teeth. Just as she started her electric toothbrush, her phone rang.

"Oh no," she told her reflection, and picked up the phone.

"I've managed to edit the photos and now we can see the two faces clear as day," Ali shouted on the other end of the line.

"What? Really?" Sara exclaimed. "I'm so relieved."

"Hell yeah," Ali agreed.

"I'm actually relieved *you* called and not the duty officer. I thought I was about to be called back to work."

Ali laughed.

"I thought you were impressed with my work."

"Of course I am. Do you recognise any of them?"

"No, but they all look the same to me. Blond, short hair, polished, black trousers, and white shirt underneath a black jacket. I don't know what else to tell you."

"This might not be as easy as we'd hoped, then . . . I suggest we go to Genarp and Staffanstorp first thing in the morning. According to Amanda Svensson, that's where these guys are based. Let's make a plan tomorrow. I really need to sleep now. So should you. Go home," Sara answered.

"I think I'll pay Greger a visit to see what he has to say about the photos."

Sara sighed.

"Can't it wait for tomorrow? I can't go on a manhunt tonight. And I've had three glasses of wine."

"You don't need to do anything. I'll handle it. If he tells me something, I'll text you. If not, you won't hear from me again tonight. There are uniformed officers on duty as well, you know? They can always arrest someone if it comes to that."

"Do whatever you want. I'm going to bed. Good night and well done."

Sara proceeded to brush her teeth and then she crawled into bed. She remembered she had forgotten to call Anders and decided to call him in the morning instead. It was a bit strange that he hadn't called her though. Great, now she was worried. After thinking about it for twenty minutes or so, she picked up her phone and called him. He answered and by the sounds of it, her call had woken him up.

58

Greger was asleep when Ali walked into his cell.

Greger didn't seem to hear him. Ali cleared his throat. No reaction. He walked over to the bed and shook the young man.

"What? What is it? What are you doing?" Greger jumped out of bed and ran into one of the corners of the cell. He was obviously frightened.

"I need to talk to you, so you'll have to come with me," Ali said, and flexed his pectoral muscles for effect.

"What? It's the middle of the night!"

"Let's go," Ali said.

Greger went with Ali, and when they walked past the guard, he looked at them with a surprised look on his face.

"Interrogation," Ali said as if interrogating a suspect at 11 p.m. was nothing out of the ordinary.

"Oh, okay," the guard answered, and returned to his sudoku. Or maybe it was a crossword puzzle? Ali wasn't sure. He didn't have time to look.

Ali left the door to the interrogation room slightly open. If anything were to happen inside the room, he wanted the guard to hear it too.

"Sit down," he ordered Greger, who did what he was asked.

"What the hell do you want? I was asleep. Am I not allowed to sleep here?"

"Yes. But not now. Here," Ali said, and threw a couple of photos across the table.

Greger looked at himself and five other men. Two of their faces were clearly visible. He flinched.

"I'm not telling you anything," he said.

"Do you recognise these men?"

"Yes, of course I do." Greger glared at the interrogating officer across from him.

"Of course you do. So who are they?"

"I'm not telling you anything, as I said." Greger's eyes turned dark. His face was tense and he looked defensive.

"So you're going to take all of the blame?"

"You don't know these guys," Greger said cryptically.

"No, I don't. But I know I would never let them walk free while I was thrown into prison for a murder they're equally guilty of. Do you get what I mean?"

"I get it, but I don't think *you* do," Greger said, staring at Ali.

"What is it I don't get?"

"We don't snitch. If you do, you're dead." Greger suddenly looked miserable. And scared.

"I see. But do you really think it's fair that they're pinning it all on you?"

"I didn't say that."

"No, but what do you think?"

"It might not be fair, but I have no choice," Greger said, looking weak and lonely.

"Okay, but this isn't what friends do to each other, is it?"

"They're not my friends like that. I ended up with them, and I think they're using me because they know I struggle. And because I can get so bloody pissed off at times. They like that."

"I really wish you would work up the courage to tell me who these guys are. It's for your own sake," Ali tried.

"Do you think I'm an idiot? I'm not. And I'd rather go to prison than die for being a rat. Simple as that."

"No, I don't think you're an idiot. I think you're really a good guy who ended up in the claws of a bunch of Nazis."

"I won't say another word," Greger said, and crossed his arms in front of him. "And think what you want."

"Do you know how devastated your parents are?" Ali decided to try a different approach.

"They're idiots." Greger wasn't interested in any detours, that was clear.

"Okay, I think we'll wrap things up here. But I want you to know that we won't quit until we know who these murderers are. And we're getting close to the answer. Trust me, we'll find a way," Ali said, and it sounded like a threat as much as it sounded like a riddle.

"I don't give a crap. Can I go to bed now?"

"Sure."

Ali walked Greger back to the custody suites, where a guard took over.

"Take this baby back to his cell. I don't want to see him again," Ali said, and shoved Greger towards the guard.

He ran up the stairs, threw the photos on his desk, put his coat on, and stepped into the freezing night.

59

Sara and Rita ran next to each other through Klostergården and past the apartment buildings that were all built during the sixties. They reminded Sara of the huge housing complexes in the outskirts of Stockholm, although Klostergården was nowhere near as depressing. There was something cosy about the area. It was a cold and wet morning, but it was still nice to get out. They ran without speaking, focusing on the road ahead. After going through the tunnel and up on Maskinvägen by Åkerlund and Rausing, they turned towards the dams at the sewage treatment plant. There weren't many green spaces in Lund, but the area around the dams was one of them. It was only 6:30 a.m., but it didn't matter. They hadn't gone for a run together in forever, so it was worth the effort.

"There," Rita said, and pointed to their left once they'd made it down the hill leading to the dams. "That's where we found Reza Mahmoudi. Can you imagine how scary it must have been for him? I'm having a hard time taking it in. What did he do, really? Nothing. He became a random victim of their sick ideology. I wonder if these young men choose violence or if they're lured into it by peer pressure and the feeling of belonging to something bigger than themselves."

"Either way, it's horrible. And sick. I thought about the election yesterday. I'm worried about how things will turn out. The Nordic Resistance Movement is being more and more accepted as a political group. I don't understand what's going on in people's minds. Do they even think at all?" The thought of the boy who was beaten so badly and then left face down in the water to die made Sara feel sick to her stomach. The boy who would have died anyway, according to the medical examiner.

"Come on," Rita said, and the two women kept running.

The thirty-minute run felt great, especially once they'd arrived at the police station, showered, and changed into their professional personas. Because that's what it felt like. Once they slipped into their work clothes, they became officers of the law.

When they walked into the department, Beatrice Larsson approached them with loud and dramatic steps. Her high heels demonstratively hit the floor hard with each step.

"Do you let your team behave however they like?" She was obviously talking to Sara, and it looked like she was tempted to slap her in the face.

"What do you mean?"

"Greger Johansson, that little shit, has filed a complaint about, and I quote: 'a dirty Muslim cop,' dragging him up in the middle of the night to interrogate him."

"Well, I don't think it was in the middle of the night. It was around 11 p.m.," Sara answered calmly.

"That *is* in the middle of the night if you ask me," Beatrice snapped.

"Either way, who cares about him? He's just whining," Sara said with a crooked smile. "Ali had finally managed to save these photos and wanted to show them to Greger to see what he had to say about them. If Greger had agreed to talk to us, we'd have more people in custody right now. Do you think that was a mistake?"

"Oh, I see. I wasn't informed about this." Beatrice blushed.

Sara patted her arm and kept walking with Rita right behind her.

"We've got to get to work now. Some of us have a lot of work to do, you know?" Sara said, glaring at her boss.

Beatrice didn't answer her, and her heels didn't hit the floor as hard on her way back to her office.

"You're so cool." Rita laughed before taking Sara's hand and kissing it.

"And you're not right in the head," Sara said, and pulled her hand back.

Sara's office felt empty without Kabhat. The chair she'd used was put back in its normal spot. Sara dumped her stuff on her desk and went to see Torsten in his office. She asked him how the interview with Greger had gone. Torsten shook his head.

"He's impossible. He's too scared. And too simple," he said. "And Ali couldn't get a word out of him last night either. But the photos are great, and we can see two faces. Ali is on his way to return the phone to its owner, by the way. If you're wondering where he is."

"What? This early? Okay, let's have a look at the photos and draw up a plan for what to do next," Sara said, and walked towards the conference room. She started the projector and pulled out a big presentation notepad on wheels.

She wrote down a list of all their leads and another list of what they needed to do next. The surveillance unit had sent her an email telling her nothing had happened in Staffanstorp during the night. Sara wasn't surprised. If anything would have happened, she would have heard about it. But she wrote them back and thanked them for their help.

As she wrote, a question popped into her mind. She called Torsten over. He poked his head into the room with a smile on his face.

"What can I do for you, madame?"

"I heard you talking to Kabhat yesterday and I want to tell you that it's also occurred to me that Wilhelm Karlsson might have had someone with him. He might not even have anything to do with the murders at all. But above all, I'm pretty sure he had nothing to do with the murder of Reza."

Torsten nodded.

"Good, then we're on the same page. But how did we come to that conclusion?"

"I'm not sure, but something about the way Wilhelm acts and talks makes me unsure. And I'm not sure how to interpret his reaction when we told him he was suspected of murdering his parents. It was as if he hadn't quite accepted the fact that they're dead. And his explanation for why he was in the house makes sense. It doesn't sound unbelievable that he found them dead and got nervous about being seen as a suspect. I don't know, but my gut tells me we're on the wrong track here."

"I agree," Torsten said. "Something doesn't feel right. But I don't know what."

A moment later, everyone but Ali had gathered in the conference room.

"Åke, how are we moving forward with Wilhelm Karlsson? He's in custody suspected of murdering Tom and Carola, but he's not suspected of murdering Reza."

"No, they didn't think we had enough evidence to accuse him of that. And they're right. His lawyer is very stubborn. So now we only have a couple of days, as you know. I think we should schedule more interviews with him. Moreover, Greger has to face the fact that he's the only one being charged with Reza's murder here. I'm not sure he gets that yet."

Ali entered the room.

"Wait until you hear this," he exclaimed before anyone could comment on what Baum had just said.

"Wait one second. Let me just comment on what Åke just said," Torsten said.

"Oh," Ali said, "sorry."

"It's okay," Torsten continued. "I'll talk to Wilhelm again today to try to make sense of things. But I won't interrogate Greger again for a while. I need someone else to do it."

"I think it's important to interrogate him again and keep pressuring him. But I guess it's good to try another interrogation officer."

Ali waved his hands eagerly.

"I've got the photos," he said, "but I have to admit I couldn't get anything useful out of Greger last night. He's bloody hopeless. Scared and stubborn. Do you want to have a look at the photos now?"

Applause filled the room.

"Great job," Jonny said, and sat down.

"How was your date yesterday?" Torsten asked, and although he wasn't trying to be mean, they all saw how much he enjoyed putting his colleague on the spot.

Jonny blushed, looking quite upset.

"What the hell, Torsten? Why would you ask me that here? Not cool. Not cool at all."

"Oh, come on. I wasn't trying to be a dick," Torsten said, feeling embarrassed.

Torsten's blunt behaviour surprised Sara, and she was reminded of what Torsten and Jonny's relationship had been like a while back, when it wasn't as good as it was now. She didn't want things to go back to what they once were so she raised her hand to stop the situation from escalating.

"Let's look at the photos now. I also want to go through a list I've made of different ways to possibly move forwards," she said. "Go ahead, Ali."

Ali connected his computer to the projector and showed everyone the photos.

"This is Greger," Ali said, and pointed to one of the photos with a laser pointer. "We can only see the backs of these two guys and their hoodies are covering their heads. As you can see, they're all dressed alike. We can only see the faces of these two as they haven't pulled up the hoods on their jackets. I know what the jackets look like because Greger has one just like them. We still don't know who's holding the camera."

"We'll get to that later," Sara said to stop them from getting stuck.

Everyone stared at the photo on the whiteboard.

"Don't they look young?" Baum asked.

"Yes, but we think they're all about as old as Greger. In their early twenties, that is," Ali clarified. "It seems as if this is the average age of those who decide to move on from the Nordic Resistance Movement to more extreme breakaway groups. At least that's what my contact tells me. Speaking of my contact . . . he hasn't been able to find more information about Action Now! I want to tell you that he defected from the Nordic Resistance Movement. That's why I've kept his identity to myself until now. But he told me it's okay to tell you. He's been my contact for about two years. Very useful. He tells me this group is great at keeping things secret and staying off the radar. And considering how hard it is to reveal the identity of its members despite having access to their private chat, I believe he's right. They're meticulous, but not careful enough as they let a guy like Greger join them. He's the one who exposed them."

Torsten leaned back in his chair and balanced on its back two legs. It looked like he was miles away, but that wasn't the case at all. Sara knew he was listening.

"I think it's a bad idea to publish their photos in the newspaper or anywhere else for that matter. They're probably on their way into hiding as it is and we don't want to let them know we're on to them, right?" he said, and lowered the chair down with soundless precision.

"I agree," Ali said. "And so does my contact. If we don't want these guys to disappear forever, we better move carefully."

"I have to admit that I never thought about it like that. On the contrary, I was ready to go to the media. But let's not. So what's our next move, then?"

"We could always start by showing Wilhelm the photos. At least it'll let him know we're aware of a lot more than he might think," Torsten suggested.

Good old Torsten, Sara thought, *always so wise.*

"Good idea," Baum said.

"Then I think we should drive to Staffanstorp and Genarp as these guys have obviously been spending a lot of time in the Åkershus area," Rita suggested. It was the first they'd heard from her since the meeting started.

"Great idea," Sara said.

"Let's do it. But shouldn't you question Wilhelm first, Torsten? That way, we'll hopefully have more information to go on once we get there," Ali said, and turned to Baum for his approval.

"Ali can talk to him about the photos," Baum said. "Then Torsten can question him after lunch."

"It's only 8:30 a.m. We can get a lot done before lunch. I'll go talk to him about the photos right away." Ali grabbed the stack of photos and rushed off.

60

"Can I talk to you for a couple of minutes?" Rita asked a young man standing by the car park next to the grocery store. He looked like a regular guy and wasn't dressed in anything that could be considered a Nazi outfit, so she felt safe talking to him.

"Why?"

"I'm with the police and I want to show you a couple of photos," she said, and flashed her badge.

"I don't talk to the police," he said, and took a step back.

"Okay, but you're not the one I'm after here. I just want to know if you recognise anyone in these photos," she said, and he suddenly seemed curious. He leaned closer to her to have a look, but she turned the photos away from him.

"Sure, I'll have a look," he said.

Rita suddenly felt hesitant and wasn't sure if she should ask the man for his name or not. She decided to leave it. It wasn't really important.

She showed him the photos. He looked at one of them.

"What did they do?"

"I can't tell you that. All I need to know is if you recognise any of these men. We need to find them. That's all."

The young man looked at the next photo and flinched. Rita paid close attention to his body language.

"That guy," he said, and pointed at one of the faces in the photo. "I know him. Or, I knew him. Before he became a Nazi."

Rita felt excited and couldn't believe her luck.

"I hate Nazis," he said. "That guy's name is Danny. Or, Dan Fagerström."

"How do you know him?" Rita said, and cleared her throat before correcting herself. "How *did* you know him, I mean."

"I was friends with his brother back in school. Danny is three years younger than me so we never went to school together. His brother, Niklas, died in a car accident four years ago. Danny lost his mind after that. And then he joined some Nazi group. The Nordic Resistance Movement, I think."

"How old is he?" Rita felt out of breath. *Must be the adrenaline*, she thought.

"Three years younger than me, so twenty-three."

"Thanks. Do you recognise any of the other men?" Rita tried to maintain her patience. She wanted to call Sara immediately but realised the man might have information about the others as well.

"That's Greger," he said, and pointed at the third photo. "Everyone around here knows who he is. He has a tattoo of a swastika. Sick fuck."

"What do you mean?"

"He can lose his temper pretty badly. He doesn't seem very smart. But I think he's really a nice guy. When he loses his temper, he goes crazy though. I've seen him in more than one fight. Ugly stuff." The young man seemed happy about helping Rita, especially for someone who claimed he didn't want to talk to the police.

"And the third man whose face you can see?"

"No idea. But considering they're all wearing the same clothes, I'm assuming he's a Nazi too."

Rita didn't answer him. She felt happy—ecstatic, even. She had bumped into the right person by chance. *How lucky can a person be?* she thought to herself.

"Thanks a lot," she said. "What's your name? Could you please tell me your date of birth and maybe even give me your phone number?"

"Hell no," he said, staring at her. He leaned closer. "I told you I don't speak to the police. I've told you what I know. That's enough." He turned his back to her and jumped into his car.

He started the engine and backed out of his parking spot. Once he had turned the car around, he stopped next to Rita and rolled his window down.

"You're hot, by the way." He rolled the window up again and waved at her while he drove off.

Rita wrote down the car's plate number, just in case. Then she called Sara to tell her about what had just happened.

Sara cheered so loudly that Rita had to hold the mobile phone half a meter away so that her eardrum wouldn't burst.

"Dan Fagerström. Twenty-three years old. He obviously lives here in Staffanstorp. Or at least he has lived here before. The name is unusual enough for us to find him without too much of an effort. The man I talked to knew Greger as well. I can't believe how lucky I was."

Sara cheered again and told Rita to call the operations centre to get Dan's address. Neither Sara, Torsten, nor Ali had met anyone who could tell them anything of importance. Sara told Rita they'd barely seen a single person around.

"I'll call you back once I've asked the operations centre for the address, then. Where do you want to meet?"

"See you at the car park in Åkershus. We need to make a plan."

Rita put the phone down and called the operations centre.

They promised to get back to her as soon as possible.

Rita got in her car and drove to Åkershus, where the others were already waiting for her.

Then she got a call from the operations centre.

"Wait," the operator said. "It looks like Dan Fagerström has multiple addresses. And according to our reconnaissance register, he's linked to Ola Jensen."

He gave Rita a list of addresses and Rita wrote everything down in her notebook.

"Did that help at all?" the operator asked.

"Absolutely! We might have a third suspect now," Rita said. Then she got out of the car and handed the addresses over to Sara.

Torsten, Jonny, and Ali couldn't believe it.

"This is amazing," Sara said.

Torsten and Jonny lifted Rita up in the air.

"Are you out of your minds? Put me down," she ordered, and they listened.

"I need to go back to the station and interrogate Wilhelm one last time," Torsten said, and waved to them before walking over to his car.

"Remember that we have another name now. Ask him if he recognises it," Sara shouted after him.

"I will," Torsten promised, and sat down behind the steering wheel. He closed the car door, then opened it again. "There must be something else. Something more that connects these murders. I just know it in my gut." Then he closed the door again and took off.

"Torsten is probably right. He usually is," Sara said. "Let's get to work. It's time to find Dan Fagerström." She laughed. It relieved a lot of tension and made the others smile. Even Ali.

Jonny clapped his hands together.

"There is nothing I like better about this job than a good old manhunt," he said, and clapped again.

The others discreetly agreed.

61

Greger Johansson and Wilhelm Karlsson were both locked up in the custody suites. That way, there was no risk of them bumping into each other and Torsten could safely get Wilhelm from his cell and into the interrogation room. Wilhelm looked even greyer than the last time. He inhaled deeply, but it sounded as if he couldn't get enough air into his lungs.

Torsten paused.

"Are you okay?" he asked.

"I'm tired," the young man said.

"I understand."

"I don't think you understand a thing," Wilhelm answered. "Did you ever get accused of two murders at the same time as you found out that your mother—who's dead and who you're accused of murdering, by the way—isn't really your mother at all?"

It was a relevant question. Torsten shook his head.

"You were shown photos today, and as far as I understand, you recognised the men in them. But you don't know their names?"

Wilhelm nodded.

"Would you mind telling me again what you know about them?"

The young man didn't look happy about being forced to repeat himself. Torsten recognised the defeated look on his face.

"Fine, I'll tell you how I came in contact with them. I knew about this site as my father . . . Tom . . . was a Nazi. He'd shown me the site a bunch of times and offered me the opportunity to go to some kind of a training camp. Or—he wanted me to go. But I didn't want to. My mother . . . Carola . . . had my back. She told me I didn't have to. But I knew how to access the site. So I connected with some people there and was invited to their private chat room. Nobody used their real name in there, as I told you before. I started talking to them. I knew they were Nazis, obviously. And we shared the same views about Muslims and people from MENA. Do you know what MENA stands for?"

"Middle East, North Africa," Torsten answered.

The young man nodded.

"They told me we should meet, and I met with them. I told them about that study group for Muslims—because all students in the study group were Muslim. And as I said, I'm not a fan of Muslims. I don't care if they're young or old."

He stopped to catch his breath. Torsten realised he was struggling. He probably had a lot of emotions to process.

"But now when I've given it some thought, I'm not sure why—or if—I feel this way. I'm voting right, but I'm not a fucking Nazi. I'm not sure about anything anymore. What am I? Who am I? Something like that."

Once again, he had to take a second to catch his breath. And he looked sad. Torsten still couldn't figure out exactly what part Wilhelm played in it all.

"We met somewhere, in a basement. And then we decided to go scare the students. I'm not sure what I was thinking. I'm a law student and I realise this was the dumbest thing I could possibly do. You don't shit where you eat, you know?"

Torsten noticed how well spoken the young man was. He was impressed with how clearly he could articulate his thoughts and how critical he was of himself. It was quite unusual for a person in his position.

"Yes, what were you thinking? Why did you feel it was important to do this to your fellow students—and to the unaccompanied refugee youths?"

"I thought they didn't have a right to be here. I thought Muslims like them make our country filthy. And I don't know . . . I don't even know if I agree with my own opinions anymore. Maybe Tom's opinions rubbed off on me. But I never wanted to kill anyone."

"So, did you?" Torsten took his chance.

"No. I've told you that already. I would never kill anyone, but I admit to hanging out with scumbags." He started crying. "I've put my whole future on the line, and for what?"

"I don't know. Why don't you tell me what your thoughts were?"

"I obviously didn't think at all. If I had thought about it for a second, things would look very different today. I wouldn't be in police custody, that's for sure. But I'm telling you . . . I would never kill anyone. Not even a fly."

"How was your father? Tom, I mean?"

"He was the devil. And bloody stupid. He was abusive, but my mother wasn't afraid of him. He was all she had though. I've thought about it a lot. She was quite crazy, actually."

"What did you think of them?"

"How do you mean?"

"You speak about your parents in quite the condescending manner. You know now that they're not your biological parents, but you didn't know that before."

"I always felt like a stranger. I was a good student and politically active. But I was never a Nazi, I need you to understand that. I pretended to be one in front of Mum and Dad though. Or, I mean . . . Tom and Carola. Can you imagine how confusing it is to be raised by a mother and a father who turn out to not be your biological parents? And now they've been murdered, to top it all off. I feel completely lost." He clenched his jaws.

"I understand if it's confusing, but I guess I'll never understand how you feel," Torsten said, and copied Wilhelm's body language as he leaned back in the chair.

"But then I started visiting that site where they showed pictures from camps and other activities. It looked like they were having fun. But I despise them, really. I was quite lonely in law school. I don't come from the same background as most of the other students there. But I guess it turns out I do, after all. Most of them didn't care too much about studying. They were more interested in partying. I had nowhere to go. You know?"

"I get it." Torsten felt for the guy. Everything seemed so hopeless for him.

Wilhelm looked at him and shrugged his shoulders.

"I don't think you get it. You didn't grow up in a weird family and you're not the one suspected of murder. So no, I don't think you get it."

"No, maybe I don't," Torsten said honestly.

"My brain is about to explode," Wilhelm exclaimed, and tapped his knuckles against his temples.

"Take it easy," Torsten said. "It won't explode. But you know what you're accused of here. And now you need to tell me the truth. I can't help you if you don't tell me what happened. But we'll talk about it another time."

Wilhelm's face contorted as he started sobbing. Hot tears streamed down his face.

62

They were driving towards Genarp, where Dan Fagerström lived with his fiancée and their young daughter. It was never a good feeling knowing a child was involved and it was never fun creating chaos, but it was part of the job. Sara hated it, even if she loved hunting down the bad guys. It always felt very instinctive and gave her an adrenaline rush, which in turn made her heart race. It was intoxicating, and when she was in the middle of it, nothing else mattered. But Sara couldn't help thinking about how sad it was that a child would get caught up in it all. And then she thought about her own children and everything they had been forced to deal with over the years. And then Anders popped into her mind. She forced herself to stop thinking about her family. She needed to focus. Instead, images of children in need took over. Children in the middle of the Mediterranean Sea. Drowned children on beaches. Children who were forced to live in the horrendous world the adults had created for them. And she realised something. This child would be better off without a father who was a violent murderer with detestable Nazi sympathies. She instantly felt better and could focus on the task ahead.

They parked their car at a safe distance from the house and walked the last bit. They had all agreed the two women should approach the house first as they looked the least like police officers. Ali and Jonny would join them later. They tried to look natural and blend in, as if there was nothing suspicious at all about two women knocking on your door.

They walked up to the house and were just about to ring the doorbell when a young woman stepped out with a baby in her arms. She was wearing a coat and was obviously on her way out.

"Oh," Rita said, and smiled, "we were just about to ring your doorbell. Are you on your way out?"

"Yes, I'm meeting my fiancé," she explained. The baby was screaming and the mother sighed. "I can never go anywhere. There is always something that makes her scream. What do you want?"

"We just want to ask you a couple of questions. Nothing serious. How are you planning to travel to wherever you're meeting your fiancé?" Sara asked with a plan in the back of her mind. But the young woman with the bleached hair didn't know about that plan.

"I'm taking the bus," she said while a bead of sweat trickled down her forehead. The baby kept screaming. "I really need to hurry up. The bus leaves in five minutes and I need to get the pram out."

"We can drive you," Rita suggested.

"Shit, that's nice of you," the woman said without asking who they were or why they needed to talk to her. It surprised both Sara and Rita that she accepted their help without hesitation. Maybe it was the stress combined with a screaming child.

Hormones, Sara thought, and remembered what it was like to be a young mother.

"Okay, let's head over to our car. It's parked right over here," Rita said, and pointed.

"Thanks, that's really nice of you." The young woman was chewing a piece of gum and suddenly, she blew a big bubble that popped outside of her mouth.

On the way to the car, they saw Jonny and Ali drive by. Rita discreetly signalled to them to follow her. Jonny nodded.

"Where do you need to go?" Sara asked once they had put the pram in the car.

"Malmö. Lantmannagatan. That's where he is. He's at a friend's house."

"Let's go to Lantmannagatan, then," Rita said. She had called Jonny up on his mobile phone and now he could hear every word she spoke inside the car. And now he and Ali knew where they needed to go.

* * *

The young woman nursed her daughter in the back seat and after a little while, the baby fell asleep. They didn't have a car seat for the baby, so she was resting in her mother's arms. A couple of minutes later, the young woman fell asleep too. It made things easier. They didn't have to tell her anything if she didn't ask any questions.

They drove all the way in silence to avoid waking her up. When they arrived at Lantmannagatan, Sara parked the car while Rita woke up the sleeping mother.

"We're here." Rita turned around and put a hand on the woman's knee.

"Oh, I must have fallen asleep," she said, looking confused.

"Yes, I think you did. You probably needed the rest," Sara said.

The young woman sure seemed innocent. Rita helped her out of the car. Then she helped her with the pram and started walking her down the street. Sara got out of the car and caught up with them.

"We'll ask you our questions at another time," she said, and waved.

They watched the woman walk away, and when she entered the building, Rita ran up to the entrance door to see where she was going. The young woman left the pram on the other side of the entrance door and started walking upstairs. Rita followed the woman as silently as she could and watched her disappear behind a door on the second floor. Just as the door closed behind her, Rita heard a scream. She waved at Sara and saw Ali and Jonny run towards them a bit further down the street. Rita ran up the stairs, opened the door, and rushed in. Sara followed her. The young woman was lying on the floor. Her face was covered in blood. The baby lay on the floor next to her, seemingly unharmed.

A man towered over her—one of the men in the photo. He had obviously punched his fiancée in the face and now he was standing with his foot on her chest. The baby was screaming at the top of her lungs.

Rita rushed over to him and wrestled him to the floor. He didn't stand a chance. Sara handcuffed him.

The woman sat up and, with blood streaming down her face, picked up her baby.

Dan Fagerström didn't say a word.

A second later, Ali and Jonny came running up the stairs.

"Here, get this piece of shit out of here. Take him to Lund," Rita said, and pushed Fagerström towards her male colleagues. He hissed at her.

Jonny grabbed one of his arms and Ali the other. Together they dragged him down the stairs. Rita and Sara helped the woman up and sat her down on a chair. Rita tended to the wound on her forehead while Sara held the baby.

Sara was overwhelmed by a warm feeling she hadn't felt in years. The little body and the tiny hands and feet. The baby babbled and put a finger in Sara's mouth. It gave Sara a sense of hope in all the misery.

63

Torsten was exhausted but felt energised when he heard Dan Fagerström had been arrested. For now, he was in custody for assaulting his fiancée as they couldn't prove he'd been at the scene when Reza was murdered. But Wilhelm had confirmed that he was one of the men who harassed Bella and Klara, which was enough for them to suspect him of the murder. The prosecutor had issued them a warrant for his arrest, but it didn't matter. The assault was enough to bring him in.

Sara called Åke Baum to tell him she and Rita were driving Dan Fagerström's fiancée to the hospital. Afterward, they would show the photos to Klara, Bella, and the rest of the students in the study group. It would be quicker than asking them all to come to the station.

Torsten was preparing to interrogate Fagerström, but he wasn't nervous. According to him, it was one of his best traits. His ability to rest in what was. He'd had some time to think about everything that had happened. Maybe he would even find some time to think about his own life. It wasn't as interesting, of course, and somewhere he suspected the key to why he felt so lonely was that he never took the time to think about his own choices and who he really was. It came so naturally to him to focus on his job. But in reality, that's all it was—a job.

He forced himself to think about something else and laughed a little at his own thoughts and how obvious it all seemed when he only gave himself some time to reflect. It was so typical.

But then again, he was who he was. Maybe there was no use trying to teach an old dog new tricks. Why else would it even be a saying?

He sighed.

He grabbed a pen and his notebook and started writing about his day, just like he did every day. It was something about the way the pen moved across the paper that made it easier for him to follow his own thoughts. As he had just told himself, you can't teach an old dog new tricks.

Judging by Greger's reaction when he saw the pictures, Torsten was reasonably sure Dan Fagerström was one of the men who murdered Reza. But who was the leader—the Führer? Torsten felt quite sure it was a man—a man older than the rest of them. But who was he? And what was that strange feeling in his gut?

His thoughts changed direction and he pictured his daughter, Victoria. He wished she would move back to Sweden one day, but he knew the chances were slim. He hated the fact that he never got to see her. At least he'd gone to London to visit her a couple of times. But she worked a lot and so did he, so he rarely had time to fly over. It pained him. There were two people in the world that he loved more than anyone else—Victoria and his wife. Or, well, ex-wife. He struggled to get over the fact that she, who had loved him so deeply, had just up and left one day. She was tired of him constantly working. They had slowly grown apart and had less and less in common. He had lost count of all the times he had cursed himself for being so unobservant. But it was too late.

"You can't keep dwelling on this," Veronica had told him once. "It's beginning to look pathetic."

Her words had really stuck with him. He didn't want to be pathetic. And he didn't want her to think he was.

What am I doing? Even if I rarely talk about it, I haven't stopped dwelling on it, he thought, and ran his fingers through his curls. Then he realised it was a habit that could probably be considered pathetic too, so he pulled his hand out of his hair.

His thoughts were all over the place and not even his notes seemed to help. He decided to take a brisk walk to clear his mind. There was no panic and he knew it would feel good to get some fresh air. Someone had once told him that you move forwards mentally when you move forwards physically. In his experience, it was true.

It was a bit warmer out now and the sun shone in the blue sky. Torsten inhaled deeply through his nostrils and could smell spring. He instantly felt happier. Maybe he should go on a date? But with whom? He had no idea. But there were dating sites online. He decided to give it a try. *It can't be worse than any other kind of dating*, he thought, and smiled.

When he bumped into Jonny on the stairs leading up to their department a while later, he was feeling much happier

"What an idiot," Jonny said.

"Who?"

"The guy we just brought in. I've never met anyone as aggressive as him. Greger is nothing in comparison."

"I suppose that's typical for Nazis?"

"Yeah, maybe. He really beat the shit out of his fiancée. And he was going to kick her while their baby was on the floor right next to her. What kind of person does that?"

They walked up the stairs. Jonny was so upset that he wasn't even panting.

"Studies have been made on members of the Nordic Resistance Movement, and it turns out many of them are actually convicted criminals. In the majority of cases, we're talking violent crimes," Torsten told his colleague.

"Hmm, and still they're allowed to operate. Sometimes I think humankind isn't as intelligent as one might think." Jonny muttered.

Torsten put a hand on his shoulder in an attempt to comfort his colleague and friend.

"Don't lose hope," he said. "Most people are good."

64

He sat with his back straight across the table from Sara and Torsten. His face was pale and stiff. The only part of him that showed any kind of emotion was the look in his eyes. It alternated between hatred, boredom, and something that wasn't as easy to identify—grief, perhaps? *The eyes are the mirror of the soul,* Sara thought, although she hated clichés. But there was really something to that one. The look in the young man's eyes was the only thing he couldn't control.

Torsten let Dan know that he'd been arrested on suspicion of murder—or possibly accessory to murder. Then he told him he was also suspected of assaulting both his fiancée and his daughter, as well as harassing the study group, which was classified as a hate crime considering the circumstances. Then he asked him if he wanted a lawyer.

Dan Fagerström declined.

Torsten explained the importance of having legal counsel present, but Dan refused.

"I'll be fine on my own," he said. "You can never trust a lawyer."

Sara wondered where he had learned to be such an eloquent speaker. He came across as having been groomed. She wondered if Torsten saw it too.

"Okay, then," Torsten said. Instead of asking Dan what he had to say about the accusations, he asked him why he had beaten his fiancée.

"She's an idiot who keeps provoking me," he said. "She deserves to be beaten."

"Do you have the same attitude when it comes to your daughter?" Torsten asked, and Sara saw a glimpse of disgust in his eye.

"I never hurt Saga," he said.

"What would you call it, then?"

"I didn't realise that bitch was holding the baby."

That's it, show us your true personality, Sara thought, and almost felt happy. It was easier to read people who talked the way they behaved.

"Are you telling me you didn't see your own baby?" Torsten showed no mercy.

Dan nodded.

"Please speak into the microphone."

"Yes, that's what I'm telling you," Dan said without hesitating.

The interrogation went on for almost two hours. Dan refused to give them a straight answer. It was tiring.

"If you don't cooperate during the interrogation, we won't get your side of what's happened here, which might not be in your best interest," Torsten said before ending the interrogation and handing the suspect over to the guards.

Everyone could tell Torsten was angry, and Sara could almost physically feel his frustration.

They walked silently side by side. Sara thought about what she could say to calm Torsten down, but realised that maybe he needed to be angry. He hadn't even been angry when his wife left him. Only sad. Sad in every way. Instead of saying anything, she put a hand on his arm for a moment before they headed upstairs. She loved the trusting nature of their relationship. It made her feel safe in critical and sometimes dangerous situations. They both knew they would have each other's backs, no matter what.

"How did it go?" asked Jonny, who had also been quite upset earlier. He glanced at Torsten and realised exactly what had happened. "Oh, I see," he said, and left them alone.

Sara called Baum, who made it official that Dan Fagerström was suspected on reasonable grounds of murder and on probable grounds for assaulting his daughter and fiancée, as well as for taking part in the harassment.

"Torsten did the right thing telling him we have reasonable grounds to suspect him of abusing the child as well," Baum said. "He's simply a great officer."

Sara told Torsten what Baum had decided.

"Do you want me to tell Fagerström?"

"No, let me do it. I want to look this man in the eye when I tell him." Torsten was clearly still angry.

"Go ahead," Sara said just as her phone rang. It was from the custody suites.

"Greger Johansson wants to speak to an inspector. He tells me has something to say."

"Thanks, we'll send someone over to talk to him." She turned to Torsten. "Greger wants to speak to an inspector. Do you want to go, or should I send someone else?"

Torsten looked a bit happier.

"Finally, a breakthrough," he said, and laughed. "I'll talk to him once I've talked to Fagerström."

Just like every other time when they were about to solve a case, they were all starting to feel excited. That was the best part of the job. More and more often, Sara thought about how much she loved her job.

65

Greger had finally had enough. His lawyer had pointed out how strange it was that he was prepared to take all the blame for a murder he hadn't committed alone. It simply wasn't right.

Now Greger was sitting on the edge of the chair in his cell. He had suffered from panic attacks lately and he felt trapped. Because trapped was just what he was. It frightened him. He knew his situation wouldn't change if the others were arrested too, but at least then they would all suffer. *We all helped kick that Muslim boy's ass*, he thought. *Why am I the only one being locked up for it?*

He wasn't allowed to have any contact with the outside world, but at least his lawyer had gone to his mother's house to tell her he was in police custody. The lawyer wasn't allowed to tell her why though. Greger had been very clear about that. He wasn't sure what she would do if she found out he had killed a human being—Muslim or not.

He had made up his mind. He would talk. He would tell them everything. There was a risk it would get him into trouble, but his lawyer had told him he was most likely facing life in prison anyway, so it didn't really matter. It was simply unfair that he was the only one paying for a crime he hadn't committed on his own. He was done being their errand boy.

Now, he waited for the inspector to show up. He hoped it would be the male officer with the curly hair. He was quite nice.

Sweat trickled down his face and under his arms, his hair was dirty, and he felt the nervousness clinging to every cell in his body. He paced back and forth in his cell, counting his steps.

As he was counting, he heard his cell door open. A girl popped her head in.

"The inspector is here. Come with me, please."

The girl was also nice. Not rude like the rest of the guards. And she was quite cute too. She reminded him of his first girlfriend. Thinking of her made his heart ache. He forced himself to think about something else.

Greger was relieved to see it was the curly haired officer who was waiting for him in one of the interrogation rooms.

"Torsten, but you already know that," the officer said, and reached out his hand with a smile on his face.

Greger shook it and said hello.

"I hear you want to tell me something?" Torsten said.

Greger nodded.

"I want to tell you what happened. And who was there when we bothered those people at the university and when we killed that guy."

"Go ahead," the police officer said.

Greger started to talk. He talked and talked and for some reason, it made him feel relieved. The fog in his head cleared and the weight on his shoulders felt lighter.

He told Torsten about when they crashed the study group. Wilhelm was there too but didn't really fit in. They didn't want him in the group after that. Luckily, they never told him their real names.

"Wilhelm was acting quite aggressively towards those twins. I could tell he scared them and he seemed to like it. But afterwards it was as if he regretted his behaviour. And then he left. We never saw him again after that."

"Why weren't you given a code name?" Torsten asked curiously.

"I'm not sure. I don't think they thought I was good enough. All I was good for was running their errands."

"But do you consider yourself a Nazi?"

"I don't know. I don't know much about politics."

"I understand. And what happened next?"

"We were ordered to kill that boy after he stood up to us that time," Greger said, and realised he'd forgotten to call him a Muslim. It surprised him.

"Who are you referring to when you say 'we'?"

"Danny Fagerström, Ola Jensen, Nils Gren, and Totte. I don't know his surname."

"And Wilhelm?"

"No, we didn't trust him. I told you we didn't see him again after we bothered the girls and their study group. But I think I accidently told him about our plan to kill the Muslim."

"Who gave you the orders?"

"Our leader. We call him the Führer."

"Who is he?"

"That's the one thing I can't tell you," Greger said.

"Why is that?"

"He's a scary dude. And brutal. I know he's had others killed. Every time he's worried about someone talking, he tells us he'll 'take care of them.' I assume this means he kills whoever snitches."

"Who has he killed? Do you know?"

"I'm not sure, but I think he killed some people up north. He was super upset and told us he would never let them get away with exposing him. That's all I really know."

"Do you think this could have been in Falun?"

"Where is that?"

"Up north," Torsten said.

"Right. That might be the place. I know the man who was murdered used a code name too. The Romanian. He was the only one who wasn't using one of Hitler's men as inspiration for his code name."

"Why do you think that is?"

"They're reading some stupid book, written by someone in Romania. We looked up to him for some reason. I can never remember his name." Greger was sweating. This was harder than he had imagined it to be.

"Codreanu?"

"Right. That's it. I think that's why he called himself The Romanian. That man that the Führer killed, I mean."

"I need to step out for a moment. Stay right here. I just need to quickly visit the toilet," Torsten said, and left the room.

Greger found it strange that the officer didn't seem happier.

A moment later, he returned and shook his wet hands in front of him.

"Out of towels," he said, and sat down again.

Greger felt immensely tired, as if he were completely empty inside.

"I understand why you're scared of the Führer, but he can't get to you in here," Torsten said. "I would really like to know who he is. And if he's the one who decides who you should kill, don't you think he deserves to be punished too?"

"He's dangerous. I won't tell you. I've given you all the other names."

Torsten shrugged his shoulders and tried to look like it didn't matter. But Greger knew it did and came to the conclusion that the officer was just trying to hide what he was really thinking.

The interrogation continued for a while longer before Torsten thanked him and left.

A moment later, a guard took Greger back to his cell.

66

The team had gathered in the conference room, which was full of energy. They could all see how immensely satisfied Torsten was. Now all that was left to do was to organise the search for the rest of the men in the group that killed Reza. Sergeant Malva Gran had joined them. As soon as Sara heard what Greger had to say, she had asked for backup from the uniformed officers, and Malva had been chosen for the task. They all knew her as they had worked cases together before.

Sara walked up to Torsten and put a hand on his shoulder.

"As you can probably tell, we've mobilised since I talked to you on the phone. And we've found addresses for all the men Greger named. Even that guy Totte."

"Greger told me that when anything like this happens, they all get strict instructions to go into hiding," Torsten told the others. "So there's a risk they'll be tricky to find. But he also told us most of them don't really have anywhere to go, which means they're forced to move back in with their parents or crash on someone's sofa. Or they might find a basement like the one we found in Åkershus. It doesn't seem very organised."

Ali cleared his throat to get everyone's attention.

"I've looked into the group's members and although none of them have a criminal record, they've all had their run-ins with the law. They haven't been charged with anything yet though—mostly thanks to how loyal everyone in the group seems to be. Until now, of course. One of them has been seen together with Amanda Svensson. She's helped us before, so there is a chance she actually doesn't know what these guys are up to. But there is also a risk she might know more than she's telling us."

"As I already told you on the phone, Sara, their leader is called the Führer. Greger told me this man had some people up north murdered. The man who the Führer murdered called himself The Romanian. Greger told us it was an alias inspired by Codreanu, the author of that book we talked about before. I asked him if he thought these murders could've happened in Falun and he told me it was possible. So I'm assuming he's talking about Tom and Carola. Everyone fears the Führer. Greger refused to give me his name. But if we can get the rest of these guys in here, I'm sure one of them will talk."

Torsten looked satisfied and Sara felt happy for him.

Rita was anxious to get going. She squirmed in her chair, like a restless child.

"Baum has issued a warrant for these three men's arrest, so let's go get them," Sara said, and raised her hands to get everyone to calm down. "Ali has sorted us out with a number of addresses to check out. Let's take three cars and go to the different addresses at the same time. We don't want to give anyone a chance to warn the others. If you find any of the suspects, I want you to inform the rest of us immediately. Okay?"

"Okay," her colleagues shouted in unison.

"Ali and Jonny, Rita and Torsten, Malva and I," Sara said, splitting the team up in three groups. When she realised she wouldn't have felt comfortable pairing Rita and Ali up together, she sighed at how silly and unprofessional it was of them to even consider a relationship. But then she remembered her own history with Matsson and regretted her sigh instantly. *Those who live in glass houses shouldn't throw stones*, she thought.

They got suited up with bulletproof vests, sturdy shoes, and firearms. Then they headed out.

Malva was driving while Sara started the radio.

"You have no idea how excited I am about coming with you guys," Malva said, and sounded just as happy as she looked.

She was a good driver and respected the speed limit in the city. Once they got out on the highway towards Malmö, she stepped on the accelerator and stayed well above the speed limit.

Sara, who loved driving fast, didn't mention it.

They talked about all the different scenarios they might encounter and planned for how to handle each one. It felt safe. Although Malva looked sweet and nice, she was tough. She was known for never running from a fight and equally known for doing everything in her power to avoid violence. She was smart and rarely acted in a way that riled people up. On the contrary, her approach was gentle and had a calming effect on people. Sara thought Malva would make a great detective on her team as she reminded her of Torsten in many ways.

Malva effortlessly parked the car in a tight spot on the street next to the apartment building they were about to enter. Sara let the others know that they were at their address and had no idea what to expect.

Torsten told them to be careful.

"You never know what to expect. We're at our address now, too," he said.

"We've arrived as well," Jonny said.

"Let's do this. Only use your radios when absolutely necessary."

Sara took a couple of deep breaths. She wasn't worried, but she wanted to get her heartrate down slightly as she could literally hear her pulse. They walked as casually as they could up to the entrance door. Sara knew the entrance code. *Thanks, Ali*, she thought.

There was an old lift in the house that looked loud and rickety.

"Let's take the stairs," Sara whispered. She didn't want to risk being trapped, and if someone saw them in the lift, they would easily be able to escape down the stairs. In other words, the lift seemed like a bad idea.

On the way up they met a man who gave them a suspicious look. Sara didn't really look like a police officer, but it wasn't hard to guess Malva's profession. She had a look in her eye that was typical for young police officers. Even her choice of shoes gave her away. *I'll teach her one day*, Sara thought. They were now on the third floor and only had one set of stairs left to climb.

Sara's heart started beating faster again. But this time she didn't mind. She needed to be focused. Focus meant the ability to react and without it, you were doomed to fail.

They got to the fourth floor and stopped outside the right door. Malva and Sara inhaled deeply. This was it.

Sara reached for the door with her left hand while holding her gun in her right. Malva stood next to her with one foot down the stairs. Her other option would've been to stand on the other side of Sara, or behind her, where she wouldn't be able to see a thing. If she stood behind Sara, she wouldn't be able to use her weapon, and if she stood on the other side of her, she would risk being blocked by the door—or hit in the head by it when it opened. Sara rang the doorbell. It didn't work. She waited for a second, then she knocked on the door.

She heard footsteps and tried to determine if the person on the other side of the door was a man or a woman. Men normally put their heels into the ground before their toes, or they dragged their feet. Women's footsteps were almost impossible to hear. It sounded like the person approaching the door was wearing shoes. *Woman*, Sara thought just as the door opened. A man opened the door and when he spotted the armed women outside, he tried to close it again. But Sara managed to get a foot in the door and stopped him. Malva grabbed the door and pulled at it while the man did his best to stop them from getting in. When they finally managed to get the door open, the man ran into the small flat again. He positioned himself by a table and aimed a gun at them. Malva fired her weapon. The shot made Sara's ears ring and the man collapsed. Just then, another man came rushing out of the bathroom. He pushed Malva to the side and tried to get to the door.

Malva regained her balance and grabbed him before he made it out and quickly brought him down onto the floor.

Sara had rushed over to the man who'd just been shot. He was alive, but his breathing was shallow and fast. She glanced over at Malva to make sure she was okay. There was no doubt she had the situation under control. The young man was still lying on the floor on his stomach. Malva had pulled his arms behind his back and handcuffed him.

"Bloody hell, you're fast," Sara exclaimed.

Malva smiled.

"How's he doing over there?"

"I'm calling for an ambulance," Sara said.

67

W ho is he?" the ambulance driver asked as they carried the stretcher out of the flat. They had performed CPR on the man, who was still alive.

"I'm not sure, but I think he's the leader of a Nazi group," Sara said. She had come to that conclusion as the man was twice as old as the rest of the men in the group. She picked up the man's gun from the floor and wrapped it in a piece of kitchen towel. A unit from Malmö arrived to pick up the arrested youth.

Documents and photos were spread out across a table in the flat.

Sara had a look at the material and gasped when she saw a photo of two people with bullet holes in their foreheads and swastikas carved next to them.

"What the . . ." she exclaimed. "It's all here."

"What is?" Malva wanted to know.

"Photos, notes, and a bunch of Nazi propaganda. A lot of photos."

"I'll call for Forensics," Malva said.

"Yes, but let them know we're bringing all this material as well as the man's gun with us as evidence. In other words, they're mostly looking for DNA."

Sara listened as Malva made the call. Just as she expected, the sergeant followed procedure perfectly. Backup had arrived at the scene and Malva's weapon was taken care of.

Malva knew they would take her gun from her. That was what happened every time an officer had used their weapon. Both Malva and Sara were asked some questions. When they were done, they waited outside the flat until the forensics team arrived. The flat was cordoned off.

Sara and Malva packed up everything they wanted to bring with them and drove back to Lund.

When they walked into the police station, they were showered with hugs, applause, and questions.

Neither of them felt especially up for the attention as they wanted to meet with the rest of their team as soon as possible to tell them what had just happened. Sara thanked everyone for their support but asked for a moment to process it all.

They were both shaken up by the experience. Everyone understood that. Torsten put a hand on Sara's cheek. It was such a nice gesture that her eyes welled up. She pulled herself together and showed him all the material they'd found. They had brought the man's gun back with them and it needed to be taken straight to the forensics department. If they were lucky, it would be the same gun that was used to shoot Tom and Carola.

"Who was the man that Malva shot?"

"We don't know. He wasn't carrying an ID. We'll see what Forensics can tell us. But I think it's the man they call the Führer as he's significantly older than the rest of them. And he's alive. But look what we found," Sara said, and threw the bag of documents onto the table.

Torsten put on a pair of plastic gloves and had a closer look.

"What on earth!" he exclaimed when he saw the photos of Tom and Carola. He put a hand on his forehead. "What a sick bastard!"

Beatrice Larsson came running into the room.

"What is this I'm hearing? There's been a shooting?"

"Yes," Malva said, "I shot a guy who aimed his gun at us."

"Jesus, that could have ended horribly . . ." Beatrice was clearly relieved.

"It only ended horribly for the Führer," Malva said laconically.

"I need a cup of coffee and something to eat," Sara said. "How about you guys?" she asked the rest of them.

"I'll take care of it," Beatrice offered without asking anyone what they wanted. But it didn't matter.

"How did you guys do?" Malva asked the others.

"They're all in custody," Torsten said with a big smile on his face.

"Wow, what a day," Sara said, and clapped her hands although she was tired enough to fall asleep on the spot. There was no time for a nap though. There were reports to write and they needed to pay a visit at the hospital. A guard had been placed outside the wounded man's room. They felt like the biggest winners in the world. The best thing of all, they'd broken up an underground Nazi group. At least they thought they had.

"Do we have enough inspectors to interrogate everyone we arrested?"

"Yes, I've gathered up some colleagues who are willing to help," Jonny said.

"Great, because we need to have a meeting and draw up a new plan based on the latest development," Sara said, relaxing a little.

"Do you think we can ask Malmö to get us the identity of the leader we shot?" Torsten asked.

"I'll call the operations centre and ask," Malva said, and left the room. She returned in just a couple of minutes.

"Sorry, they can't help us. And the guard isn't a police officer, so we can't ask him to do it. I called the hospital as well, and they told me he'll survive. He's badly wounded but he'll make it."

"Okay, I guess I'll go over there and see what I can find out," Torsten offered.

"That would be great, but let's eat and have coffee first. And have a little talk. We need to go through all the new material before you go to the hospital. Perhaps you could stop by there in the morning as well, on your way to work?" Sara said.

"No way, I'll go after the meeting," he said. "It's only a short drive."

"It's up to you," Sara said.

Just then, Beatrice returned.

She had popped down to the Thai restaurant right around the corner and she was still wearing her fur coat.

"Here is some water as well," she said, and put six bottles on the table. "There is coffee in the machine."

"Thanks a lot for the food, Beatrice," Sara said. "And for the water."

She opened one of the bottles and had a couple of thirsty gulps.

They sat down around the table and tucked into the food. They were all laughing and enjoying each other's company while they took turns talking about their day. The others hadn't experienced anything out of the ordinary and they were all curious to hear Sara and Malva's story.

68

They had never seen anything like it. Detailed plans to attack journalists and politicians nationwide. Maps and a lot of photos. Unfortunately, not a single photo of the Führer, but of everyone else in the group. Most of the photos were of the targets for the planned attacks though. Underneath the photos of the journalists and politicians who were clearly on the group's kill-list, they had written things like "traitor to the nation," and "race traitor."

The man's weapon was in the lab and the flat had been combed for evidence. The forensics team had found even more documents as well as a computer full of information. The IT technician told her over the phone that the computer seemed to belong to a company in Lund called Microtech. They had called the company to ask if they were missing a computer, which they weren't. The man they'd talked to asked for the computer's serial number, but it had been filed off. All that was left was a sticker with the company's name on it. The company hadn't been able to explain it. Finally, the technicians had asked the company to give them a call if they realised a computer was missing after all, and they had promised to do so. Sara thanked him for the new information and went back to her colleagues. The mood was still great when she returned.

"Now we have reports to write," Sara said, and told her team what the technician on the phone had just told her.

"Unfortunately, I can't remember the name of the company now," she said, and excused herself.

"Maybe it's an old computer that the company has thrown out? You never know," Ali said. "And right now it doesn't really matter, right?"

"No, maybe not. They promised to send a report over tomorrow. I'm sure it'll work itself out."

They all sat down to write their reports. Each team needed to leave a written account of their version of how the arrests had been made and report the identities of everyone except the leader—or the supposed leader. It was boring, but it had to be done.

A sergeant called to tell them all three arrested men were being charged with the murder of Reza Mahmoudi. They were all in police custody in Lund and Malmö, and a guard had been placed outside the wounded man's room at the hospital. They still hadn't been able to identify the man.

Sara and her team were all free to go home. Torsten changed his mind and decided to save his visit to the hospital for the next morning. It was 8:30 p.m. and he probably wouldn't be allowed in to see the man anyway, considering how serious his condition still was. A guard would stay outside his room all night, so he would still be there in the morning.

Instead, Torsten went home and called his daughter on Skype. He was tired, but he really missed her. He felt grateful when he realised how happy she was to hear from him.

"Are you tired, Daddy?" she asked, and he could see in her eyes how much she cared about him.

"Yes, but I feel better now when I talk to you," he answered.

He wanted to hug his daughter, but all he could do was place a hand on the screen.

"Shouldn't you try to find someone to share your life with?" she asked. "I don't like that you're so lonely."

"Honey, I don't want you to worry about me. I'm fine. I've got you and all my colleagues. They're my friends too," he said, trying to sound cheerful.

"But hey, I'm all the way over here. And you can't centre your life around me."

"I know, and I don't. You know, the other day I was thinking about signing up for one of those dating sites online."

"That's great! Do it!" she said, and let out a little laugh full of love and support.

"I will, but we have to solve this giant case first."

"But, Daddy, you're always working. Don't try to get out of this now. Do it tonight. You don't have to date if you don't find anyone interesting enough, you know? Promise me to sign up after we end this call." She squinted her eyes and tried to look stern.

Torsten laughed.

"What would I do without you?" he said, and smiled. "You really know how to take care of your old man."

"Yes, what would you do without me?" She winked.

He winked back.

"Well, I need a bath," he said.

He knew what she was going to say and beat her to it.

"I'll sign up for the dating site right after my bath. I promise."

"Fine. Bye, Daddy. Talk to you soon."

"Bye bye, darling. Talk to you soon."

He took his sweaty, dirty clothes off. It had been a rough day. But a good one.

He filled the tub, put a glass of wine next to it, and stepped into the bath. It was scalding hot but felt great for both body and soul. He had a sip of his wine and sang to himself. He suddenly felt very sleepy.

He woke up with a start. The water was cold and he shivered. He instantly realised he would have to postpone signing up for the dating site for another day. He emptied the bathtub and had a warm shower, still sitting down in the tub.

He slept like a baby that night.

69

It was just before 8 a.m. when Torsten arrived at the hospital in Malmö. He knew exactly where to go and showed his badge to the nurse who opened the door for him.

"I'm here to see the unidentified man who was shot yesterday."

"He's not doing so well," the nurse said, "but it would be fantastic if we could find out who he is soon. Nobody has called here asking for him, which is strange as people normally realise it quite quickly when a loved one or family member is missing. Maybe he's not Swedish?"

"I definitely think he's Swedish. But I'll see what I can do to help," Torsten said, and followed the nurse through a long corridor.

There was a guard sitting on a chair outside the room. He looked tired.

"Did you sit here all night?" Torsten asked.

"Nope, I got here an hour ago. I just had a bad night's sleep."

"I can't remember the last time I had such a *good* night's sleep," Torsten said, sounding cheerful.

The nurse opened the door to the patient's room. The man was lying on a bed, connected to tubes and wires. It looked like he was in a deep sleep.

"Is he asleep?" Torsten asked.

"No, he's sedated."

"Oh, I see."

"I'll leave you alone with him. You'll be safe," she said.

Torsten approached the bed but stopped when he saw who was lying in it. He rushed out of the room, ran down the stairs, and hurried to his car. He spotted a parking ticket on the windscreen, put it in his pocket, jumped into the car, and took off.

As he was driving, a memory popped into his mind. A memory that he saw with new eyes now.

Torsten heard the front door open and the woman stood up with tears streaming down her face. Torsten and Jörgen stayed seated while she walked towards the hallway. A young man entered the kitchen with confident steps. Torsten already knew how old he was, but he noticed that he looked very adult. Tall and muscular. His hair was of medium length and his beard was trimmed and quite impressive. His blond hair fell in soft waves and framed his powerful face perfectly, but it didn't look deliberate. Torsten stood up and Jörgen did the same.

"Staffan Ehn," the man said calmly, and looked at Torsten with sad eyes as he shook his hand. Then he shook Jörgen's hand too.

Molly stood next to him. She didn't look clingy, but independent. She was still crying.

"Why can't you find Karl-Axel?" Staffan asked after taking a seat at the table. Torsten felt relieved that there was nothing accusing in the way Staffan formulated the question. Torsten had always had a hard time dealing with angry people. Even if he was an experienced officer, he still found it uncomfortable to handle people who were aggressive.

"There is a simple answer to your question. We don't know where to look," Torsten said after thinking about it for a moment. "That's why we're here. We're hoping to find a clue."

"Ask your questions and I'll do my best to answer them," Staffan Ehn said, and locked eyes with Torsten. Honest, but not cocky.

"How come you ended up in Lund? You lived in Falun before you moved here, right?"

"That's right. But I was accepted to the Faculty of Engineering, so I moved here. Simple as that." A slightly smug smile played on his lips for a second.

"Right," Torsten said, and aimed a crooked smile Staffan's way as he was having a hard time interpreting the smile. "Can I just ask you what's so funny? You just smiled . . ."

"Did I?"

"Yes."

"I don't know, I guess I thought the question was pretty stupid. I mean, what's so strange about moving? I've moved around my whole life," Staffan explained, and Torsten found it hard to determine if he was acting superior or friendly.

"For how long did you live in Falun?"

"I moved there when I was fourteen and moved away right before I started uni."

"Did anyone ever threaten you?"

"Threaten?" Molly asked with her eyes wide open. She had finally stopped crying.

"No," Staffan answered without hesitation.

But Torsten had seen something. A look on his face. Was it loathing? Or superiority? Either way, it had disappeared in the blink of an eye. But he had seen it.

As Torsten approached the gate to the police station, he couldn't help thinking that the tiny movement he'd seen all those years back had probably been a sign of how satisfied Staffan was about fooling the police.

He hurried up the stairs and rushed into Sara's office. He was out of breath and had to take a second to collect himself.

"Do you . . . do you know who . . . Malva shot?" Torsten asked, and saw that he had caught Sara's attention.

"No, who?"

"Staffan . . . Ehn," Torsten said, panting. "I knew it, I knew it. I just couldn't believe it was him."

"What are you talking about?" Sara exclaimed, and stood up.

"Staffan Ehn. Molly's husband. The father of her daughter. Karl-Axel's stepfather. Can you believe it? Right in front of our faces."

"Oh, wow. What are we doing now?" Sara was baffled and wasn't sure how to react.

"We must tell Molly. We have to. He's been shot and admitted to hospital. She needs to know."

"You're right. Do you want to tell her or do you want me to do it?"

"We'll talk to her together, but didn't you recognise him?"

"No, I never met him. It's never been at the top of my list, if you know what I mean . . ."

"No, you're right. Let's go straight away." Torsten spoke loudly. Sara had never seen him so worked-up before.

"Calm down. We have to tell the others first."

But it turned out they didn't need to. The rest of the team had all heard Torsten and now they were waiting for them outside Sara's office. Baum, who was visiting, had also heard it all.

As always, he came across as calm and professional.

"I wonder why he shot Tom and Carola," he said.

"Because we were on to them, of course," Torsten said after calming down slightly.

"On to them about what?" Baum asked, and raised his eyebrows.

"Well, we were starting to investigate the family regarding their son. Considering the tip we received, I think he knew we would find them. And Tom and Staffan obviously knew each other. My guess is he helped them get their hands on Karl-Axel as he didn't want to take care of someone else's child. Or maybe it was a way for him to get rid of Carola? I don't know."

"Oh, I see," Baum said, and lowered his eyebrows.

"He probably knew that if we could get Carola to talk, all his plans of murdering journalists and taking over the country would be crushed. My guess is there was something going on between Tom and Staffan as well. Maybe Tom threatened to expose him?"

"Let's find out."

"This whole story is bloody unbelievable," Jonny said, waving his hands around.

"I couldn't agree more," Sara said. "Rita, can you call Kabhat and let her know about this? We need to compare the weapon with the one that was used to murder Carola and Tom. Torsten and I will go talk to Molly Altenius now. And shouldn't we let Wilhelm go?"

"Yes, of course. And take this opportunity to tell Molly Altenius that her son has been found," Baum said, looking stern but happy. "He'll still have to face charges for harassing the study group, don't forget about that. But he's free to go as of right now."

70

Molly opened the door and looked at Sara and Torsten. Judging by the expression on her face, she realised something serious had happened.

"Can we come inside?" Torsten asked.

"Yes," she said without hesitation. "Did you find my son?"

"Yes, we did," Sara said. "That's the good news."

Molly stepped to the side to let them in. Then she showed then into the kitchen. She turned towards them with eyes full of tears.

"You found Karl-Axel. I can't believe it, even if I hoped this was the case when you asked for my DNA before."

"Yes, unfortunately things have turned out to be more complicated than we could have imagined," Sara said, "but you'll get to see him soon. I promise."

"That's amazing news. But how will it be? We don't know each other." She looked to them for help.

"I'm sure it'll be fine. But we do need to share some bad news with you too. Your husband, Staffan, has been admitted to hospital in Malmö. He was shot last night . . ." Sara was talking too fast and had to pause to compose herself. "He's badly wounded."

"Shot?" Molly repeated. "Who shot him and why?"

"He aimed a gun at a police officer who was forced to shoot him to protect her own life."

"That can't be true," Molly said. Her eyes wandered from Torsten to Sara and back to Torsten again as she was trying to take in all the information.

"Unfortunately, it is. He's under arrest, and as soon as he's strong enough, he'll be brought to the police station. But . . . you won't be able to see him. You will see your son though."

Sara realised that what she had just said probably didn't make Molly feel that much better, but there was nothing else she could say.

"But what should I tell our daughter?"

"I'm afraid I can't tell you what to say to her. If I were you, I would tell her the truth." Sara placed a hand on the woman's arm. She didn't seem to notice it.

"Do you know anything about your husband's political views?" Sara asked.

"I thought I knew everything about him, but apparently not."

"Did you know that he was the leader of an underground Nazi group?"

"What? How is that even possible . . ." she said, gasping.

"No idea," Sara said honestly.

"But he's an engineer," Molly said, opening her eyes wide. "Was this what he was doing on all those business trips? I don't understand."

"How often did he travel for work?" Torsten asked.

"Once per month, maybe. And he plays chess too. Or at least that's what he says he does. I'm not sure if I should believe what you're telling me."

"I think you should," Sara said. "We have no reason to lie to you. I think you know that."

Molly nodded. She was obviously shocked. *Who wouldn't have been in her situation*, Sara thought.

Suddenly, it was as if Molly realised something.

"Do you know something strange?"

They both shook their heads.

"I never told Staffan that you asked me for a DNA sample when you thought you might have found Wilhelm. I'm not sure why I didn't tell him. Maybe I suspected something wasn't right? I don't know." She shivered as if the realisation made her feel cold.

Molly stopped talking but looked reasonably calm.

"Maybe Wilhelm is still alive because of it," Torsten said.

"Yes, maybe," Molly said. "Will you let me know when I can see Karl-Axel. Or—Wilhelm. I should probably get used to that name," she said.

"It won't be very long. I suggest that you contact a therapist who specialises in treating trauma," Sara said, and decided not to tell Molly that Wilhelm had been a murder suspect until very recently. It would have to wait.

Molly nodded.

"Good," Sara said. "You'll most likely need help processing this. I'm thinking about your daughter as well."

"Thanks, I'll contact someone," Molly said.

"I also think you should contact family and friends for support through this. We normally don't leave people by themselves after giving them bad news like this. But I have a feeling you'll be okay."

"I'll call my parents. I'm going to be fine," she said, and walked them to the door.

The whole way back to the police station, Sara thought about what it would feel like to find out what Molly had just found out about her family. And she wondered how she would have handled it. Maybe the shock protected Molly Altenius. *Things normally happen for a reason,* she thought, trying to make herself feel better. But she couldn't help feeling sad. It was incomprehensible and heartbreaking that people could become such monsters.

71

S ara walked through the garden gate and towards her her home and her family. She felt so happy that she couldn't stop herself from giggling a little. And she was so incredibly tired. She looked through the kitchen window and saw Anders and Bella standing by the stove. Candles were lit on the kitchen counter. Judging by how Johannes and Klara were moving around in there, they were busy setting the table.

Sara was overcome by an infinite and overwhelming feeling of satisfaction. Joy.

She suddenly felt wide awake and rushed up the stairs. She opened the door and let her family know she was home.

Four warm voices full of love welcomed her. What could be better?

Anders and her three children met her in the hallway. Anders was dressed in an apron. They all took turns hugging her.

"We love you," they said in unison while Johannes helped her take off her coat. Klara pulled a little stool out and ask her mother to take a seat. Sara laughed at their display of care.

She took off her shoes and put on a pair of slippers that Bella had brought her. Then she let herself be guided into the kitchen.

It was so beautiful. There was a huge bouquet of roses in the middle of the table, which was beautifully set.

They had even pulled out the gorgeous, handmade candleholders from Georg Jensen.

The first course was already served. The serviettes were folded beautifully.

"You're all wonderful," she said, and walked over to her usual spot by the table. Johannes pulled out the chair for her and she sat down.

The rest of them also sat in front of the beautiful plates of food. Sara was so happy she could barely eat. Anders raised his glass.

"Cheers to Sara, he most beautiful woman there is."

"Cheers to the best mother in the world," the three children said, raising their glasses too.

"Cheers to the most amazing man and to my incredible children," Sara said, toasting them.

She had a sip of wine. Then she tucked into the starter, followed by the main. Life couldn't be better.

After dinner, she wasn't allowed to lift a finger. She felt relaxed and happy.

When the table was cleared and the kitchen clean, the children had other plans. Klara and Bella were heading out to meet up with some friends. Johannes was going to his girlfriend's house. Before they left, they kissed her forehead as she was half-lying on the sofa.

Anders had a seat next to her, put her legs across his lap, and started massaging her feet.

"You're amazing," she told him. "You're not only amazing, but you're also truly wonderful. In every way. I barely deserve you."

He smiled but didn't say anything.

"Hey," she said.

"Yes?" he said, smiling.

"I love you."

"That's a relief," he said, and leaned in for a kiss. He stroked her forehead, cheeks, and nose and ran his fingers gently over her lips. "And I love you more than I can say."

"That's a relief too," she said. Then she closed her eyes and drifted off into sleep in his warm embrace.

He woke her up gently.

"Time to go to bed," he said.

She forced herself to go to the bathroom, but she felt just as reluctant as a child. She didn't want to brush her teeth. She wanted to sleep. But she brushed her teeth anyway because that's just what you do. Then she stumbled over to the bed.

A couple of minutes later, he joined her.

"Do you know if the children are coming home soon?" she asked, and yawned.

"Yes, it's a school day tomorrow. Or—university day." He kissed her and she fell asleep with a smile on her face.

72

Luckily, Staffan Ehn survived. It didn't matter that he was the most detestable person Sara had ever met. They needed some clarity. If he died, they would never get their answers.

Once he was strong enough to talk, they went to the hospital to interrogate him. During their first interviews, he was impossible to get through to. He kept his mouth shut. They couldn't get him to open up and therefore, the interviews were kept short.

For the first time since she met Torsten, he refused to interrogate the suspect. He told Sara that he was afraid of bringing his private emotions into the interrogation room. Sara understood him and decided to interrogate Staffan herself. She could see that Torsten was at the point of breaking and she suspected it wasn't only because of the case with the missing boy.

She decided to leave him out if it and turned to Rita to prepare for the interrogation instead.

During the fourth interview, Staffan let his guard down slightly. He was finally strong enough to leave the hospital, so Sara interrogated him at the police station.

"The weapon you were carrying when you were shot is the same weapon that killed Tom and Carola Karlsson. And the only fingerprints we've found on it are yours. Also, we found pictures of the murder victims in your possession. What do you have to say about all this?"

He gave her a smug look.

"I'm not stupid, you know," he said. "Of course I shot them."

He looked proud. Sara looked at him and felt disgust.

"So, yes. I admit murdering the two dumbest people I've ever met. Stupid, unintelligent, uneducated. What more do you want me to say?" He aimed a sardonic smile their way.

"Well, for example . . . Why did you shoot them?"

"Once you received that tip, I knew you would find them and I knew they would talk. They weren't smart enough to keep their mouths shut. I got there too late though. You had been there already."

"How do you know?" Sara sounded surprised.

"Carola told me, before I shot her. She promised she hadn't told you anything, but I knew she would—eventually."

"And why did you carve the swastikas into their foreheads?"

"I thought it would confuse you. Why would a National Socialist shoot other National Socialists? Seems pretty odd, don't you think?"

"Maybe," Sara said. "But what was it you didn't want them to tell us?"

Staffan threw his head back and laughed.

"You don't understand a thing, that much is clear."

"What don't I understand?"

"Tom Karlsson was an idiot. He wanted to join my group, but I didn't want him there. He was too dangerous. Too weak," Staffan said without answering the question.

Sara let him speak. It seemed as if he was more than happy giving her all the information she needed without her even asking for it.

"I understand," she said.

He shook his head.

"As I said before—you don't understand a thing. My group didn't need another member who wanted to be in charge. Tom was like that. But he was far too stupid to be in charge of anything at all."

"What happened to their biological son?" Sara asked. She was getting bored listening to Staffan and his ideas.

"Tom got angry when he wouldn't stop screaming, so he threw him across the room. Not very smart. The boy died. I know Tom beat him as much as he beat Carola. She was scared of him, but what could I do?"

"So she never stalked you?"

"I guess it depends on how you see it. She was a nag. I was relieved when she met Tom. But then that thing happened with their son. I wanted to get rid of Molly's son. So I basically gave him to them," Staffan Ehn said as if a child meant nothing.

Sara was shocked and felt like throwing up. But she did her best to hide it.

"Did you take him?" she asked, and tried to sound and act like she was unaffected by the situation. But she wasn't. Her instinct told her to kill the man in front of her. He felt like a threat to humanity. But she stayed professional.

"No, Carola did. But I made sure she knew when he would be outside and then I told her how easy it would be to get him to come with her." He seemed pleased with himself.

Sara didn't really want to go on, but she kept asking questions. She asked about Reza's murder and who ordered it.

He answered her questions as if he got a kick out of telling her how smart he'd been. As if the murder of Reza was just an example of what they were capable of. The only thing he regretted was letting an idiot like Greger join the group. It was his biggest mistake.

"Did you know Molly's son studied in Lund and that he interacted with your group?"

It was the first time her questions threw him off balance, which told her he didn't know about it. It also meant his allies hadn't told him about Wilhelm. Staffan Ehn didn't answer. But it didn't matter.

When Sara was finally finished interrogating Staffan Ehn, she left the room with his last sentence ringing in her head.

"You think you can kill National Socialism, but you'll see," he had said while looking confident in a way she had rarely seen in people who were about to be sentenced to life in prison. Even if it was obvious that Staffan saw himself as quite an important person, the cause was clearly more important to him than one man's fate as an individual.

Sara was so exhausted that she could barely move.

Once she got back to her office, she grabbed ahold of Rita and asked her to come to dinner with her. Rita came without hesitating.

They sat together for a long time, chatting about life, death, the case, society, and love. They both needed a good talk.

"I've been thinking about something," Sara said. "A boy went missing twenty years ago. Staffan Ehn destroyed his life. And he used his horrific Nazi beliefs to brainwash a bunch of boys who were led to believe in all the craziness of this narcissistic man. He ordered them to kill Reza to gain more power, but in the end, they all lost everything. Now there is only one of these boys who has a shot at a future, and it's the boy that everything started with."

Rita stroked her cheek. It was a gesture full of love.

"That's one way to look at it," she said.

Rita wasn't a very philosophical person. But Sara didn't mind. They complemented each other. Things were different with Torsten. He was a thinker, which was nice too.

They left the restaurant.

73

Something happens, and the world is never the same again. A sullen group sat in the conference room. It was a cold morning and Sara had just briefed them about the last interview with Staffan Ehn. They had all read the transcript, which was frightening and gave them all the feeling that the world was turning into a darker place. Murders happened all the time. But it was the recent social development that scared them all.

"The only positive thing about this is that Molly and Wilhelm have been reunited. Maybe they'll be mother and son again, for real. He has nobody else. Well, he has a sister, of course. So he does have a family. I spoke to Molly last night. She seemed quite optimistic, despite what she found out about Staffan."

Sara looked at her colleagues and saw a glimmer of hope in their eyes.

"Everything started to make sense once we figured out what he was really doing when he said he played chess or went on business trips. In reality, he was busy with Action Now! and his grandiose Nazi dreams that involved taking control of Sweden," she continued in front of her silent team.

"I can't believe it takes so little to get people to commit murder," Jonny said.

"Yes, it's absurd," Torsten said.

"I witnessed this throughout my childhood, back in Afghanistan," Ali said. "My mother is Hazara. My father was French and went to Afghanistan to work as a doctor. My mother was one of few Hazara women with an education. She's a nurse and worked at the only hospital in the area. My father worked for Doctors Without Borders. When the hospital was bombed by the Taliban, we had to escape. We went to France, and then my father got a job as a doctor in Sweden. I was forced to face racism every single day, and I still do. But I'm strong because my parents have always been strong." Ali kept his head high while he told his story and when he was done, he leaned back in his chair again.

"Yes, maybe that's one thing we can learn from this. Children are at risk of becoming easy targets for ideologies like this, if their parents can't be there to support them," said Sara. "But you know, I think we'll take the day off tomorrow. It'll be the first Saturday in ages when we can relax a little. At least that's what it feels like. All our suspects are in custody and we've earned a weekend off. We probably deserve more time off than that, to be honest. You know what? I think we should go home right after lunch. I'll run it by Beatrice, but I doubt she'll say no." Sara stood up and left the room.

After a couple of minutes, she returned.

"Let's go home after lunch. Beatrice will cover for us."

The team cheered when they heard the news.

"And I invite you all to my house at 4 p.m. for a glass of bubbly and some snacks. What do you say?"

Her team cheered again.

It made Sara happier than she thought it would. She felt grateful working with such an amazing and capable team. She thought about Jörgen and hoped he was okay.

Lunchtime came and Sara grabbed her jacket and left the police station. She inhaled the scent of winter turning into spring. There was still hope after all.

THANK YOU

Without a Trace has been the most difficult book to write. If I hadn't been surrounded by so many wonderful people, I'm not sure if I would have been able to finish it.

I want to aim a thank-you filled with love to my beloved Torgny, my star children Anna and Mika, and my dear mother. You always fill my sky with light.

A big thank-you to my dearest and most lovely Camilla Ländin, who has read my script and given me positive and encouraging comments along the way. You are my anchor.

For all the expert help, I would like to especially thank a couple of people. Lena Körner, who has patiently answered all of my questions from a prosecutor's perspective. Henrik Andersson, police officer and dog handler, who has helped me understand how police dogs work. And finally, Jonathan L, who has helped me with questions about Nazism.

An equally warm thank-you to Eva Klang Vänerklint, who keeps encouraging me to grow. I also want to thank all my beautiful friends who keep sending me loving comments and hearts from all over the world. You have been a huge comfort to me when things have felt difficult.

And to my dear father, thank you for cheering me on from a place far away.

Finally, I want to thank both my parents for giving me the most valuable gifts I can imagine: the gift of social competence, a rich emotional life, creativity, and energy. And last but not least, stubbornness and patience. *Without a Trace* is for you!

Cecilia Sahlström
Lund, 19 February 2019

ABOUT THE AUTHOR

Cecilia Sahlström is a popular Swedish crime writer based in Lund, in southern Sweden. Sahlström worked in the police force for twenty years before becoming a writer. Her first novel, *White Lilac*, has been praised for its gritty realism and authentic portrayal of police investigations.

DISCOVER
STORIES UNBOUND

PodiumAudio.com